# Once Upon True Love's Kiss

## An Enchanted Realms Novel

### MICHELLE MILES

ISBN:   9798224054275 (ebook)
ISBN:   979-8-9898542-1-9 (paperback)

Mysti
Kin
King Rufus
Dark Wizard
DUNMEADE
BAY
Hollow Glen
Kingdom
EN
WO
King

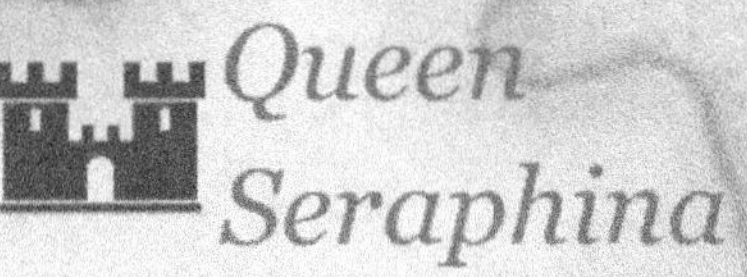
Queen
Seraphina
Brookdale
Lighthill
Westfall
Faradill
Elven
Village
Wyldwood
Forest
SEA OF
MARA
...ale
...om
...IANTED
...DLANDS
Clayharbor
Bridgefort
Feywood
Kingdom
King Egber...
Ellewood
Kingdom

*For Helen, aka Georgie. Her brilliant smile will be forever missed.*

# PROLOGUE

*Spring, Present Day*

Rain dotted the concrete as Hilde hurried across the parking lot clutching her umbrella. The overcast sky threatened dark, stormy clouds and she wanted to be inside before it broke loose and poured. Despite the coming Spring, it was still chilly, making her shiver under her thick pea coat.

She hustled up the steps of the children's hospital entrance, retracting her umbrellas as she crossed the threshold of the double sliding doors. She made her way to information, leaving a trail of raindrops. The receptionist gave her directions to her niece's room. She headed to the elevators at a brisk pace.

When she found the room, her sister, Linnea, was dozing in the chair beside the girl's hospital bed. Her chin was on her chest, her hands limp in her lap. Marigold was curled on her side in the bed hooked up to all sorts of contraptions. It hurt her heart to see her little niece like that. But the one thing that gave her comfort was seeing the blue scarf wrapped around her. The scarf she gave her for Christmas when she was six.

She'd just celebrated her eighth birthday and then immediately came down with some sort of respiratory infection. The doctors ran every test they had but never discovered the cause.

The door closed with a soft snick behind her and she paused there in the half light of the room. Outside, rain began to pour.

Linnea startled and lifted her head. Her eyes opened and fixed on Hilde standing at the door. Confusion flickered over her face for a moment, then she gave her a nod of hello. She yawned and stretched and rose, walking around the end of the bed to greet her. She wrapped her in a tight hug.

"Any change?" Hilde asked when she pulled away.

Linnea shook her head. Her eyes were bloodshot. Dark circles had formed under her lower lashes. Exhaustion lined her face.

"I'm glad you came." Her voice was low so as not to disturb Marigold.

Hilde clutched her sister's arm, squeezing it. "Why don't you go home and get some rest? I'll sit with her for a while."

Linnea glanced back at Marigold, the hesitation evident in her body language. "Are you certain?"

"Yes, of course. She's my favorite niece. I don't mind."

"She's your only niece," Linnea pointed out.

They shared a chuckle.

"I could use a shower," her sister said.

"Then go. How's Jack?" she asked, inquiring about her brother-in-law.

"He's staying busy at work. I think he's trying to be strong for all of us."

"As he should." She hugged her again. "Go on. She'll be fine. Take this. You'll need it." She handed her the umbrella.

Linnea gave her a tired nod as she took it with a glance to the window. Rain sluiced down it in rivulets. "Thank you."

She grabbed her purse from the chair and left. When she was gone, Hilde perched in the chair next to the bed. She clasped her hands in her lap, watching Marigold sleep. Her round, cherub face was in repose, her long lashes brushing her cheeks. She looked thinner than when she saw her at Christmas. Her cheeks were not quite as rosy. Her blonde hair was flat against her head.

She stirred and her eyes fluttered open. Even with the illness, her blue eyes were still bright and clear.

"Where's Mummy?"

"She went home to get some rest." Hilde leaned forward, placing her hand on the girl's cold one. She gave it a quick squeeze. "I'll stay with you until she comes back."

Marigold shifted in the hospital bed, eyeing the water jug across the room. "I'm thirsty."

"I'll get you some water."

Hilde rose and moved to the other side, pouring a cup of water for her. Then handed it to her. She sipped it, then handed it back. Hilde placed it on the side table and sat again.

She hated seeing Marigold like this. She looked and sounded weak.

"Auntie, will you tell me a story?" she asked, blinking her wide blue eyes.

How could she resist? "Of course, I will, sweet girl. And I have just the one for you."

"What's it about?"

"Why, it's about a princess who was the fairest in all the land. But the evil queen was so jealous of her, she exiled her from the castle when she was the same age as you. The queen hoped she would never return."

The girl's eyes went round. "What did she do?"

"The princess ran into the forest," Hilde said. "She was scared and alone. As night fell, she needed a safe place to sleep. She found a village hidden deep within the forest populated by forest elves. They took her in and let her stay with them."

"And then what happened?" She scooted to a sitting position.

"I'll tell you. Once upon a time, there was a lovely young woman named Snow White..."

# Chapter 1

Deep in the Wyldwood Forest of the Enchanted Woodlands, the first twitter of a morning bird sang out. A blue bird, by the sound of it. Its happy song echoed through the woodlands. A breeze rustled the treetops and whispered past, tickling her skin and lifting her hair. The first stirrings of the woodland creatures were beginning. And deep in the forest, a brook babbled its way over rocks and logs winding its way northeast to spill into Dunmeade Bay.

Snow White sensed all of this as she sat cross-legged, her hands on her knees, on the moss-covered ground, her back against the ancient oak tree, her eyes closed. She was attuned to the forest and its magical creatures around her. The energy thrummed through her, singing through her veins. It was peaceful and joyful all at once.

The flapping of delicate wings came close to her face and she remained still. A smile wanted to erupt, but she managed to keep it at bay as the fluttering buzzed her once again. Another buzz.

This time, Snow cracked open an eye. She caught a glimpse of the gossamer wings fluttering so fast, it was an iridescent blur. The creature was so quick, it was a tiny body zipping back and forth.

In the heart of our enchanted glade so bright, Snow White, a vision in the morning's light.

The high-pitched voice lilted through her mind. She smiled and opened her eyes all the way to see the forest sprite dancing in front of her vision. She held up her hand, palm flat, and the tiny thing landed. Her bare feet were light as she alighted.

"Good morning, Annilen," Snow said.

The forest sprite was one of her first friends when she came to the Wyldwood. She was barely six inches tall, with long, flowing golden hair, bright blue eyes and coppery skin that sparkled in the morning sun. She had a tiny, pert nose, high cheekbones, wide lips. Her wings, both upper and lower, were delicate, catching all the colors of the rainbow. Her outfit was formfitting, the leaf skirt hitting her above the knees. She was barefoot, as most sprites were.

"Good morning, my lady." She gave a low curtsy in the palm of her hand.

Snow stretched out her long legs. After sitting cross-legged for so long, they had started to cramp. She leaned against the old oak, who gave a bit of a resigned sigh. She craned her neck to look up at the branches and leaves far overhead.

"Sorry, old friend, but I have to rest my back."

As you wish, my lady, the oak replied. The oak was named Faradill. He stood in this forest for over a hundred years, but even at that age he was still one of the youngest trees.

In her palm, Annilen bounced back and forth from one foot to the other. "Snow, are we going to walk today?"

"Don't we walk every day?" she asked, in return.

"It's just that...with the Springtide festival..."

"Oh, the bloody moon! I forgot!"

Snow leapt to her feet so quickly, it jarred Annilen. She fluttered away, hovering near her head. Before she dashed off, she turned to Faradill and placed her palm flat on the trunk.

"Bless this tree with life and roots that go deep," she whispered, reciting the blessing to the tree for keeping her safe.

"As in your shade we find solace and keep," Annilen added.

Faradill's voice rumbled, deep and low, through her mind. So, mote it be.

And then Snow was off, picking up her skirts and hurrying through the forest back to her home. She leapt over fallen logs. She knew this forest better than anyone. Knew where the trail was, even though most travelers would not. Knew where she would find the yarrow root or bloodroot or mandrake or the monkeyflower. Annilen kept pace with her, fluttering close to her head.

"You don't...have to...come with me," Snow panted as her breath see-sawed in and out of her.

"I do," Annilen said, as she flew next to her. Flying gave her an advantage. Flying meant she was never out of breath.

Snow was a bit envious of that. When she realized what the sprite said, she halted. Her chest rose and fell with every heaving breath.

"Wait," Snow said. "Did Elator send you?"

Elator was her woodland elf father, though that wasn't the right term. He was more of a father figure, a protector, and the one who had raised her from the time she was eight and exiled from her own castle. Yirrie was his wife who was giddy at the prospect of raising a human child. They took her in without question, gave her a home, loved her, raised her, and treated her as though she were one of their own.

Though she wasn't. The only thing she had left of her royal life was a necklace she wore day and night. It was a pendant with the royal symbol of the Mystic Vale—a rose and crown.

Annilen fluttered around her head in an agitated state. "Not exactly."

Snow put her hands on her hips, tipping her head to one side in question. "Then who did?"

When the sprite failed to answer, Snow held out her hand in an invitation for her to land. Heaving a sigh, Annilen settled in her palm, her wings coming to rest behind her and drooping.

"It was Yirrie."

Snow frowned. That wasn't good. "Because...?"

"Because you forgot about your fitting."

Snow rolled her eyes to the heavens. She had forgotten about that, too. "Hurry on ahead. Tell her I'm on my way and will be there soon."

Annilen dipped a little curtsy. "Yes, my lady."

Now that Annilen was headed to Yirrie with her message, she took her time walking back to the village.

She hadn't meant to spend so much time in the forest that morning, but she was drawn to it. Unable to sleep, with the moon bright and beckoning, Snow left her bed, climbed out the window and made her way into the forest. The earth, the wind, the sky all called to her. Even the nocturnal animals sensed her and spoke to her as she walked through the bracken. She was safe here, she knew. Not even Seraphina's evil could reach here.

And so, she found her way to the foot of Faradill, perched on the forest floor, and attuned herself to the world around her. When the sun started to peek over the horizon, she should have headed home. But the world around her called to her, calmed her, made her feel as though she were a part of it. She had to be a part of it. And she was unable to stop her feet from carrying her farther and farther away from the elven village.

The Wyldwood Forest was populated with all sorts of mystical and magical creatures. From the forest sprites, to the tiny pixies that made their beds within the confines of flower petals, to the wisps that were nothing more than dances of light in the night, to even the wild endangered unicorns. They greeted her as she made her way.

Stepping over a fallen log, a mournful sound echoed through the trees. She halted, her gaze narrowing as she tried to pinpoint where it came from. It sounded again and then a shout which sounded like a man's voice.

Clutching her skirts in her hands, she ran toward the sound and opened her senses. Something was in trouble, the baleful sound vibrating through her and telling her she was headed in the right direction.

Through the trees, she saw the glint of morning sun off the spiral horn of a unicorn. Around the unicorn's neck, a rope yanked by a tall, brute of a man. The unicorn's eyes rolled back as it jerked its head, stomping its hooves and trying to pull away.

Snow stopped, releasing her skirts. She clenched her fists at her sides and closed her eyes, connecting to the nature around her, asking the plants for help.

A thick ivy unwound itself from the forest floor and moved toward the man, wrapping around his legs. Another vine glided down from the trees to slide around his upper torso. And a snake slithered from the underbrush to hiss at him.

He cried out, dropping the rope, his eyes wide with fear as he looked down at his bindings. Snow opened her eyes, satisfied with her handiwork. She took slow methodical steps toward the man who had a thick beard, a wide feral face, dressed as a hunter. She knew these types. Sometimes, they would wander into the forest looking to hunt the creatures that inhabited it. He saw her at last, his terrified gaze landing on her.

"Help me!" he said.

"And why should I do that?" She reached the unicorn and slipped off the rope from around its neck. The horse nuzzled her in thanks.

*He was going to steal my horn*, the lilting voice said in her mind.

*And he was going to kill you for it*, she said. She cut a glance back to the man.

"You are a hunter, aren't you?"

He didn't answer as he struggled against the vines and the ivy, trying to free himself while keeping a watchful eye on the snake at his feet. The snake that had grown in size and lifted its head up to meet his gaze. He didn't have to answer because she already knew.

"P-please, miss. Will you help me?"

*What do you think? Shall I release him?* she asked.

Its gaze landed on the man, still struggling. *If he promises to never return, then yes.*

She looked back to the hunter, brushing a hand down the animal's neck. The hair was soft under her palm. "Will you promise to leave this forest and never return?"

"Y-yes! I promise!"

She continued to brush the animal, trying to sense if the man told the truth or if he lied to escape his bonds.

"Can I trust your word?" Snow asked.

"Yes! You have my word."

She gave a quick nod. "Very well."

With a twitch of her hand, she released him. The vines and ivy retreated. The snake returned to its normal size and slithered away.

"Now, be gone and warn your fellow hunters this forest is not a hunting ground," she said.

He nodded as he stumbled backward, tripping over a fallen log before turning and running. She stood with the unicorn, listening to his footsteps crashing through the forest as he headed away from them.

"You're safe now," she said.

Thank you, my lady.

The unicorn nuzzled her neck making her giggle. "I must go." She patted its nose in farewell.

It gave one last snort as it trotted away from her through the forest. It wasn't the first time she had run off hunters. She doubted it would be the last. Those who hunted unicorns, though, were the worst ones. They would do anything for the mystical beast's spiral horn. There were very few of them left in this forest. She felt it was her duty to protect them.

Just like her duty was to be fitted for her Springtide gown. With a sigh, she hurried through the forest to home.

# CHAPTER 2

High in her castle, Seraphina stood on her balcony over-looking the far reaches of the Mystic Vale kingdom. *Her* kingdom.

She had risen through the ranks of court, garnering the eye of the king, and schemed her way into his arms. From there, it was easy to use her magical abilities to convince him to marry her.

But his daughter was a problem. Even from her young age, Snow didn't like Seraphina. She tried on numerous occasions to come between her and the king.

The queen did what she had to do to dispose of the king by using her magic. Knowing the girl was too young to rule yet, her plan was to step in as regent and then make sure Snow would never ascend the throne. However, Seraphina discovered the king made sure the rule of the Mystic Vale would pass to Snow White upon his death.

Seraphina did not want to hand over rule to an eight-year-old child. Why should she? In a document outlining the king's final wishes, there was no mention of a regent or a steward. It merely stated Snow would ascend the throne and rule.

Naturally, there was much talk among the high council that there should be a steward. None of those on the council deemed her worthy. They voted to uphold the king's final wishes, effectively casting her aside and ending her rule. So, they thought.

As the months passed, Snow prepared for her coronation. Seraphina realized there was one truth above all—the people loved her and would never want to see anyone else ruling the kingdom or sitting on the throne. This did not sit well with the queen who was now a widower.

She did what she had to and invited the girl for a walk in the castle gardens under the guise of getting to know her better. When they arrived, she told Snow White all those who lived within the keep hated her and wanted her gone. She used a bit of dark magic to make the girl believe and then cast her out into the night, banishing her forever from the castle.

The girl, crying with despair, fled. The queen had never seen her again. Her hope was that the girl fled into the dangerous Wyldwood Forest and it would swallow her whole.

When she banished Snow White, most of the castle staff left. So be it. She didn't need them if they were not loyal.

Heaving a sigh, she shoved away those memories. After all, it had been ten years since the girl's disappearance. Surely, she was dead by now.

As she stood looking at the land gripping the handrail, her mind plotted. There were three other kingdoms in the Enchanted

Woodlands. Three kingdoms that could be under her rule and only her rule. Three kingdoms she needed to bend the knee to her.

Feywood was to the south and ruled by King Alfred. He had a large army and so he would be difficult to defeat. He would be a formidable foe. Further south, Ellewood. A smaller kingdom ruled by a smaller man, King Egbert, who was as flamboyant and ridiculous as his name. To the east, Hollow Glen, ruled by yet another king by the name of Rufus.

Kings. Alfred, Egbert, Rufus.

She scoffed.

Useless men. All of them.

Why should the kingdoms be ruled by men, when she was as worthy? She had a crown *and* magic.

Regret sifted through her now as she thought of Snow White. She should have used the same destroyer spell on her but something held her back. Instead, she banished her from the kingdom.

Turning from the balcony, she walked across her immense chamber to the secret door hidden behind a tapestry. She shoved it aside and pressed the stone which was a lever. Stone scraped against stone as the door slid open for her.

Once inside, she whispered an illumination spell, lighting the two torches on either side of the Magic Mirror. A mirror that was full of darkness and shadow. A mirror that held secrets and dark magic. She consulted it from time to time to give her guidance and advice.

It was one of three on the entire continent, though the one Malvina possessed, the Dark Mirror, was destroyed. Pity. With its destruction, the three were no longer connected. Only the Magic Mirror and the Enchanted Mirror remained.

The oval mirror in a silver frame was large enough to fill the whole wall. She paused a moment, admiring her reflection. Her black hair was over one shoulder. Onyx eyes peered back at her out of her youthful face that belied her true age. She raised taxes on the land more than once to maintain her extravagant taste for high fashion that included fairy silks from the Eternal Court and velvet from Rothbridge on the other side of the continent.

"Magic Mirror, in your silver sheen, who's the one with dreams so keen? In this vast world where hopes do roam, tell me, mirror, who calls it home?"

The mirror came to life, the visage appearing as nothing but a featureless face. "It's you, my queen, who holds no fear."

She smiled, well pleased with the mirror's response. "Tell me, mirror, who is the one to control all the land?"

A pause, then, "You, my queen."

She smoothed a hand over her shiny hair. "Tell me, mirror, who is the fairest in all the land?"

She asked this question every now and then to make sure she still reigned supreme. That no man would be able to resist her charms when she marched across the land to take down other kings and kingdoms.

The mirror said, "With dreams that sparkle and passions that enthrall, in your heart, you're the fairest one of all."

That response gave her pause as she stared at her wavering reflection and the face in the mirror that gave her the answers she sought. But this answer was not the one she wanted to hear.

"In my heart?" That phrase sent a cold chill through her. "Is there another? Tell me, mirror."

It was silent for a long moment, and then, "It is a fair maid I see. Lips red as the rose. Hair black as ebony. Skin white as snow."

She gasped, pressing cold fingers against her lips. "Snow White. She was supposed to die in the forest. The girl still lives?"

"She still lives, my queen. Deep in the forest she has made a home, where the elves have allowed her to roam."

"The *elves*?'"

The elves were a reclusive sort. But what she knew of them was they inhabited the Wyldwood Forest. She sent a hunter there to bring back the horn of a unicorn. She needed it for a particular spell. One that would help her conquer the remaining kingdoms in the Enchanted Woodlands.

"Yes, my queen. She lives among them and follows their ways. She's learned their magic in the moonlit forest where enchantment plays."

Fury rose through her breast in a burning sensation. It was not the news Seraphina wanted to hear. She shoved away all thoughts of conquering the rest of the realm. Now, the only thought she had was of destroying Snow White, for while the princess lived, she was a threat to her and her throne.

"Thank you, mirror." Her voice was but a whisper.

She turned from the room, closing the secret door behind her once more and returned to the balcony in her chamber. Once there, her hands gripped the handrail as she glared with deep regret and fury at the treetops in the distance. Somewhere out there the princess dwelled.

Seraphina had been a fool to think she would perish deep with the forest. Perhaps it was time to conjure a spell for the elves in the Wyldwood Forest. A spell that would, ultimately, reveal the princess's location. One thing she knew for certain, Snow White could not be allowed to live.

Snow White must die.

As Snow approached her woodland village, she saw the preparation for the upcoming Springtide Festival, the celebration of the vernal equinox, was already underway. When she slipped out early that morning, no one was stirring in the village. Now, several villagers hung cascading colorful string lights going up on the lowest tree branches. Others wrapped the base of the trees in lights to match.

Long tables covered in white tablecloths for feasting were placed under the trees. Down the length of the table were clusters of candles in three different sizes. In between the candles were square vases with fresh cut flowers of the season.

The festival was held every year to celebrate not only the coming spring, but also the romantic pursuits of the young elven men and women. When the seven-day festival was over, there were always couples announcing their intentions to marry.

As she approached the village entrance, a couple of the men hoisted a large arbor into place under the strict supervision of one of the women Elders. Her long silver hair hung in waves over her shoulders. Her gown was also silver trimmed in white fur. Her sharp blue eyes took in every detail. When she saw Snow, she gave a broad smile and a wave.

"Snow, Yirrie is looking for you," she called. "Best hurry along, dear."

She gave a nod, then picked up the hem of her skirt off the ground and hurried through the bustling village. A pang of guilt swept through her as she realized she was late for her solstice gown fitting. Yirrie would not be very happy with her for slipping out before dawn. So, she hurried, waving and smiling to the few who greeted her along her way. Not everyone in the village accepted Snow's presence.

At last, she reached her woodland home and burst through the front door.

"Yirrie?" she called.

Yirrie, who raised her since she was eight years old, was the closest thing to a mother she had. Her own mother had passed away when she was small. She had no memory of her.

"Ah, there you are. Where have you been? Why is there dirt on your face?" Yirrie emerged from her bedroom looking frazzled.

"Did Annilen tell you I was on my way?"

Yirrie was tall and elegant and carried herself with aplomb, something Snow had always wanted to emulate. Her brown hair was long and straight and always had two plaits on either side of her head showing off her pointed elven ears. Her eyes were a mystifying shade of copper with gold flecks that gave a charmed look about her. She had high cheekbones, a pointed chin with a cleft, dusty pink lips, and was quite possibly one of the most beautiful elven women in the village.

Ignoring her question, she huffed out a breath at Snow's appearance and shook her head. "You've been deep in the forest again, haven't you?"

"I—"

"And yes, Annilen told me. Come now. The dressmaker is waiting."

She grasped Snow's elbow in a firm grip and led her through the house to the bedroom where Yirrie had emerged. The dressmaker was an elderly woman and, by elf age, that meant she was more than two hundred years old. No one was quite sure how old Zaliya was, after all, but she had been the dressmaker in the village for decades. She knelt at the base of a gown on a dress form, pins in her mouth, as she pinned up the hem of Yirrie's gown.

"She's here, mistress," Yirrie announced.

"Ah," she said around the pins on her mouth. She waved Snow forward, then removed the pins. "Where is the gown?"

"Here, mistress."

Yirrie had somehow disappeared into the other room and quickly retrieved Snow's solstice gown for her final fitting. The shiny blue and silver material was draped across her arms. She shoved it at Snow.

"Get changed quickly."

Snow took it and disappeared into what served as the dressing room. She pulled off her day dress and shimmied into the gown, the smooth fabric hugging all her curves. The sleeves were a bit too long and the hem dragged the floor but that was why the dressmaker was here. Snow was also concerned about the plunging neckline that showed a significant amount of cleavage and intended to bring that up during the fitting.

When she emerged from the dressing room, both Yirrie and Zaliya gasped with delight and then smiled.

"Such a lovely vision," Zaliya said on a sigh.

Yirrie clasped her hands together, a wistful smile on her face. "Snow, you look beautiful."

"I'm not sure about the neckline—" she started.

"It's perfect, dear. Now stand still and let me pin the hem," Zaliya said as she dropped to her knees. The pins were back in her mouth as she scooted around Snow.

"But, it's too—" Snow tried again.

"What's wrong with it?" Yirrie moved to stand in front of her, looking her over with a critical eye. "It's the new fashion for all the maidens."

"Ye will be sure to catch the eye of one of the young men," Zaliya added helpfully.

Something shifted inside Snow at those words. She wasn't sure that's what she wanted. While she was a member of the village for the last ten years, she wasn't exactly looking for a husband. Though she knew that most of the young maidens in the village *would* be doing just that. The Springtide Festival was all about finding one's soul mate, dancing and singing around the bonfires, sipping honeywine, and feasting until one could no longer feast. The banquet hosted a twenty-course meal that included several roasted meats, vegetables, different kinds of breads, all sorts of delectable desserts, and dancing and singing from the moment the sun set to the moment the sun rose.

Suddenly, a sense of exhaustion pressed through Snow as she thought of the coming evening. Her shoulders slumped a little.

"Snow, do stand up straight," Yirrie said when she noticed. She pressed a hand into her back between her shoulder blades to force her back straight.

Once Zaliya was finished with the hem, she rose, her knees creaking as she did. Then she went to work on pinning up the end of the sleeves so they would fit her properly.

"Is there nothing you can do about the neckline?" Snow asked.

Zaliya stopped what she was doing to give her an incredulous look. "What's wrong with it?"

"It's just…" Snow made a gesture with her free hand up and down. "Too…"

"It's fine, dear," Yirrie said. "This gown will turn all the heads."

She sounded so happy about that it was hard for Snow to argue. She had to admit it was a lovely gown. Blue with shimmering silver whorls that twisted and turned up and down the bodice and the skirt. For a moment, the thought it made her feel like a princess skittered through her mind. Then she quickly pushed that away. She was no longer a princess. She had lost her kingdom years ago.

"It's just that it feels a bit plunging," Snow tried again.

Zaliya finished with her second sleeve, all the pins removed from her mouth now. "It's perfect, dear. Now if you'll let me have the gown, I'll have it finished and back before you know it. Be careful of all the pins."

Nodding, Snow returned to the dressing room and slipped out of the gown and back into her day dress with the dirt smudged along the skirt. In her mother's room, she handed off the dress and wondered when she could make her escape back into nature.

Zaliya took the gown with a nod and told Yirrie she would return in a few hours with both gowns—which meant her mother already had her final fitting.

"Now that you're back, I need your help in the kitchen."

Yirrie had other plans for her. Snow should have realized solstice day was a busy one. She wouldn't likely get another chance to visit the forest until tomorrow. Sighing, she gave a nod and followed her.

# CHAPTER 3

Yirrie was known for her breads. Every year, she made more than a dozen loaves of different kinds—from acorn bread to oat cakes to their traditional elven bread. She was also known for her mini vegetable pies. Over the years, she'd taught Snow how to bake them.

It wasn't the only thing her elven family taught her, though. Even at the age of eight, Snow had the ability to connect to nature around her. It was the reason she managed to survive that first night alone. She had conjured a bed out of leaves and vines and conversed with the local wildlife, asking them to keep her safe. At the time, she didn't know about the sprites who made the forest their home or even the elves who dwelled deep in their tree village.

By the second night, she made her way deeper into the forest. She'd made friends with a squirrel and an owl who followed her on her trek through the trees. By nightfall, exhausted and hungry, she made another bed at the foot of a tree. Faradill.

The next morning, Yirrie found her. To this day, she wondered if the ancient tree had something to do with that. He had never told her, but it seemed fitting that he would call to the elves and beseech them on her behalf.

Yirrie and Elator took her in. And though she already had elemental magic, they taught her how to hone and use it. Yirrie herself was connected to the earth. She could grow anything from the tiniest seed. That's why her vegetables pies were so unforgettable.

All of this crossed Snow's mind as she kneaded the bread, then placed it in a bowl to rise. Why she remembered it now, she didn't know. It was almost as though she sensed something. Perhaps it was merely a feeling deep in the pit of her gut. A feeling that told her everything was about to change. That her peaceful existence would be no more.

It didn't help the Springtide Festival loomed ahead of her. Most of the elves accepted her as one of their own. There were a few who didn't. Her stomach was a mess of butterflies at the thought of a romantic pursuit. She was content to live with Yirrie and Elator for these last ten years. But now, at eighteen, the expectation was that she was to find a mate. It was, after all, the elven custom.

"Snow, dear, are you all right?"

Yirrie's question snapped her out of her thoughts. She realized she still held a ball of dough in her hands and had yet to knead it.

"Oh. Yes. I'm fine."

Yirrie glanced at her askance as she slipped the dough from her hands. "You look tired. You spent most of the night in the forest, didn't you?"

Guilt washed over her as she wiped her hands on a blue and white kitchen towel. She pressed her lips together trying to decide how to answer.

"You don't have to answer. I know the truth of it." She gave her a surreptitious wink.

Snow blew out a breath. "I was. I'm sorry, Yirrie. The moon was so bright and full and it was hard to resist. It was a perfect evening. The forest was quiet except for a few of the nocturnal creatures."

"I think you're a bit nocturnal yourself," Yirrie said, good-naturedly. She placed the dough on the counter and started to knead it. "Are you sure it's safe for you out there?"

When Yirrie and Elator found her at the foot of Faradill, she had told them she'd run away from home. That she was no longer wanted by her family. She had never told them she came from the castle and was, in fact, the princess and heir to the Mystic Vale throne. Yirrie often worried her family would eventually come looking for her and force her to return with them.

But Snow knew differently. Seraphina wasn't interested in her return since she was ruling the kingdom now. She wouldn't send anyone to come looking for her, so she felt safe deep within the forest. And Snow had no interest in returning to dethrone her stepmother.

Perhaps her need to visit the forest last night stemmed from the knowledge it was the anniversary of her father's death. She found solace in the night sounds around her.

"It's perfectly safe," she answered at last.

Yirrie's pinched expression, though, said she still worried about her.

"Besides," Snow continued, "I have all the forest to protect me." She gave her a reassuring smile. "Faradill and Annilen and all the others."

Yirrie finished kneading the bread and put it in a bowl next to the others to rise. Then she turned to the oven and pulled out her tray of a dozen mini pies. The delectable smell of vegetable pie permeated the small kitchen making Snow's stomach grumble. Her mother placed the tray of pies on the counter and then turned to her, taking her by the shoulders and looking deep into her eyes.

"I do worry," she said.

"I know, but there's nothing to worry about." Even as she said it, that niggling sensation shifted through her. She shoved it away almost as quickly as it appeared. "I promise."

Her surrogate mother patted her cheek and gave her a small smile. "If you're certain."

A quick knock sounded on the door. Yirrie used the same kitchen towel to wipe her hands.

"That must be Zaliya with our gowns."

She bustled to the door, Snow right behind her. When she pulled it open, there was the dressmaker on the other side holding the two gowns draped across her arms.

"All finished!" the woman announced, her face beaming. She handed the gowns to Yirrie. "It's some of my best work, if I do say so myself." Then she gave a chuckle.

"The gowns are perfect," Yirrie said. She handed them off to Snow.

"Snow will be one of the loveliest maidens at the festival." Then she waved and was off.

Snow flushed hot. The last thing she wanted was to be one of the loveliest maidens at the festival. The other elven girls were not so impressed with her elemental magic or the fact she was actually human. She hadn't many friends. And it was why she chose to spend her time among the forest sprites and creatures rather than forge friendships with them. Perhaps that was another reason why her nerves were suddenly on edge. The first night of the festival was when elven girls would seek out the attentions of the eligible boys.

"Oh, goodness. It's getting late. I best get the rest of the bread in the oven." Yirrie hurried back into the kitchen. "Snow, will you take care of the gowns?"

"Yes, of course."

With slow steps, she headed first to her mother's bedroom and laid out the gown on the bed. Then she went to her own. She draped the gown over the back of her dressing table chair and stared at it, her gut churning. As dread swept through her, she pressed a hand against her stomach.

The front door opened and closed with a bang, then Elator's boisterous voice called out to his wife. He said something that made Yirrie laugh and then chastised him for sneaking one of her pies. His booted footsteps headed toward the bedroom but he paused to stand in her doorway.

Elator was tall and elegant like Yirrie. And like Yirrie, he wore his long brown hair with two plaits on either side of his head. Sometimes, they were pulled back away from his face. His blue luminescent eyes sparkled with life and mirth. He had a big, booming laugh and a voice to match which was sometimes strange coming from him.

"Are you ready for the festival?" he asked.

She dropped a hand and forced a smile, watching him take another bite of the small pie. Crumbs trickled down from his hand to the floor. When Yirrie saw, she would fuss at him as she grabbed the broom.

"I am," she said, though she wasn't sure she believed it.

"You look worried," he said.

Elator was always able to read her emotions, even though she tried her best to keep them off her face and bury them deep down.

"I'm not," she replied.

One dark brow raised in question. Snow puffed out a heated breath.

"All right. I am a little."

"Why?"

"It's just that...the first night of the festival is the night where—" She clamped her mouth shut before she said what she was thinking.

"Where a girl is chosen?" he finished for her.

Her shoulders slumping, she nodded.

"And you're worried about that?" he asked.

"A little."

He gave her a smile. "I don't think there's anything to worry about. You are a lovely vision. Any elven man—"

"That's just it, Elator. I'm not an elf."

That never mattered to Elator or Yirrie, but Snow worried it would matter to others. He popped the rest of the pie in his mouth, brushed the crumbs from his hands, and gave her a thoughtful look as he chewed.

"You're right. You're not. But that doesn't matter to any of us here."

It mattered to her, though. Elator stepped into her room and gave her a peck on the cheek, then granted her a smile. He said nothing more as he left her room and headed to his own to prepare for the festival.

Heaving a sigh, she perched on the edge of her bed and eyed the gown with increasing trepidation. As much as she wanted, she could not avoid the Springtide Festival. She moved to her bedroom door and closed it so she could change. As she paused there in the middle of her room, she eyed the window, longing for escape.

It was not an option. Taking a deep breath, she began to dress.

34

# Chapter 4

Snow stood in front of her full-length mirror and stared at her reflection with dismay.

Her black hair hung loose down to her waist. She'd plaited a length on each side to frame her face in the elven way. Her lips were naturally rose colored and there was color high in her cheeks, due to the heat swarming through her.

And then there was the dress. The neckline that plunged downward toward her navel. The long sleeves. The form fitted bodice. The flared skirt. The silver swirls shimmered with every movement.

She was not the kind of girl who attended fancy balls or festivals looking for romance. She was the kind of girl who snuck out of her bedroom window in the dead of night. She was the kind of girl who spent an evening under the full moon visiting with forest sprites and tiny garden gnomes.

Lifting a hand, she held her right palm flat in front of her and closed her eyes. She imagined a length of vine with tiny pink flowers blooming along it, wrapping around her wrist and climbing its way up the length of her arm to her shoulder. When she opened her eyes, it was there. She smiled.

Then she used the same elemental magic to allow the floral vine to spread from her shoulder, across her bosom to the other side where it wound its way down to her left wrist. The floral vine was the perfect camouflage to hide the daring neckline she so disliked. She opted to leave her pedant on her dressing table for the evening.

A swift knock on her door startled her. Yirrie popped her head in. She started to say something then paused, her mouth forming a round o-shape as she peered at Snow from the doorway.

"What have you done?" she asked.

"Do you like it?" Snow held her arms out and did a slow turn.

"Snow, the vines—"

"Are perfect," she interrupted. The last thing she wanted was for Yirrie to insist she remove them. She plastered on a bright smile.

"But they hide the beauty of the dress." Yirrie pushed the door open wider and stepped in. She reached for Snow, prepared to pluck them away.

Snow batted her hand away and gave her a hard stare. She took a step back out of reach. "I like the vines and the flowers."

Elator popped into the doorway then, a small package in his hands. He peered, uncertainty in his eyes.

"Ah, Snow, you look lovely," he said.

"Elator, the vines are—"

"Perfect." He gave his wife a stern look. She clamped her mouth closed with a snap.

A small victory. Perhaps he had some understanding at how she felt in the revealing gown. Or perhaps he merely wanted to shush his wife's nagging about her appearance. Either way, Snow was grateful and grinned at Elator as he moved past Yirrie. He stepped into the room, holding the box out to her.

"For you," he said.

Snow took it, opened it and gasped when she saw the silver circlet resting on a bed of white satin. The scrollwork was delicate. Elator lifted it and placed it on her head. She turned to look at herself in the mirror and stared with appreciation at the lovely silver band. It dipped to a point on her forehead. For a moment, she belonged. The only difference between her and the others was her rounded ears.

"I love it," she whispered.

"Fit for a princess," he said.

Her heart skipped at that. She realized he was saying it as a thought of affection, but it still sent a shiver through her. He didn't know who she was, nor did she ever want him to know. She cut a glance to the pendant resting on her dressing table. The rose and crown symbol gleamed in the half light.

"Happy Springtide." He kissed her on the cheek, then took Yirrie by the elbow. "Now, come you two. It's time for the festival."

Snow paused a moment longer, giving herself a once over. Satisfied with the vines trailing over her, she smiled. Yirrie picked up a large basket loaded with her freshly baked bread and handed it to Elator. She picked up yet another basket full of her mini vegetable pies. Remnants of her baking frenzy still lingered in the kitchen, leaving it with a heady, earthy scent.

Snow followed them out into the early evening air. Even though winter was giving way to spring, there was still a chill in the air reminding her that though flowers bloomed, the frost could return.

Elves gathered under the twinkling lights of the trees. One of the Elders walked the length of a nearby table lighting every candle as she went. The evening air was redolent with honey beeswax—the scent of the candles—and the scent of fresh cut flowers. Laughter filtered through the village and somewhere in the distance, the sound of a lute followed by the soft lilting voice of an elf in song.

Snow paused at the edge of the table, watching as Elator and Yirrie melded with the growing crowd. Smiles were on their faces as they greeted their neighbors and friends. Yirrie took to placing her mini pies at every place setting until she ran out. Elator placed loaves of her fresh bread on the tables, going down the line until his basket was also empty.

"Hello, Snow."

The voice next to her made her jump and her heart kick into a rapid beat. She pressed her hand against her chest as she looked over to see Ardan standing next to her.

"Apologies. I did not mean to startle you."

"It's all right." She dropped her hand and tried very hard not to look at him.

Ardan was handsome. His pale blue eyes twinkled with starlight. His white hair was cropped in short layers that floated around his head, barely brushing the collar of his pale blue tunic with silver buttons. She didn't want to notice his perfect white pants tucked neatly into his shiny black boots. Nor did she want to notice how close he stood to her or how pleasant he smelled. Like patchouli. Spicy and sweet all rolled into one.

He clasped his hands in front of him and remained next to her in congenial silence. Still, it made her uncomfortable to have him standing so near. She shifted from one foot to the other, scanning the crowd and wondering when it was appropriate to make her escape.

"You look lovely this evening." He sounded unsure.

She cut him a glance. "Do I?"

Color rose in his pale cheeks. "You do."

His gaze wondered over her, pausing on the tiny flowers she'd conjured on the vines. He reached for one on her shoulder, his finger grazing the delicate petals. Her eyes met his, making her stomach flutter. All the surrounding noise dissipated. For a blissful moment it was only her and Ardan. And for that moment, she was lost in the depth of his dreamy eyes.

"Would you care to dance with me later?" he asked.

Oh, dear. She didn't know how to answer that without sounding rude. Yes, she most definitely wanted to dance with him later. But common sense told her to refuse.

"I—"

"There you are!"

The shrill voice rose, breaking into their intimate moment and shattering whatever magic was forming between them. It was his sister, Valda, charging toward them. Her gown was the same blue as his tunic with a high neck collar. She had the same pale blue eyes as he did and the same white hair, though hers was much longer and braided in an elaborate braid that crisscrossed the back of her head and then hung down in one long plait down her back. Disdain crossed her face as she glanced at Snow and then took her brother by the hand.

"*Emya* is looking for you." *Emya* was the elvish word for *mother*.

He gave her a sheepish glance as she led him away. "Bye, Snow."

So much for her dance with Ardan. She sighed. It was the way things were and she was used to it.

She watched as they melted into the crowd, talking and laughing with others their same age. They never invited Snow to join in. Valda glanced her way as she said something to the others, then they laughed. One of the girls hooked her arm with Ardan's. He gave her a surreptitious glance full apology.

The Elders called for them to gather at the tables. It was time to feast. Snow took her place between Elator and Yirrie in the middle.

Ardan, his sister, and a few of the others took seats further down on the opposite side. Though they were down the length of the table, Snow still caught his eye every now and then. The girl who had hooked her arm in his sat next to him, scooting close and beaming with a bright smile. At least she had Yirrie and Elator to keep her company.

One of the Elders, a woman by the name of Tasnia, stood at the head of the table, her arms outstretched and palms up as she delivered the Springtide blessing.

"Greetings, friends and fellow kin. You are all welcome here on the first night of our Springtide Festival. Let us break bread together and feast and dance and sing under the glow of the silvery moon. For tonight, we revel in the warmth of the coming days. Huzzah!"

"Huzzah!" everyone said in unison.

The feast began. The elderberry wine flowed. The first course was served—a succulent meat in a cream sauce. Snow tore off a piece of Yirrie's crusty bread and spread it with a healthy dollop of butter. Though she tried not to listen, she attuned her ears to the laughter down the length of the table.

All around her, there was chatter and laughter and a sense of happiness as they looked forward to the coming spring. Though the treetops were too thick to see through, she lifted her gaze skyward hoping to catch a glimpse of the full moon. It had been big and beautiful the night before and she wondered if it was the same for this night.

The second course made its way around. This time a hearty vegetable soup to go with Yirrie's vegetable pies. The lilting sound of a harp drifted on the breeze and moments later, their voices were lifted into an elven blessing that was meant to be sung. Though she understood their elvish language and could speak it just as well, she remained silent. After the third course, there would be music and dancing until the sun broke the horizon. Already she was weary of it all.

Something strange began to happen. The elven voices around her faded into nothing more than a muffled hum. Her senses came alive, attuning to nature around her. Her back stiffened and she straightened as she glanced around the area, but no one else seemed to sense it. In the distance, she heard a faint buzzing sound.

She shot to her feet so suddenly, the dishes on the table rattled. Her hands clenched into fists at her sides as she peered into the darkness and tried to make sense of what she was hearing.

Annilen's voice suddenly burst into her mind with one word. *Snow!*

"Snow, what is it?" Yirrie asked.

She didn't answer. She spun from the table, hurrying the length of it to the end. The buzzing grew louder. Her heart rammed hard as she gathered the length of her skirt. At the edge of the trees, she broke into a run. She thought she heard Yirrie calling her name but she ignored her and dove into the darkness of the forest, leaving the light and the laughter behind.

The path she took was the one she had taken to return home that morning. As she leapt over the log, something caught her skirt. She stumbled forward, almost tumbling to the ground but managed to keep her footing. She tugged her skirt free but not without it ripping. She only paused a moment and decided to deal with that—and Yirrie—later.

The sounds of the festival faded as the space expanded behind her. All around her, the forest came alive with a humming that thrummed through her veins. She halted suddenly, her heart beating wildly as she stood there surrounded by trees and nocturnal creatures. Sweat beaded her forehead and dampened the back of her neck. There was an underlying sense of fear vibrating there.

But fear of what?

She slowly turned, narrowing her eyes and peering into the shadows. She saw nothing. But that faint buzzing was still there.

*I know you're out there. I am coming for you.*

The voice burst through her mind with such a force she stumbled back a step. It was a warning. A cold chill skittered through her. But she didn't have a chance to process what it meant. A frantic flutter of wings erupted near her face.

"Snow!" Annilen said her name on a breath.

"What is it? What's wrong?" She held up her hand so the tiny sprite could land.

"Do you sense the buzzing?"

"Yes," Snow said.

"It's coming..." she whispered.

"What is it?" Snow asked.

Before she could answer, Elator's voice rang out. "Snow?"

"Annilen, what is it?" she demanded.

"Dark magic," she whispered. And then she was gone in a flutter of wings.

"Snow, where are you?" Elator called.

He had followed her. She flushed hot as she glanced down at her torn skirt. The faint buzzing was still in the air. Dark magic, she said. But she didn't sense magic. She forced her feet to turn and head back to the festival, dreading facing Yirrie when she discovered the torn dress. Mostly she dreaded seeing the disappointment in her eyes.

She hadn't made it far into the forest. Elator was standing on the edge, his hands on his hips. And though his face was shadowed, she knew he must have a look of disdain in his face. As she neared, the lights dangling from the treetops gave enough illumination for her to see the worry creasing his features.

"What happened?" he asked as she approached.

She had no explanation. "I thought I sensed something. I—"

His brows drew together in question and concern. He would never understand what she sensed or that she heard a voice in her head threatening to find her. It was a woman's voice. That much she knew. But whose?

"It's nothing." She plastered on a bright smile. "Let's go back to the party."

Then she hooked her arm around his. They started back into the village. The cursory glances and the stares from the others did not escape her notice. As they reached their table, Ardan stared at her while his sister giggled, clearly amused at her disheveled appearance. Yirrie's expression told her everything the woman thought about her in that moment—disappointed with an underlying hint of anger. Snow hoped she would not see the torn skirt until much later.

They rounded the end of the table, heading back to their seats, when that buzzing sound increased. Snow jerked her arm out of Elator's and spun around, looking for that sound. But no one else seemed to hear it. She sucked in a sharp breath, her chest heaving and the vines along her torso shuddering. Somehow, they had managed to remain intact during her race through the forest.

"Snow?" Elator asked.

"Don't you hear it?" she asked, turning to meet his gaze.

"Hear what?" He shook his head.

Yirrie, who had clearly had enough of her nonsense, joined them. "Snow, whatever you're playing at must stop."

"I'm not playing at anything."

The sound was so loud now, she clapped her hands over her ears and stumbled backward away from them both. She had garnered the attention of Tasnia at the head of the table. The woman slowly rose to her feet, a strange expression on her face. She pinned Snow with her fierce gaze.

*I am coming for you.*

That voice again. She shook her head, continuing to step backward away from the table.

"I shouldn't be here," she whispered, though it was difficult for her to hear herself over the buzzing.

Yirrie's face had gone pale. Elator pressed his lips together in a thin line. The girls continued to laugh at her. Ardan remained seated staring at her with pity. That was the thing that bothered her the most—that he pitied her.

Suddenly, the world around her fell away. Everyone around her was frozen in time like a statue. All that remained was the horrible buzzing sound.

She saw it then. The black mist seeped through the trees and spilled into their cozy festival. It came from all directions, blotting out the light, the buzzing now louder than ever.

The black mist formed into a silhouette which was nothing more than an opaque shadowy outline. Snow dropped her hands to her sides, her heart in her throat, as she scurried around the end of the table.

A misty hand reached for her.

# CHAPTER 5

L ong wispy tendrils wrapped around her throat, squeezing the breath out of her. She gasped as she clawed at the spectral fingers. Again, she heard that voice in her head.

*I am coming for you.*

Her eyes started to water. She tried to suck in a breath but it was useless. Whatever held her was not letting go until it crushed the life out of her.

Light glinted off a blade as it slashed downward through the black mist. A hissing sound and then it released and retreated back into the shadows, disappearing. The buzzing stopped. Snow crumpled to the ground in heap. She sucked in long breaths, forcing air back into her lungs. A pair of shiny black boots stood next to her. She tilted her head back and looked up to see Ardan standing next to her, his sharp gaze on the trees around them.

"Snow!"

It was Yirrie who crouched next to her. "Are you all right? What happened?"

She tried to answer but it was Ardan who spoke.

"There was a black mist."

As Yirrie helped her to her feet, Snow saw Arden held a sharp dagger in his hand. A dagger that had likely saved her life. A dagger with the most unusual shimmering blade. Tasnia moved into their circle of light, concern pinching her aged face.

"You saw this black mist?" she asked.

"I did." Ardan turned to Snow then. "It was trying to kill her."

Yirrie gasped and then whimpered, wrapping an arm around her shoulders and pulling her tight. Elator made his way over to them, then.

"Where did it go?" he asked.

"Back into the shadows," Snow said, her voice weak and rough.

"What was it?" Yirrie wanted to know.

"Magic," Snow whispered. "Dark magic."

"Where would dark magic come from?" Elator asked. His gaze was firmly on Tasnia.

The first thought that came to her was that it was Seraphina. As far as Snow knew, though, she didn't know she was still alive and living in the Wyldwood Forest.

Or did she?

How could she have discovered this truth?

And did she use Snow's friend, Annilen, as bait to flush her out of the elven village and find her?

*Annilen?* she asked, sending the thought toward the forest sprite.

There was no answer.

Tasnia's eyes glinted hard as she looked at Snow. "There hasn't been dark magic in these woods in a very long time. These woods are safe."

"Well, they are no longer and the dark magic is back," Elator snapped. "We must do something to protect ourselves."

"To protect Snow," Ardan corrected. "The black mist came for Snow."

She cut him a glance. He had a firm look on his face as though he was certain he knew what he saw. But how did he when all the others were frozen in time?

"Then Snow White must leave this place," Tasnia said.

Snow stiffened, sucking in a sharp breath as she peered at the woman she had known most of her life. Tasnia's hard gaze was on hers and there was something about her stance that told Snow she was not willing to budge. How repulsive it was to see the woman was so willing to throw her out of the village.

"No!" Yirrie said, her voice hard and firm. She squeezed Snow tighter. "I will not allow it."

"She is—" Tasnia began.

"She is part of this village and my daughter," Yirrie insisted.

"And mine," Elator added. "We will not allow you to send her away."

Snow flushed hot at the vehement words from her adoptive parents who were determined to keep her alive and safe within the confines of their village. She knew, as Tasnia did, that she did not belong. She was, after all, human. The pendant with the rose and crown was a stark reminder of that and her true identity.

Tasnia's eyes flickered from Yirrie to Elator, then back to Snow. It was clear the Elder was not enamored with Snow. If it was up to her, Snow would have never been allowed to stay in the village in the first place.

"We, the Elders, will use our magic to protect the village. But only if Snow White promises to remain within its borders. It is the only way to safeguard her and our people."

"She promises," Yirrie said, her tone taut.

A hot flush went over her as Snow shifted from one foot to the other and Yirrie squeezed her tight. There was no way she would make such a promise. The forest called to her. It made her whole again to return night after night and be a part of nature and with all the nocturnal animals that inhabited it.

There was still that hard, unforgiving glint in Tasnia's eyes. Finally, she gave a stiff nod.

"Very well. I will gather the rest of the Elders. We will do what we can to protect our village from more of this...dark magic. For now, I think it best we end the night and return to our homes."

There were grumbles from the other guests, but most of them already slipped away and returned to their homes. Yirrie held tight to Snow as Elator came to her other side. He eyed Ardan who still held the dagger in his hand.

"You can put that away now," Elator said, his voice soft.

Ardan, as if realizing he still held it, sheathed the weapon into its holder attached to his belt, which was concealed by his tunic. Snow met his gaze and gave him a nod of gratitude. He reciprocated her silent appreciation with a small but genuine smile. It made her stomach flutter.

"You saved her?" Elator asked.

"I did," he said.

"How?" Snow demanded. "All the others were frozen in time."

"I was, too, for a moment. But I focused on your vines." He reached a hand out. The tip of his finger brushed down the delicate petals of one of the flowers on her shoulder. "The flowers were shriveling. I realized something was terribly wrong."

She glanced down at the flowers that were, indeed, shriveled all along the vines she had conjured. Their petals were puckered into nothing more than dried up wrinkles.

"How did you break free?" Snow wanted to know.

He shook his head. "I don't know. Only that I was compelled to reach for my dagger. I did the only thing I knew to do. I slashed through the black mist. That's when it released you and disappeared."

Yirrie released Snow long enough to wrap Ardan in a fierce, tight hug. "Thank you, Ardan."

When she released him and stepped back, he gave Snow a weak smile, as though he was not sure what to make of Yirrie's sudden affection.

Valda made an appearance then, taking her brother by the hand. "We're going, Ardan."

As she tugged him away, she flashed Snow a look of displeasure, as though she were unhappy he was speaking to her now. Snow ignored her, though, and kept her attention on Ardan whose focus never left hers as he walked away. A delightful fluttering danced within her chest as her heart skipped a beat.

She immediately squelched that feeling. While Ardan's attention was lovely, she knew the Elders would never allow their courtship.

"I think we should be going, too," Elator said. "The Elders are using their power to protect the village."

Yirrie nodded. She returned to Snow's side, putting an arm around her shoulders as they walked back to their home. She glanced down and noticed the tear in her skirt.

"Oh, Snow. Your gown…"

"It can be repaired, my wife," Elator said, sounding weary.

Snow glanced at him as he rubbed a hand down his face and sighed. She almost laughed. So Elator found his wife just as exhausting as Snow did on some occasions.

"Yes, of course. I'll have Zaliya repair it."

And that was the last they spoke on the short walk back home.

That night, Snow laid in her bed curled on her side peering through the window. Moonlight slashed through the trees, sending blue-white beams to the ground. There was something mystical about it. Something that seemed to call to her.

Unable to sleep, she pushed off the bed covers and rose, placing her bare feet on the plush rug. She perched on the edge of her bed, plotting. She should not be thinking about slipping out into the night, especially after what happened that evening at the festival.

And yet, she could not stop thinking about Annilen. The forest sprite had not responded to any of her calls. She needed to know her friend was all right.

She slipped out of bed and, rather than dressing, pulled on a dressing gown over her nightdress. At the window, she pushed it open and paused, taking in the verdant scents of the evening as they wafted to her. Inhaling, she closed her eyes. As the wind fluttered by, she smelled the nightingale flower blooming somewhere nearby, damp leaves from a recent rain, and the woodsy scent of trees.

Perching on the window ledge, she swung her legs out and, after taking one more deep breath, she hopped out of her window. Her feet landed on the cool grass and then she headed around the end of the house toward the edge of the forest. She needed to find Annilen.

She took her time as she made her way along the path, her feet silent as she placed slow, methodical steps. The path she had come to know as well as anything.

In the clearing, she saw the unicorn again grazing in a pool of moonlight. It lifted its head, the spiral horn luminous in the shimmer of pale light and its white coat gleaming. It peered at her for a long moment and then, deciding she was no threat, went back to grazing.

Snow watched it for another moment, smiling as she watched the peaceful sight of the animal. Then she was off again, heading deeper into the forest. Her senses were open to her surroundings, but she was unable to locate the sprite.

Finally, she came to the foot of Faradill. She placed her hand on the massive trunk, closed her eyes, and said a brief blessing.

*Hello, my friend,* he said in her mind.

*Faradill, where is Annilen?* she asked without preamble.

His reply was cryptic. *She was here. And then she wasn't.*

What did that mean? And where had Annilen gone?

Snow sank to the ground, crossing her legs in front of her. She placed her hands on her knees and waited, leaving her senses open to all that surrounded her. Something nearby rustled the underbrush. It was nothing but a tiny red fox that popped out. Its dark eyes met hers.

*Have you seen Annilen?* she asked the fox.

Its nose twitched. *No, my lady.* And then it was off.

Snow closed her eyes, concentrating on the location of her friend. At last, she sensed the fluttering of wings near her face. A smile crossed her lips as she opened her eyes, relieved to see Annilen dancing on the wind. She held up her palm to allow the sprite to land. When she did, she sank down, drawing her knees up and wrapping her arms around them. Her wings stopped fluttering and dropped behind her.

"You're all right," Snow said. "I was worried."

"Snow, something dreadful happened," the sprite said.

"Tell me. What is it?"

"A darkness crept into the forest," she said. "Unlike anything I have ever seen before. It was...it was looking for you."

Snow knew this already, of course, because the dark mist found her. "I saw it."

"I shouldn't have called to you," she said. "It's what it wanted."

"What was it?" she asked.

But it was Faradill who spoke in her mind. *A Shadow.*

Snow turned her head to glance upward at the massive tree. "A Shadow?"

"Yes," Annilen said on a rough whisper. She quickly got to her feet and glanced around as if worried something or someone heard her.

*A creature of the dark*, Faradill explained.

"Where did it come from?" Snow asked of both Annilen and Faradill.

Annilen shook her head. "All I know is that it appeared sudden-ly. It used whatever power it had to convince me to call to you." She hung her head. "I'm sorry, Snow."

It was as she thought. The Shadow used Annilen as bait to flush Snow out from the village and into the forest. Leaving the safety of the elves' magic and the security of the village was a risk, but one she had to take to make sure her friend was safe.

"It didn't hurt you?" she asked.

The sprite shook her head. "No, my lady." Then her gaze snapped up to Snow's. "Did it hurt you?"

"No," she said. There was no reason to alarm the little sprite about the attack on her. She didn't want the girl to feel guilty for falling under the Shadow's dark magic.

*The darkness has crept back into the forest,* Faradill said. *It will return.*

Chills skittered up her spine. Gooseflesh bloomed along her arms and legs. Though the ancient tree did not say it, she under-stood he meant the darkness would be back for her.

"I should return home," Snow said. "Before I'm missed."

Annilen took flight, her wings moving so fast they were nothing but a colorful blur. Snow climbed to her feet, placed her hand on Faradill's trunk and said her blessing.

*Stay safe, my lady,* the tree said.

Annilen flitted back and forth around her head with a sort of nervous energy. "Can I come with you?"

"You want to return home with me?" Snow asked.

She nodded her tiny head. Snow sensed her nervousness and underlying fear. She was afraid to be in the forest tonight. She understood.

"All right," she said. "But just for tonight."

"Just tonight, my lady," she said with a nod.

Together, they headed back through the forest and into the village. Snow climbed back through the window, allowing the forest sprite to enter behind her before closing it with a snap. Then she settled back into her bed, pulling the blankets up to her chin.

Annilen curled on her side on the pillow next to her, her tiny wings curved around her back and her knees drawn up to her chest. Moments later, she was fast asleep. Smiling, Snow settled under the coverlet, allowing her eyes to drift closed.

# CHAPTER 6

Seraphina stood on her balcony and glared out at the Wyld-wood Forest with dismay, watching the sun rise higher and higher into the azure sky. At this elevation, the wind was cold and whipped through her hair, fluttering the many layers of her gown. She tried, unsuccessfully, to destroy Snow White with her Shadow spell. The only good thing that came of it was finding the girl deep within the forest.

What a fool she'd been to think the girl was dead after all this time. Her deepest hope was when she banished her to the forest years ago was that she would perish. Though she had to admit she was impressed the girl managed to stay alive and find a way to convince the elves to take her in as one of their own.

Even the forest creatures seemed to love Snow. It had taken a great bit of magic to flush out the forest sprite and convince her to call out to the princess. And when she did, she warned Snow of the impending magic. Clearly, she was loyal to her.

Seraphina clenched her hands into fists. There was something else troubling her, though. The elven boy somehow severed the connection of the Shadow to Snow, releasing her from the clutches of death. How did he do it? She had never seen anything that had the power to dissolve a Shadow's connection.

She turned from the balcony and stepped back inside her chamber where a fire burned hot and bright in the hearth, the flames reaching upward so they disappeared within the chimney. She stalked across the room, shoved aside the tapestry and pressed the stone to open the secret door.

"Magic Mirror, in your silver sheen," she began.

The face appeared in the oval.

"Tell me, mirror, what I seek."

"By your command, my queen."

"The Shadow spell did not work," she said. "It was destroyed by an elven boy who used a dagger."

There was a long pause as the face floated within the confines of the mist. Then, it said, "Tell me more about the dagger."

"A shiny blade was all I saw through the Shadow."

There was more silence. "The only blade that can sever the connection of a Shadow is an enchanted one."

"Where would this boy get an enchanted blade?" she asked, more to herself than the mirror.

The mirror responded. "Seek the master blacksmith in the town of Bridgefort, my queen."

"Bridgefort?"

The town was in the Feywood Kingdom and was on the other side of the Wyldwood Forest, which meant she would have to travel through the forest to get there. It was also the home of King Alfred. It would be quite the journey, especially since her home was far north in the Mystic Vale.

Unless she used a portal spell to transport her there. She had used one before when she stole the mirrors from the elves. The mirrors she shared with her soul sisters, Malvina and Gerda.

"There you will find him in his forge," the mirror said.

"Who is this master blacksmith?" she asked.

There was no answer from the mirror as the face faded from view and went dark. That was all the information she was going to get from it. With a huff, she dropped the tapestry back over it.

Just as she did, a rap sounded on her chamber door.

"Come," she called.

Her Captain of the Guard, Erick, pushed open the door and gave a swift bow. "Apologies for the early morning intrusion, my queen, but the hunter has returned from the Wyldwood Forest. He waits for you in the great hall."

"Ah, yes. He has returned with the item I've been waiting for. Lead the way."

She followed him out of her chamber, down the winding staircase to the great hall where the man waited. She sent him to retrieve the horn of a unicorn several days ago and had been waiting not so patiently for his return. She had plans to turn the horn into a deadly magical weapon and had yet to acquire one.

"You will remain," she said to Erick.

He gave a nod and paused inside the great hall, his stance at ease and yet ready to do her bidding should she need it. It was one of the reasons why she liked him so much.

In the great hall, the man's haggard appearance was the first thing she noticed. A shadow of a beard graced his cheeks and chin. Dark circles were under his eyes, as if he had ridden all night to get back to the keep. His clothes were dirty and wrinkled, his boots caked with mud.

"Your majesty." He bowed low when she entered the great hall.

"I trust you have what I sent you to retrieve," she said, skipping the pleasantries.

He shifted from one foot to the other, his hands twisting in front of him.

"You do have it?" she asked.

His face visibly paled. "I went to the Wyldwood as you commanded. I found the unicorn."

"Good. Where is the horn?" She held out her hand, waiting.

"There was a...girl in the forest, your majesty. She..." His voice trailed off.

"A girl?" Her brows drew together as the hairs on the back of her neck prickled with suspicion. She dropped her hand to her side. "What did this girl look like?"

"She had dark hair and red lips and skin the color of moonlight. And she had magic. She used it. She...she..."

When she heard the girl's description, a dark punch of hot fury scalded through her. The hunter's constant stammering infuriated her. "She *what*?"

"Vines wrapped around me and she made me promise to leave and never return to the Wyldwood." His voice wobbled with the last words as he stared at her, hoping for forgiveness and understanding.

He would get none of that from her. She narrowed her gaze, her voice low. "And did you?"

"It was the only way she would release me. I feared for my life. I—"

"You failed me, then," she snapped. "You did not bring the unicorn horn, did you?"

He shook his head. "No, your majesty, I—"

"Take him to the dungeon," she said to Erick, never taking her eyes off the hunter.

The captain stepped forward and grasped the man by the arm.

"Please!" he wailed. "I had no choice."

"You had a choice. Your choice was to kill the girl and bring me the unicorn's horn but you didn't. You are nothing but a coward," Seraphina said. "And you will live out your days in the dungeon."

His piteous wails were heard as her captain dragged him away, leaving her to stand there alone with her rage. The weak hunter allowed the girl to capture him, to force him to give up his hunt for the unicorn.

From the description, she knew the girl was Snow White.

Snow White who protected the unicorn from her hunter deep in the Wyldwood Forest. Who somehow managed to survive after her Shadow attacked her. Who still had the audacity to live in her kingdom even after she exiled her all those long years ago.

She thought of the mirror's command to see the master blacksmith in Bridgefort. If the mirror was sending her there, then perhaps the blacksmith could lead her to the enchanted weapons. But the journey was far too long and would take far too much time. She would definitely need to open a portal.

Returning to her chamber, she slammed the door behind her. The spell book she acquired was still hidden in the bottom of her wardrobe. She went there now, shoved aside shoes and other items, and hefted the massive tome out. She placed it on the edge of her bed.

The book was probably four inches thick. The pages were yellowed with age. On several of the pages, the charmed ink was faded to almost nothing—the sign the spell was nearly used up. Once the ink was gone, the spell was rendered useless.

Using great care, she turned each fragile page until she found the one she was looking for—the portal spell. All she needed to do was draw a circle. The text showed the sigils in which one would need to draw it. Once it was complete and the incantation said, the portal would open to the desired location.

Smiling, she began.

# CHAPTER 7

The first twitter of birds awoke Snow to morning light streaming through her window. When she returned that night, she hadn't drawn the curtains closed. Opening her eyes, she saw Annilen still curled into a tight ball on the pillow next to her. The poor little sprite must have been exhausted from the previous night's excitement.

Snow yawned and stretched and tried hard not to disturb her sleeping friend as she came to a sitting position. It was only then she realized she still wore her dressing gown over her nightdress. She hadn't bothered to remove it when she returned for the night.

As she sat there, drawing up her knees to her chest, she thought of what Faradill told her. That the darkness had crept into the forest and would be back. A cold shiver of fear danced down her spine. Did that mean the darkness would be returning for her?

She didn't know.

There was something else bothering her. The voice in her head that said *I am coming for you.* She recalled that with a sort of trepidation and was unable to shake a sense of foreboding resonating through her. The only thing she knew for certain was the voice sounded female.

A terrifying thought came to her. Was Seraphina the one? Did she know she lived in the forest with the elves?

Annilen stirred next to her with a yawn and a sigh. "Good morrow, my lady."

"Good morrow, my friend," she said. "Did you sleep well?"

"I did." Indeed, the forest sprite looked well rested as she climbed to her feet and walked down the pillow, leaving tiny footprints behind. She hopped down and then craned her neck to look up at Snow. "Thank you for letting me stay with you."

Snow held her hand down to the little sprite. Annilen stepped into her palm, allowing her to bring her to eye level.

"I'm glad you were safe with me," she said. But even as she said it, she chewed her lower lip.

"Something troubles you, my lady?" she asked, sensing her distress.

"It's just that..." She paused, trying to choose her next words. "Faradill said the darkness was here and would be returning. Do you think it's true?"

Annilen cocked her head to one side as she considered. A thoughtful look creased her tiny features. "I don't know, my lady. But Faradill is old and wise."

Which meant Snow should heed his warning. Perhaps she should stay within the confines of the village, safe behind the protective magic of the elves. That went against who she was at her core.

"It has been many years since such a darkness has touched our forest," Annilen said, almost as an afterthought. As though she remembered something.

Snow lifted a brow in question. "What do you mean?"

She tapped her chin with her forefinger, a thoughtful look crossing her features. "There is a legend about a wizard. A dark wizard who lived somewhere in these woods."

"I've heard no such tale," she said.

"It was a long time ago before you came to live with us," Annilen said. "I don't recall the story. All I do remember is that the elves cast him out."

"What happened to him after that?" she asked.

Annilen shrugged. "No one knows." With that, she launched into the air, her wings fluttering behind her. "I must be off, my lady."

"Of course."

Snow slipped out of bed and padded to the window where she opened it. Annilen bid her farewell and fluttered off into the early morning. As she watched the little sprite disappear, Snow wondered about the wizard. Perhaps there was some mention of him in the elven archives. Perhaps she needed to find out what she could about this dark wizard. She didn't know if the shadow creature was connected to him, but she had to find out.

She pulled on a dress and crept to her bedroom door, listening for movement in the cottage. When she heard none, she opened the door. She expected to see Yirrie hard at work baking for tonight's festival. Now was her chance to slip out and go to the elven archives.

As she hurried to the door, though, Yirrie's voice stopped her.

"Where are you going?"

Snow turned to see her standing in her bedroom doorway, her hands fisted on her hips and a look of dismay on her face. There was no sense in lying to her. She'd eventually find out anyway.

"I'm going to the archives."

Yirrie dropped her arms to her side. The dismay was replaced with confusion. "Why?"

"There's something I need to look up," Snow said.

"I need your help with the baking today," Yirrie said, a warning note in her tone.

"I won't be long. I promise." Snow reached for the knob.

"You aren't going to leave the village, are you?" There was a hint of worry in her voice.

Snow froze, her hand on the knob. She didn't dare turn to face her because she feared her expression of guilt would give her away. Yirrie had a sense about things and likely already knew Snow had slipped out last night.

"No. I'm just going to the archives." She kept her voice steady and strong. "I'll be back soon."

Before Yirrie replied, she stepped out into the fresh morning. Closing the door behind her, she hurried across the village to the edge where the archives were housed. It looked small on the outside, but that was merely an optical illusion. Inside, there were rows and rows and rows of books and scrolls documenting the history of the elves in the Wyldwood Forest. They had been here for hundreds of years and every detail about every harvest, seasonal festival, births, deaths, and other events were penned for historical reference.

Snow had only been there once with Elator when she was a small girl. She hadn't been back since. She didn't know if she would be able to access the archives since she wasn't an elf, but she had to try.

When she entered, the bell on the door tinkled to announce her arrival. The entryway was a small, tidy room with nothing more than a desk in the center and a closed door on either side leading to the massive collection.

The Master of Archives was one of the Elders named Harwin. No one was quite sure how old he was. He'd been Master for as long as anyone could remember. The left door opened and he shuffled out, his long silver hair unkempt as though he'd just rolled out of bed. His clothes were wrinkled like he'd slept in them. He had a red mark on one side of his face as though he'd fallen asleep in one of his books. Perhaps he had. He was known for never leaving the archives unless he absolutely had to.

"Ah, Snow," he greeted. "What brings you here?" He stifled a yawn as he hobbled to the desk, leaning his elbows heavily on it and peering at her through pale blue eyes.

"I'm sorry for the early hour, Master," she said. "I didn't mean to wake you."

He stood straight, smoothing a hand over his disheveled hair.

"Did you fall asleep reading?" she asked, and gave him a smile, hoping to win him over.

He looked abashed. "Is it obvious?"

"Not terribly." She grinned. "I have a request. I was hoping you could help me."

He ran a hand over his smooth chin as he considered her. "You can't see the archives."

It was almost as though he'd guessed her request. She tried not to frown. "Because I'm not one of you."

"Well..."

It occurred to her that if anyone knew the story of the dark wizard exiled from the Wyldwood, Master Harwin would. An idea struck her.

"Then if you won't let me in to see the books," she said, "at least answer a question or two for me?" She moved closer to the desk so only the large piece of furniture separated them.

One silvery brow lifted in intrigue. "I heard what happened last night at the festival. Does it have to do with that?"

Of course, Harwin wasn't at the festival. He was too absorbed in his histories and diaries and logbooks to join the festivities. He lost track of time and simply forgot the revelry had begun. Something about that was endearing. She wished she could allow herself to get lost in the magic of the forest and never have to worry about joining in parties that made her feel as though she were an outcast.

Because she was an outcast. As long as she lived with the elves, she would always be an outcast.

"No," she answered. Then, "Well, perhaps. What can you tell me about the dark wizard?"

He stared at her a long, quiet moment. Curiosity faded from his eyes and was replaced with concern.

"Where did you hear about him?"

Not everyone knew Snow had a connection to the forest and the creatures who resided within it. She had to choose her words carefully. "Someone mentioned him to me in passing."

"No one mentions the dark wizard in passing, my dear. Come with me."

He waved her around the desk, then headed for the door on the right. The opposite door from which he'd entered.

She followed him. her heart doing a little excited dance as she stepped through the threshold behind him. When she was inside, he closed the door behind her.

She was in a large living room with well-worn furniture—a sofa, two chairs, a low table between them. A thick rug covered the hardwood floors. On the other side of the room was a small kitchen with enough space for a table with high-backed chairs. A curving wooden staircase led to a loft with a bed that looked as though it had not been slept in.

This was the Master's living quarters. Small and sparse yet cozy. The other door must lead to the actual archives with the rows and rows of books. She wished she could see it.

He lumbered to the small kitchen, filled a kettle with water and set it on the stove to boil. Then he got down two cups from the overhead cupboard. He placed loose tea leaves in each one. While he waited for the water to boil, he turned back to her and waved her to one of the chairs at the table.

"Please," he said.

Snow realized it was quite an honor to be here with the Master of Archives, in his home, while he made tea. Some bit of apprehension went through her as she realized the mention of the dark wizard must mean serious business.

She perched on the edge of the chair as the kettle whistled. He poured the water, making them both a cup of steaming tea, then headed to the table where he plunked her mug in front of her. With a grunt, he slid into the chair opposite her, the cup held between his aged hands.

"Now that we have tea, perhaps you tell me what you know of the dark wizard."

"Only that he lived somewhere in these woods and the elves cast him out." She gripped the cup between her hands, the warmth seeping into her palms.

He considered her a long moment. "What does this have to do with what happened to you?"

"I'm not sure," she said. "But I wondered if there was a connection between the two."

"Very well, I'll tell you the story." He took a sip of tea and sat back in his chair. "Many years ago, there was a man who lived on the western edge of the forest. He had a cottage there. He had no wife and no children. We were aware of his existence, but since he never seemed to venture far from his home, we let him be.

"But one day, things began to happen. The trees came alive. The forest inhabitants seemed to have a mind of their own. Sprites and gnomes and pixies appeared when they had never lived here before. Flowers bloomed when they shouldn't. Trees died when they should have lived. It rained while the sun was out. All manner of odd things."

He paused, taking another sip of his tea.

"Was that because of the wizard?" she asked.

He nodded. "Though we elves tried to ignore him, we discovered he was using his power to control these creatures, the weather, the surrounding nature in which he lived. And then he decided to use it as a weapon."

Snow stared at him, stunned. In all her years connecting to nature around her, it had never been mentioned. Surely, Faradill would remember such a thing happening. Unless he was merely a sapling at the time.

"He built an army using all manner of things from the forest. The living creatures, the trees, the flowers, everything. He became drunk on his power. He wanted to expand his domain, which meant he wanted to eradicate the elves and their home to make way for his new one. It did not go well for him."

He paused again to sip his tea.

"What happened to him?" she asked.

"We banded together. Light against dark. There was a great battle within the forest. But it was Tasnia who used her power to send him away, casting him out and forbidding him to return."

"What happened to him after that?" she asked.

"He disappeared. But he left behind his mark on the forest. We finally learned how to use our elemental power to make peace with the forest and all the creatures within it."

And she, in turn, learned how to connect with nature as well. She, too, had that elemental power. She would never use that power for evil, though.

"When he was expelled, we were determined to protect our village woods with our own magic and keep out any other magic."

"That seems selfish," she said.

He chuckled. "Perhaps it is. But it has been that way for years. We've kept the peace and kept our people safe. Recent events have reminded us of the dangers of other magic." He gave her a pointed look.

She understood what he meant. Safe from dark wizards and other magic. The elven magic Tasnia and the Elders used to surround the village would, no doubt, keep out whatever darkness lurked beyond the borders of their small village.

Still thinking of the dark wizard, she asked, "Do you think he was destroyed?"

"No one knows for certain. He never returned to the Wyldwood. Even if he wanted to return, he couldn't because elven magic would never allow it. After he was gone, we searched the wizard's isolated cabin and discovered he had magical items there he used to help him control nature. We took them and hid them away."

Intrigued, she asked, "What sort of magical items?"

He smiled, his lips thinning.

"Ah. You can't tell me. I understand."

The elves held their secrets closely guarded. She would have to find out another way. She did wonder if the wizard's home still stood. She smiled, then met his sharp blue gaze.

She had more questions, but she didn't want to take more of his time and she really did have to get back home to help Yirrie with the festival baking. She took a healthy swig of the warm tea and slid off the chair.

"Thank you for your time and the tea."

"Leaving already?" he asked.

"Yes, I have to get back."

Harwin moved off the chair and followed her to the door. "Did you get the answers you were seeking?"

Though she hadn't, she said, "You've been quite helpful."

As she left the Master's home, she had more questions than answers.

# CHAPTER 8

The day dragged on. She went through the motions of helping Yirrie bake throughout the day, distracted as she thought of what Master told her about the dark wizard.

Nothing made sense to her. She had a difficult time making the connection between the dark wizard and the Shadow that tried to kill her the night before. In fact, there was nothing connecting the two.

"Are you all right, Snow? You seem preoccupied," Yirrie said.

Snow realized she had been kneading a ball of dough absently. At Yirrie's question, she placed the dough in the bowl and covered it to rise.

"Yes, I'm sorry. I am a bit."

"Worried about anything?" she asked.

Snow managed a smile. "Nothing. I'm preoccupied as you said."

"I'll finish up here. Why don't you get ready for tonight?" she suggested.

It was her polite way of telling Snow to get out of the kitchen.

In truth, she was relieved to be released from duty and scurried to her room, closing the door behind her. Tonight's festival event would be less formal than last night's. She wouldn't have to wear a fancy gown. Though there would be dancing, she wouldn't have to worry about a boy asking her.

Thinking of that, though, made her think of Ardan. Her cheeks warmed at the thought of him and she wondered if she would see him tonight.

It was ridiculous to even entertain. She shoved away those thoughts and went to her wardrobe where she pulled out one of her older gowns in green silk. She dressed, then brushed out the length of her black hair. She tied it at the nape of her neck with a matching green ribbon. As she peered at herself in the mirror, she noticed the pale purple bruises along her throat. Bruises that looked like fingerprints.

She leaned closer to get a better look. The Shadow that had attacked her must have left the marks. Where else would she have gotten them?

Not wanting anyone else to see the marks, she decided to change her dress into something with a high neck. She exchanged the gown for a deep royal blue one that would conceal the marks.

As she left with Yirrie and Elator for the second night of the festival, apprehension swept through her.

The long tables were set as before. All the candles lit. The lights dangled from the trees, illuminating the area of the village where the revelry always took place. Normally, Snow enjoyed this time of year. But this year was different. This year dark magic tried to kill her.

In past years, the first night of the celebration went into the wee morning hours. The second night was when the couples who formed the previous night would dance after the feast. It would go on well into the night. She dreaded that because, undoubtedly, she would never be picked.

After the feast, the music and merriment began. Much to her astonishment, Ardan appeared at their table with a shy look on his face that told her he wasn't sure what he was doing. Surprise flickered through her. Tonight, he wore a dark blue brocade jacket trimmed in silver with silver buttons, black pants and black boots. She had to admit he looked quite handsome.

"Hello, Snow." His hand rested on the hilt of his dagger belted at his waist. Tonight, he wore it in plain sight.

"Hello, Ardan." She kept her voice strong and sure, but deep down her nerves jangled through her. What was he doing at their table?

Yirrie and Elator were both riveted, watching their awkward exchange. Finally, Ardan held out a shaking hand to her and cleared his throat.

"Would you do the honor of granting me this dance?"

Snow's mouth went dry as she stared, dumbfounded, at him. "You want to dance with me?"

He glanced at Elator who gave him an encouraging nod. Something struck Snow then and she wondered if he had something to do with this sudden invitation from the young elf.

"Yes," he said, keeping his hand extended to her.

"Are you sure?" Snow's brows drew together.

Yirrie elbowed her. "Go on, Snow."

"I'm sure," Ardan said, sounding confident.

Even though she was uncertain about his intentions, she rose from her chair and walked around the end of the table with slow, methodical steps to give him time to change his mind. He didn't. He turned toward her with his hand still outstretched, his fingers slightly shaking. Trepidation slipping through her, she placed her hand in his. He whisked her off to the dancefloor where one warm hand landed on her waist and the other gripped her hand.

Snow looked everywhere but into his eyes, a sudden uneasy shyness plaguing her. The music was soft, encouraging the newly formed couples to dance closer and closer to each other.

"You look lovely tonight," he said, his voice wavering a bit with his nerves.

Her cheeks heated as she watched their feet. "Thank you."

His hand tightened on her waist. Finally, she met his gaze and realized he was smiling at her. She smiled back. As they twirled around the makeshift dance floor, she caught Valda's acid gaze. Clearly, his sister was not happy Snow was dancing with him.

"Your sister doesn't like me," she remarked.

"My sister doesn't like anyone," he replied with a chuckle.

She noticed, then, he was leading her away from the other couples to the edge of the forest.

"I don't much like these festivals," he said, then. "Would you like to take a walk with me in the forest?"

She chewed her lower lip as she thought about leaving the elves' protective magic. "I shouldn't…"

"I'll keep you safe." He flashed an irresistible grin. "We don't have to go far. We can stay within the circle, if you like."

It was as if he sensed her apprehension and why.

She gave him a nod. "All right."

They stopped dancing. He took her by the hand and led her toward the edge of the forest. The music faded to nothing more than a din as they stepped out of the puddle of light and into the trees shrouding them in darkness. He led her to a fallen log and perched on the edge of it. She did the same. They sat there in amicable silence for a long moment, watching the light from the festival flicker in the distance and listening to the faint lilting music.

"I didn't have a chance to thank you last night," she said. "For saving me."

"You don't have to thank me," he said.

"Yes, I do. If it hadn't been for you and your blade, I might be dead."

She thought of the bruises along her neck and how the Shadow tried to choke the life out of her. A cold tingling sensation skipped down her spine as she remembered.

Silence descended between them as they both considered this.

"I think I know why I was able to do it," he said.

She cut him a cursory glance full of question.

"To save you, I mean." He reached for the dagger in the sheath on his belt. He pulled out the blade and showed it to her. "It's an enchanted blade."

"Enchanted?" She peered at it, curious and suspicious all at the same time. "Where did you get it?"

"My father brought it back for me from Feywood," he said. "He had it made there." He turned the hilt toward her, extending it to her.

"Your father was in Feywood? I thought elves never left the village."

He grinned. "Sometimes, we do. Go on. Take it."

Tentatively, she wrapped her hand around the hilt. The dagger was lightweight despite the handle being made of oak. The delicate details along the handle were elven scrollwork that only an elf would know. She turned the blade so the light caught it and saw the wavy design down the steel. The blade shimmered with an ethereal glow in the half light.

"What makes it enchanted?" she asked.

"My father said he heard of a master blacksmith who made beautiful weapons. Swords of all sizes and daggers. He makes blades for King Alfred. Blades and armor and other things."

Snow handed him back the blade. He held it up, letting the light catch along the edge. It glinted and shimmered with an iridescence, something she had never seen in a dagger, or any blade, before.

"Apparently, he has a way to forge enchanted blades. My father didn't know how. See how it shimmers?" He tilted the blade in the light again.

"Yes. It's beautiful."

"I think the enchanted blade somehow helped me break free. It was why I was able to sever the Shadow from you." As he said this, he sheathed the dagger.

An enchanted blade. Could it be possible? Had anyone ever heard of an enchanted blade before? There was only one person she thought of who could answer that question. She was certain the Master of Archives would know.

"I didn't get a chance to tell you that last night." He reached for her hand, wrapping his warm fingers around hers.

Butterflies erupted deep in her gut. Though she liked Ardan, she saw him as a friend and nothing more. The tenderness in his eyes told her he thought of her as something more.

"Snow..." His voice was soft and a little shaky. "There's something else I wanted to tell you last night."

Her stomach clenched. The custom of the first night of festival was for the young men to find a young lady and proclaim his intentions. It was the last thing she wanted to hear from Ardan. She shifted, a sudden feeling of discomfort coming over her. To save herself from turning him down and seeing his disappointment or hurting his feelings, she took her hand away from his and hopped to her feet.

"I think Yirrie is calling me." She kept her gaze pinned on the clearing ahead. "I should go see what she needs."

"I didn't hear anything." He got to his feet. "Snow—"

"Yes, I definitely heard her calling me." She spun toward him, plastering a wide smile on her face. "Thank you for showing me the enchanted blade and telling me about it."

"But—"

"I have to go."

She was off before he uttered another word, picking up her skirts and hurrying back through the trees to the table where Yirrie and Elator sat talking and laughing with others. Her heart pounded a wild beat as she approached the table, her gaze cutting over the merrymaking. Elator caught her eye and lifted his tankard in greeting, then went back to his conversation with the elf at his left. Yirrie hadn't noticed her at all.

Snow veered to the right and headed back into the village where she had one thing on her mind—a visit to the Master of Archives.

# CHAPTER 9

Snow wasn't sure if she would find Master Harwin. All she did know was that he wasn't at the festival again that night. In fact, he rarely participated in them. When he did, it was to record some monumental event that everyone knew was coming. Like the introduction of an Elder who was taking the place of another who had passed on to the Otherworld.

She pushed open the door, the bell tinkling her arrival. It was dark inside save for one lone candle in a wall sconce behind the desk. She stood there in the silence for a long moment listening to the faint tick of a clock somewhere out of sight. Finally, she approached the desk.

"Master Harwin?"

The door on the left was ajar and caught her attention. She stared it, certain it was closed before she approached the desk. It was unlike Master Harwin to leave the door open.

The door on the right remained closed. The one in which she had entered earlier that day to ask him about the dark wizard and share a cup of tea. She hesitated, unsure what to do.

It was expressly forbidden for her—or anyone—to enter the archives without permission from Harwin. At least, that's what she had always been told. She wasn't certain the archives were behind the left door but it was an assumption. Where else would he keep all those books and scrolls and histories and diaries?

She stepped up to the door on the right and gave a swift knock. Then stepped back and waited.

Her heart pounded and her pulse thrummed deep within her. Something seemed amiss, but she was uncertain as to what she was feeling.

The door on the left beckoned.

When Harwin did not answer, she took a tentative step around the desk and halted. Her heart was loud in her ears. So loud it drowned out the ticking clock.

Taking a deep breath, expelling it, she took a tentative step toward the door. Then another and another until she was standing in front of it peering through the opening into soft shadows illuminated by flicking firelight.

"I shouldn't," she whispered.

Her hands were in fists at her sides and she glanced around. The other door remained firmly closed. Closing her eyes, she connected to the world around her, reaching out with her senses. All was quiet. Nothing stirred within the confines of the Master's home.

She reached for the knob, opening the door fully. A slash of yellow-orange light filled the doorway and spilled into the quiet, darkened entryway. She blinked against the sudden brightness. From where she stood, she saw a bookshelf lined with books of all sizes.

One step and she would be inside the archives. One step and she would know what was behind that mysterious door.

She stepped inside and pulled the door closed behind her with a click. Standing there, she took in the room.

It was large. So large, her mind could not understand how it fit. On the outside, his home was tiny. But this room was cavernous and filled to the ceiling with rows and rows of bookshelves. How would she ever find the answers to her questions in this vast amount of books?

But it wasn't just books he had. He also had items on the right side of the room. Swords, armor, murals painted of battles long past, an odd-looking wooden chair that, in her mind, resembled an ancient throne. All of that was on the opposite side of the room from the shelves. As though he was not only a collector of knowledge but a collector of history. These must be the magical things Master Harwin mentioned.

Something drew her to the right where all the items were housed. She walked down the aisle, looking at each of them as she passed. Over each item was a nameplate identifying the item.

Over the sword was *Sword of the First Elven High King.*

Over the armor a similar one reading *Armor of the First Elven High King.*

The label above the ancient throne was simply labeled *Throne of the First Elven High King*.

She didn't know who the High King was. The elves had stopped using a royal hierarchy and instead had the Elders who were the most wise and the leaders.

Onward down the aisle, she paused to look at each and every artifact with wonder and amazement. She had no idea all of this was stored here. She wondered if Elator or Yirrie knew about it.

At the end of the aisle, there was an empty spot where a round object had once been. The label read *Dark Mirror*.

She gazed at it a long, hard moment, her heart beating so hard it hurt.

Where had the Dark Mirror gone? Who had taken it? Did Master Harwin know it was gone?

She stared at the empty spot, unsure what to do. She couldn't tell Harwin it was missing. Then he would know she was in here when she wasn't supposed to be.

She turned the corner at the end of the aisle and saw yet another empty spot that appeared to have been where something once resided. It, too, was gone. The label read *Enchanted Mirror*.

Another mirror missing.

Her hands shook as she took another step down the row to see yet another vacant space with a label identifying it as *Magic Mirror*.

Three mirrors. All missing. Stolen? And if so, how did someone get past Harwin to steal them? How did someone know the elves had them?

Harwin had told her they removed magical items from the dark wizard's cabin. Were these mirrors some of those items?

She backed away, then turned and ran up the aisle. She was here to find out about enchanted weapons, but now discovered another mystery. At the front of the room, she paused to catch her breath. Did she dare stay to find out about the enchanted weapons, or leave and try again another day?

Knowing she shouldn't be in there, she decided to do the right thing and leave. Twisting the knob, she pushed open the door and peered out. All was as she had left it when she entered the room. Stepping out, she softly closed the door.

Turning, she nearly jumped out of her skin when she came face to face with Master Harwin. He stood behind the desk, still in the same state as earlier that day when they shared tea. He held a candle in one hand, the faint light flickering over his face pinched with a cross between fury and disappointment.

"Snow, would you like to tell me what you were up to?"

"I-I…" She didn't know what to say.

Her heart was throbbing so hard, it made her lightheaded. Her head pounded with a sudden shooting pain. She pinched the bridge of her nose between her thumb and forefinger to make it stop.

"Well?" he prompted.

"I had a question for you," she began.

"At this time of night? Shouldn't you be at the festival?" His tone had a hard edge.

"I don't much enjoy the festival," she said without thinking.

Some of the anger faded from his face. "Neither do I. That's why I never go. Well, come on then. Since you woke me up and you have questions, you may as well have some tea." He sounded more weary than angry.

He shuffled back through the door on the right into his cozy home. Stunned, it took her a moment to follow. She stumbled after him, closing the door behind her. He was already putting a kettle on to boil. The candle he had carried was placed in a holder in the middle of the table.

There were only a few candles burning in the place, giving it a warm glow. She perched on the edge of the seat she had occupied earlier that day and waited while he prepared the tea.

"I'm sorry, Master Harwin. I didn't mean to intrude."

"Something must be very urgent for you to be here in the dark of night." He brought over the tray with two cups, creamer, sugar, and teapot. He placed it on the table, then poured a cup.

"I did knock," she said, accepting the cup he offered. "But there was no answer."

He gave her a curious glance full of question. She rushed on.

"I didn't mean to go in the archives, but, I...well, I..." She placed her shaking hands in her lap. "I'm sorry." She blew out a breath, her shoulders slumping.

He poured himself a cup and sat in the chair opposite. "The archives are sacred. They represent our history. There are documents and books there that were written thousands of years ago."

"I know. That's why I thought you might have the answer."

"About the dark wizard?" he asked.

"About enchanted weapons," she said.

He gave her a tight smile as his brows drew together, his eyes full of doubt as he stared at her a long moment, then took a sip of his tea. "Where did you hear about enchanted weapons?"

"From one of the young elven boys, Ardan," she said. "He said his father brought him an enchanted dagger from another kingdom."

"And you wanted to know if he was telling you the truth?" His voice was neutral tinged with uncertainty.

"Is it possible to make an enchanted blade?"

He sat back in his chair, holding his cup in his hands as steam did lazy curls upward in front of his face. There was deep contemplation in his eyes.

"It is," he said at last. "They were once called Artificers. They had a type of elemental..." he paused, searching for the word, "...ability. They knew how to manipulate fire, air, and the iron deep within the earth to enchant the steel."

Her brows drew together. "What sort of ability?" Then it struck her. "Magic. You're talking about magic."

She understood, then. Artificers were elementals. Typically, elementals only harnessed one ability. But Artificers harnessed three, sometimes all four.

She knew from a very young age she had the ability to connect with nature. Though she had never really thought of it as magic, she suddenly understood then she was an elemental with the ability to harness the earth. Her added gift was that she also had the ability to converse with the wildlife.

"Yes, and that type of magic died out a long time ago." He waved away the notion as if it were nothing more than a child's bedtime story.

"Ardan told me his father found a master blacksmith who made the blade. If it's enchanted, wouldn't he have to be one of these Artificers?"

He considered this, but still looked unconvinced. "I cannot believe anyone would be forging enchanted blades."

Snow pressed her lips together in a thin line. She wouldn't have believed it either, if she hadn't seen it for herself. She thought of the numerous books inside the other room and was certain there was something there that would tell her more about these Artificers, as well as the dark wizard.

She sipped her tea, debating on whether or not to tell Master Harwin about the missing mirrors.

"You said this Ardan had an enchanted blade?"

She nodded. "I saw it."

"Interesting." Still, he sounded as though he didn't believe her. Perhaps he would have to see it for himself. "It is a form of magic I have never seen."

She thought of the missing mirrors again. Placing her cup on the table in front of her, she ran her finger around the rim.

His eyes glinted with suspicion as he peered at her from across the table. "Are you going to be telling me why you were in there?"

"I wanted information on the enchanted blade," she said, which was the truth.

"Well, I gave it to you. There's no reason you or anyone else should be in that room without supervision. There are dangerous things there. Things that should never see the light of day again. Things that were hidden away for the very reason magic was driven out of the Wyldwood."

"Things like mirrors?" she asked.

He went very still as he peered at her. "Yes, things like that."

She swallowed hard, a lump suddenly forming in her throat. She had to tell him. "There is something else you should know."

He lifted a shaggy brow. "And what is that?"

"The mirrors are missing."

# CHAPTER 10

Snow and Master Harwin stood in the archive room. When she told him they were missing, he demanded to see for himself at once. Now, he stared at the empty spaces where the mirrors were supposed to be with wide, fearful eyes. He muttered, "How did this happen?" over and over again as if Snow had the answer.

She didn't.

He moved from one vacant spot to the next, paused to stare at what was left of the outline of each mirror, his hand rubbing the skin of his forehead.

"They were supposed to be safe here," he said.

"How would someone break in and take them under your nose?" she asked.

"They didn't break in through the front door." He rocked on his heels, staring at the place where the label for *Dark Mirror* had been.

"Then how?"

"There is only one way. Through a portal. This is my fault." He paced a short distance back and forth, his agitation clear.

"I don't see how it could be," she said. "You've always carefully supervised the archive room."

"And yet you were able to enter it with ease."

His piercing stare bore into her, causing an icy chill to creep up her spine. The weight of his disappointment pressed down on her, making it hard to breathe. Anxiety gnawed at the edges of her mind as she desperately searched for words to ease the tension that hung heavy in the air.

"However," he added, "if you hadn't, then I would have never known the mirrors were missing."

She wasn't sure if he was thanking her for that or not, so she remained silent.

"I must alert the Elders," he said.

"What will happen then?"

"Then? I will likely be removed as Master of Archives."

As she gazed into his eyes, she saw the weight of his sadness etched deep within them. The lines on his face seemed to deepen, revealing a profound sorrow that tugged at her heartstrings. It was as if every ounce of joy had been drained from him, leaving behind an overwhelming sense of despair.

Harwin had been Master of Archives longer than she had been part of the elves' village. Longer than Yirrie and Elator had been alive, even. She stepped toward him and hugged him. He was so surprised by that he didn't return the hug.

"What was that for?" he asked when she pulled away.

"You looked like you needed it." She glanced at the vacant space, chewing on her lower lip. "Do you have to tell them now? Maybe you should wait until after festival."

He glanced from her to the void and back again. "You want me to lie?"

"Not lie," she said. "Just wait to tell them. Only you and I know the mirrors are missing. The others don't. And, by the looks of the spaces along the walls, it appears they have been missing for quite some time."

"But..."

"Perhaps I can help," she rushed on.

He narrowed his gaze at her. "How?"

"Let me see if I can find out something."

He tilted his head to one side, question lingering in his eyes. "How will you do that?"

"I have some ideas." She patted his arm for reassurance. "Let me try. I feel like this is partially my fault."

"No, Snow, not your fault at all."

Perhaps not, but she couldn't shake the feeling that something was amiss. Something or someone had wanted her to see the archive room. She didn't tell him the door was ajar. She decided to use her nature powers to find out more information about the dark wizard and the mirrors. She wanted to find the wizard's home. If it still existed, perhaps there were answers hidden there.

She stifled a yawn. "I should go."

He walked with her toward the door and then out of the archive room. Once they were out, he shut it and tested the knob to make sure it was locked. He followed her as she made her way around the desk.

"Thank you, Snow," he said.

She turned to face him. "For what?"

"For telling me about the mirrors. For your help." He granted her a weak smile.

"You're welcome. I'll let you know if I find out anything."

He nodded and then shuffled back to his cozy home. Snow slipped out into the night and headed home.

As she walked back, though, she heard the festival was still in full swing. Lots of joyous voices, singing, music, laughter. This year, she felt more like an outsider than ever. The familiar faces seemed distant, their laughter echoing through the trees as a constant reminder of her isolation while she stood on the periphery. She knew it was because all the young couples were pairing off and looking for their own true loves.

Snow, though, knew her true love was not here in the forest.

He was somewhere out there. When she met him, she would know.

She started to make the turn for her home and then changed her mind. Since everyone was still at the festival, it would be her chance to go into the forest and see if she could find those answers.

It was a risk, she knew, especially stepping outside the protective circle of the Elder's magic. It was a risk she had to take.

She made her way from the village through the forest as she did many times before. So many times, she had lost count. She lifted the edge of her gown and stepped carefully over fallen logs. She made her way to Faradill where she knelt in front of the massive tree. She placed her palms on the trunk, closed her eyes, and whispered the incantation.

"Ancient oak, with roots so deep, guardian of secrets, wisdom to keep. In your branches, the whispers of old, reveal to me tales untold."

*Hello, my lady Snow.*

"I have a request."

Faradill was not only wise, but also intuitive.

*I will help if I can.*

"Do you know where the dark wizard once lived?"

*Quite the request.* He chuckled. *The dark wizard gave us life. The elves saved us from his wickedness.*

She nodded, knowing this already from the story Master Harwin told her.

*Indeed, I do know where he lived. His cabin is on the edge of the woods. To the west.*

Her heart thudded. That was too far to hike at this time of night and she had never gone that far alone anyway. She needed an excuse not to help Yirrie with the baking tomorrow so she could trek across the forest to the wizard's cabin.

*Why do you seek it?* the oak asked.

"I have questions about him. I hoped to find answers there."

*You are going.* It wasn't a question.

"I am."

There was a long pause. Then he said, *Tread carefully there, my lady Snow. No one has been near there in years.*

A warning. Cold shivers slipped up her spine. "Is it dangerous?"

*It is where the dark wizard began,* he said. *The elves tried to hide his cabin, but it still stands.*

"I will heed your warning. Thank you, Faradill," she said.

*Stay safe, my lady.*

She removed her palms, releasing the spell on the ancient oak. A yawn escaped her. She sank to the ground and sat with her back against the trunk, stretching her legs out in front of her as she thought of the dark wizard and his hidden cabin deep in the Wyldwood. How would she find her way to the other side of the forest? As she pondered this, her eyes grew heavy and before long she was fast asleep.

Snow awoke to the sound of faint birdsong. Her eyes fluttered open. She had fallen asleep at the foot of Faradill, curled on her side and her head pillowed on her arm. Sometime during the night, she was covered with a thick blanket woven from leaves and sticks. Annilen was in a tight ball near the base of the tree, her tiny features calm and serene as she slept. She smiled, wondering when her friend had found her. The last thing she recalled was falling asleep after chatting with Faradill about the dark wizard.

Realizing it was morning, and that she was likely missed at home, she sat up straight. The leaf blanket fell away. Her arm had fallen asleep, so when she moved, pinpricks pierced up and down her arm as the feeling came back into it.

Her sudden movement disturbed Annilen, waking her from her deep sleep.

"Morning, Snow," she said around a yawn.

Snow struggled to her feet. "I have to go. Yirrie will be looking for me."

She was going to be in trouble. A lot of trouble. Her only hope was that she would be able to sneak into her bedroom and pretend she had been there all night. The sun was just starting to peek over the horizon, so she hoped Yirrie and Elator wouldn't be awake yet.

Annilen fluttered next to her, keeping pace. "The festival went long into the night."

That gave her hope. She had spent a good portion of the night with Master Harwin and was certain no one missed her when she slipped out of his house and into the forest. Her heart, though, was still beating a rapid pace.

"How do you know?" Snow asked.

"How could we not know? Music and dancing and singing kept most of us awake."

She sounded irritated and for some reason that made Snow smile.

"When I saw you sleeping at the foot of the tree, away from all the noise, I decided to join you," Annilen said. "Some of us had to get far, far away from the village to get any rest."

She couldn't help it, she giggled at the way the little sprite sounded so cranky.

As they neared the village, though, apprehension rolled through her. What if Yirrie knew she was out all night? She told her to stay within the confines of the village, within the protective ring of magic laid out by the Elders warding off evil spirits and dark magic that might want to invade. She had disobeyed. Because she was desperate to find answers.

Though Annilen said the merriment went late into the night, something made Snow pause, close her eyes, and reach out with her senses to tap into nature. The magic surrounding the village was still intact. That was a relief.

The village was quiet. The birds, squirrels, and others were only just now coming awake, which gave her hope.

"What is it?" Annilen asked.

"Just checking the village," she said. "All seems to be well. Which means I can sneak back inside the house unnoticed. You should go, Annilen."

The sprite gave her wave and flitted off.

Snow continued on her way and entered the village. No one was up yet, which was a good sign. She hurried to her house, slipping around the back and heading for her window. She shoved it open and climbed inside, relief sputtering through her. Her room was empty and dark.

She quickly changed out of the dress she wore the previous night into a clean day dress. After she combed her hair, she stepped out of her room and ran right into Yirrie.

Her arms were crossed over her chest. A pinched expression of both anger and worry creased her features. Immediately, Snow realized she had not been so stealthy after all. Her sneaking was discovered.

"Where have you been?" Yirrie demanded.

"I was—"

"You were in the forest all night, weren't you?" Her tone was less than kind and told Snow there was no use in giving her excuses.

She flushed hot, her cheeks burning. Finally, she nodded.

Yirrie dropped her arms and huffed out a breath. "Even after what happened that night at festival? Snow..." She shook her head, unable to continue.

"I'm sorry, Yirrie. The forest called to me and I had to obey."

It was a half-truth. She couldn't tell her about visiting with Master Harwin or finding the missing mirrors or even learning about the dark wizard. She wasn't sure Yirrie would believe her anyway.

"Snow, Tasnia wanted to banish you from this village because of what happened. You promised to stay within the safe perimeter of the village."

She clenched her jaw, biting back the caustic reply that sprang to her lips. No, it was Yirrie who had promised for her. Yirrie didn't understand what it would do to her if she remained within the village.

And besides, nothing happened when she was there last night. No Shadows came for her. No dark magic or dark wizards. She was perfectly safe.

Instead, she said again, "I'm sorry."

Yirrie softened, her worry and distress melting off her face. She reached for Snow, wrapping her in a tight hug.

"After what happened, I worry."

Snow patted her on the back. "I know."

Yirrie pulled back, holding her at arm's length and smiling at her. "I'm glad you're all right. Now, let's get to our daily baking."

As Yirrie released her and hurried into the kitchen, Snow inwardly groaned. The last thing she wanted to do was more baking. But it was still festival time and she knew she had to help. Her hike into the forest to find the wizard's cabin had to wait. She trudged into the kitchen.

# CHAPTER 11

Seraphina stepped through the portal and into to the busy town of Bridgefort. She arrived on the edge of town north of the walled city. Even from her distance, she heard the hum of the busy streets. On the hill, King Alfred's castle loomed over the town, gleaming in the late afternoon sunlight, the heraldry flags flapping in the wind on the highest turrets.

How she hated that man.

She entered the town, which was abuzz with activity from all the shops and shoppers. Here she would find the master blacksmith, though she had no idea what he looked like or how she would find him. She stopped at one of the local shops and asked where she might find the blacksmith. The man at the shop did not recognize her as Queen of the Mystic Vale. And why would he? Her castle in the vale was far to the north and rather isolated. He gave her directions to the forge at the end of town where the blacksmith made weapons and armor for the king, as well as took commissions.

Intrigued by this, she headed through the crowded streets, dodging the filthy peasants. Perhaps she should have been accompanied by her royal guard, but then, she did not want to make this an official royal visit.

At the forge, she paused in the doorway. All along the walls hung all manner of weapons from axes to war hammers to swords as well as armor that included helms, breastplates, and gauntlets. The man was busy at the back of the forge.

She watched him work. He pounded out a long piece of steel on an anvil with a hammer. With every beat of the hammer, sparks flew. Then he took the sword and placed it back in the heat. He brought it out of the fire and pounded it again, trying to shape the steel. When he gave no indication he noticed her standing there, she cleared her throat.

He stopped mid-swing to look over his shoulder. His face was dirty and sweaty, but beyond that she was unable to discern much about him.

He placed aside the hammer, reached for a nearby rag and wiped his hands as he approached.

"What can I do for you?" His voice was deep and dark and slid over her like hot molasses.

It made her shudder.

"I understand you take commissions," she said.

He gazed at her with blue-green eyes. Now that he stood closer, she saw his face had sharp, chiseled features and a square chin. His hands were large and strong. Sweat dampened his shirt under his arms and his chest.

"A few," he said at last.

Still unsure why she was sent here by the Magic Mirror, she glanced around his forge once more. A long blade hanging on the wall nearby caught her eye. It shimmered even in the half light, almost as if it were glowing. There was an intricate design along the length of the blade. The handle was made of wood and richly decorated with spiral carvings.

"Do you make all these yourself?"

"Yes," he said. "That one is not for sale."

"What is it?" Her fingers twitched. She resisted the urge to reach for it.

"A special commission." He was a man of few words.

She cut him a glance. "It looks different from the others."

"Because it is." Finally, he folded his thick arms over his massive chest and narrowed his gaze at her. "Is there something you want?"

Undeterred, she tipped her head to one side. "What sort of commissions do you take?"

"All kinds." His mouth pressed into a thin line, clearly running out of patience with her.

She almost laughed. If he only knew who she was. "Tell me, blacksmith—"

"Roderick," he snapped.

Her brows lifted. "Tell me, *Roderick,* will you make one for the Queen of the Mystic Vale?"

His arms dropped to his side, his demeanor changing from resistance to interest. "Are you here on her behalf?"

She grinned. "You could say that, yes." She turned her gaze back to the shimmering blade and motioned to it. "Tell me about this one."

"It's enchanted," he said.

"It's magic?" she asked.

"In a manner of speaking." He reached for it and brought it down from the wall, handing it to her hilt first.

She took it in her hand, the smooth wood of the hilt resting against her palm. The blade itself looked as though it were a masterpiece instead of a weapon. It was lightweight in her hand. She reached for the blade, desperate to touch it.

"Don't," he warned. "It's sharp."

As she met his eyes, she saw the warning glint there.

"What makes it shimmer?"

He chuckled. "Trade secret. I can't tell you that."

The man was infuriating. "Then at least tell me what an enchanted blade *does*."

"It does what the wielder wants." Another cryptic reply.

"I don't understand."

He held his hand out for the blade. She turned the hilt back toward him, but as she was about to hand it over, a blinding flash of light erupted from its hilt. Heat burned her hand. Startled, she dropped it to the ground with a dull thud. The small forge filled with the metallic tinge of magic as she stared wide-eyed at the man, her heart racing with astonishment at the sudden display of power.

"What was that flash?" she asked.

"A warning."

He merely grinned as he bent to pick it up. "It's linked to the bearer. It can make a knight undefeatable in battle once it understands how the knight fights. This one belongs to me."

"You said it was a special commission."

"Yes. For myself." He grinned.

He replaced it back on the wall.

"You mean, it enhances skills?" She eyed it, curious.

He nodded. "A hunter would always catch his prey. A knight would always defeat his enemy."

"And a blacksmith?"

"Always forges the perfect blade."

"I suppose that's why you're a *master* blacksmith, then."

"I suppose it is," he said.

A wide smile spread over her face. The back of her neck tingled with sweet anticipation as she thought of the power of the enchanted blade. Wielding one against Snow White would ensure the woman would die. But she could not be the one to kill her. She needed an assassin. Someone she could trust. But who?

"I want one," she said. When he gave her an odd look, she smiled. "For the Queen of the Mystic Vale."

"You can speak on her behalf?" he asked.

"As I said, I do. Now, when will the blade be ready?"

"It will take several weeks—"

"The queen needs it as soon as possible."

"I have other work here—" He waved to the forge behind him.

"Five thousand gold crowns if you deliver it yourself in a week."

Astonishment flickered over his face. He appeared to be rendered speechless.

"Deliver it myself?" His voice quivered with disbelief.

"Yes, to the castle in the north of the Mystic Vale." She reached into her pocket and, though it was devoid of contents, she quickly conjured a purse full of gold. She pulled it out and handed it to him. "One thousand gold crowns as a deposit. Does that suit?"

His jaw dropped open, unable to form any coherent response. Finally, he said, "And five thousand upon delivery?"

A flicker of amusement went through her as she nodded slowly. "Indeed. If you deliver it in person to the queen, yes." She gave him a sweet smile.

He took the purse from her hands, the coins jingling inside. "I will see you in a week then."

# CHAPTER 12

Another night of festival. Snow managed to avoid Ardan and his adoring looks. The night held more dancing and more singing for the young couples.

Faint morning light filtered through her window. She sat up in bed, her knees drawn to her chest, watching as the night gave way to dawn. Her stomach fluttered, her mouth was bone dry, and her heart pounded a wicked tattoo. She took a deep breath, held it, then blew it out to calm herself.

She shoved off the blankets, both excitement and fear pounding through her. Now was her chance to sneak out of the house and begin her long trek through the forest to the dark wizard's cabin on the western side.

Part of her told her not to do it. To remain in the village as she promised Yirrie. To not leave the protective magic of the village. The other part of her drove her to seek the answers she needed to put the questions to rest. To find out the truth about the dark wizard and the missing mirrors.

Pausing a moment, she pressed a hand against her roiling stomach and took a deep breath to calm her jittery nerves. It helped a little.

Instead of her normal gown, she pulled on pants, boots, a tunic and padded vest. She pulled her hair back and tied it with a leather thong at the nape of her neck. With stealth-like grace, she cracked open the door to her bedroom and peeked out. No one was about.

Scurrying to the kitchen, she filled a flask with water and slung the long strap over her shoulder. Then she grabbed a half-eaten loaf of yesterday's bread and a couple of apples. She stuffed them in a small duffel, shouldering it along with the flask. A quick glance at Yirrie and Elator's bedroom. Their door was still closed and she hoped they were still sleeping. It was still too early for her to be up.

Snow slipped out of the house, hurrying to the familiar path that would lead her through the forest. She passed Faradill, who stood tall and silent with morning dew on his leaves. She gave him a quick bow of acknowledgement before continuing on her way. Deeper and deeper she went as the sun climbed higher in the sky. As she passed Faradill, Annilen joined her.

"Are you ready for our morning walk, Snow?"

"Not today, Annilen," she said, increasing her pace.

"Why not?" The sprite fluttered around her head in a frenzy.

"There's something I need to do."

"I'll come with you," she offered.

"No." Snow halted and turned her, holding her hand out. Annilen landed on her palm. "You can't. It's something I have to do alone."

She tilted her head to one side in question. "What is it?"

Snow looked out at the forest, sensing the restless nature around her. Almost as though it sensed her direction and her unease. But she couldn't allow the little sprite to come with her in case it was dangerous.

"I'm looking for answers deep in the forest," she said at last.

"What sort of answers?"

Snow smiled at Annilen's questions. "I'll tell you when I return."

"Promise?"

"Yes, if you make me a promise."

"Anything!"

"Stay out of the village and don't tell Yirrie where I'm going," Snow said.

Her little brows drew together in question. "But why?"

Snow considered her words before answering finally. "Because it's a secret mission. Can you keep a secret?"

Annilen gave a vigorous nod. "Yes!"

"Good. Then I'll see you after."

The little sprite took off, winging her way through the forest and disappearing out of sight. Snow resumed her trek, hoping her small friend would keep her promise.

Soon, she came to an overgrown path. At least, what appeared to be an overgrown path. She followed it through the forest, her booted steps surefooted. She was attuned to the forest around her, listening to all the creatures and inhabitants. It was a bright, cheerful morning for those in residence. The birds were singing. The squirrels were foraging. The tiny sprites were busy flittering from one flower to the next. Even the forest pixies were busy within their own little world. A few followed her from a distance. She sensed the curiosity and it made her smile.

It had been years since anyone had come to this side of the forest. She paused, reaching out to her surroundings to inquire about the cabin.

"Am I close?" She reached for the flask and took a long drink.

A vine extended itself upward and pointed northwest. She was still on the right path.

She made her way past overgrown underbrush, ducking under hanging limbs. She pushed aside another low hanging branch and took another step, then halted.

The cabin still stood, but it had been overgrown with vines and ivy. Years of neglect allowed nature to take over. The roof was caved in on one side, but the walls were still intact as far as she could see.

Here, the forest was silent, sending an eerie sensation over her skin. There were no twittering birds. Or animals rustling the underbrush. Not even a breeze fluttered past. Those who had followed her were now gone or at least keeping a large distance away from her. Faradill had warned her about the place, telling her it was where the dark wizard began and gave them life. Life that now continued to thrive throughout the Wyldwood.

But this place was different. It was almost as though there was still dark magic lingering here. She sensed a deep despair. Even the foliage was darker. Gloomier.

The urge to turn back swarmed through her. She ignored it, shoving her fear down deep. She came too far to turn back now and answers were within reach. That part of her was desperate for answers about the wizard and his mirrors.

With slow steps, she approached the cabin. Vines clung to the eaves, covering the door and windows. She pulled them away enough for her to shove open the door. It creaked, sliding across the floor with a loud scrape.

Stepping across the threshold, she paused to allow her eyes to adjust to the dim shadows and take it all in.

Faint shadows slashed across the rotting floor littered with leaves. Inside were more vines and ivy that had taken over. Remnants of broken furniture remained. The cabinets to the tiny kitchen stood open. One door hung by a broken hinge.

Taking a tentative step, she tested the floor to make sure it was sound. It creaked, but held her weight. She moved deeper into the cabin. To her left, a door stood open. She stepped into the entryway to peer inside.

A broken bed frame but no mattress was on one side. There was nothing else but dust. An overgrown tree blocked the one window with moth-eaten curtains.

She turned from the room and faced another door. This one closed. Purple flickering light glimmered around the edges.

Odd.

She stepped toward the door, reaching for the knob, her heart a wild beat. Pushing open the door, she sucked in a sharp breath at what she saw.

A bright purple ball of light spun in what appeared to be a hovering cloud within a silver cage. She halted, her heart in her throat as she stared at it trying to make sense of what it was. She remained rooted in the doorway, hesitant to step inside. A tingling sensation went over her. The same sensation she sensed when she stepped past the overhanging branches and found the cabin.

What was this light?

"Ahhh. A visitor. There has not been a visitor in many years."

The disembodied voice was that of a man. She glanced around but saw no one.

"Where are you?"

"Here. In this room. Trapped for all eternity," he said.

She regarded the purple light with questions swirling through her mind. The man was the light in the cage?

"Who are you?"

He chuckled. "The one who lived in this cabin. But now nothing more than a phantom." The light swirled as he spoke.

"*You* are the wizard?" she asked.

"I am. And you?"

Hesitation shifted through her. She didn't want to tell him who she was, so she asked another question.

"What is your name?"

A rumble of a laugh went through him. "The last time I gave up my name to someone, it was a mistake."

"I cannot call you *wizard*, can I?" she asked, determined to learn his name.

"No more than I can call you *maiden*." There was a pause, then he said, "You seem harmless enough. My name is Govan."

Govan was a name she had never heard, nor would soon forget. With her hand still on the knob, she watched the swirling light within the cage.

"How did you get like this?"

"'Tis a long story." Another swirl and a dance.

She released the knob and stepped closer to peer at the ball of light trapped within the cage made of silver. Tiny squares kept the light from seeping out. Someone had trapped him here. But who and why?

"Tell me your name, maiden, and I shall tell you the story."

Snow knew there was a power in names. She was reluctant to share hers with a dangerous dark wizard. She glanced around the room, searching for inspiration, but saw nothing she could take as her name. Then it occurred to her to take a name from nature.

"You may call me Ivy."

There was a long pause as the light swished around in its cage, then he emitted a long, low chuckle.

"Ivy. Very well. I shall tell you the story of a vengeful girl who stole my magic and trapped me here."

He told her the tale of being forced out of the forest by the elves with nothing but his wits and his spell book. Snow already knew this story from talking to Master Harwin. When he was expelled, he went north to a small village where he met a young peasant girl desperate to leave her poor, wretched life behind. She had aspirations and dreams of becoming something more than what she was and she wanted someone to help her get there.

"She wanted riches and power and love. All things I gave her. I helped her do away with the queen. I helped her marry the king. I helped her become *the new queen*. I watched as she was crowned and began her new life with all she ever wanted and dreamed. All because of me. I gave her those things."

As the light spoke and spun, Snow pressed trembling cold fingers to her lips. "Who was this woman who became queen?"

"Her name was Seraphina."

Snow sucked in a sharp breath. *Seraphina*. That was how she came to power. She killed her mother. Then her father. Then banished her from her own kingdom. All because she wanted to be *the queen*, the most powerful in the Mystic Vale.

"All I wanted in return was to be part of her court. To have a place at her side. She is a jealous, hateful shrew. I was a fool to trust her. To allow myself to think I was her faithful advisor. I should have never allowed her to charm me. She stole my spell book and used my own magic against me, cursing me. She destroyed all but what you see here. The very essence of my magic. She trapped me in this cage. As long as I'm here, her magic thrives."

"You mean, if you were to..." she paused, choosing her words.

"Die," he said. "Then she would no longer have her magic."

"*Can* you die?" she asked.

He laughed. "Only if her curse is broken."

"How would it be broken?"

"So many questions! I like you, Ivy. You are very inquisitive." There was a smile in his voice and then he sighed. "The Magic Mirror must be destroyed. It's the one keeping the curse alive."

"The Magic Mirror?" she asked, though she knew about it. She hoped the dark wizard would explain.

He scoffed. "Those elves thought they were so clever hiding them in their village. All it took was a portal spell for her to find them and take them."

"Them? There is more than one?" Again, she knew the answer to this question, but she wanted him to tell her.

"Three, to be exact. Three I made. Three I forged. One Dark, one Enchanted, one Magic. When I was expelled from the forest, the elves took the mirrors from this cabin. Oh, I knew they did it because I was still attuned to the surrounding nature and to the mirrors."

Snow understood what he meant for she, too, was attuned to the nature surrounding the cabin. It was nothing like when she was attuned to the rest of the village. These plants did not speak to her.

"They took the mirrors and hid them away. Seraphina used a truth spell on me to find them."

And she did. But why did she only have one?

As though he heard her thoughts, he said, "She took the Magic Mirror for herself and then gave away the Dark Mirror and the Enchanted Mirror."

"To who?" Snow asked.

"I know not," he said. "I only know before she trapped and cursed me, she thanked me for giving her the mirrors, which are all connected."

Snow tipped her head to one side. "You mean, their magic is connected to each other?"

"Of course."

She dragged her lower lip through her teeth wondering where to find the other two mirrors.

"Dear Ivy," he said, his voice low and serious. "I must ask a favor of you."

Her brows drew together. "What kind of favor?"

"Destroy the Magic Mirror."

"But you'll die."

"Yes, and so will Seraphina's magic. It will end my suffering." He flashed and blinked as if imploring her.

If she were to destroy the Magic Mirror, she would have to return to the castle. She had no desire to return to the castle.

"Will you try? I need to rest. My mind is exhausted. And every day that passes is another of pain."

"It's painful for you in there?"

"The cage is made of iron to keep me contained for all time."

Snow understood. And something deep within her wanted to help the dark wizard. Destroy the Magic Mirror and she would destroy both him *and* the evil queen. She took a deep breath. She hadn't any idea how or when she would return to the castle, but perhaps it was worth a try.

"I will do what I can," she said.

He breathed a sigh of relief. "Oh, thank you. Thank you, sweet Ivy."

"I must go," she said as she backed out of the room. She reached for the door.

"Farewell, my dear. And thank you."

She tipped her head to the side. "For what?"

"For helping me."

Her heart clawed its way to her throat. Now, she felt as though she were obligated to help. He didn't seem *so bad* after all. Perhaps he merely made a series of poor choices. Clearly, helping Seraphina was one of them.

"Farewell," she said at last.

She closed the door and stood there a moment, her hands shaking. Then she fled the cabin, never to return again.

# CHAPTER 13

S now hiked back through the forest, leaving the disembodied wizard and his cabin behind. By the time she reached Faradill, it was long past midday. She took respite at the base of him, sitting cross-legged at the foot of the tree and resting her back against his roughened bark. She took a long drink from the flask and ate a bit of the bread and an apple. She hadn't realized how hungry or thirsty she was until then.

Annilen found her there. She flitted to her, her wings beating so fast they were nothing but an iridescent blur.

"Snow, you're back!" She fluttered around her head, dancing back and forth. "Did you find the answers you were looking for?"

She munched on the apple and nodded. "I found answers, yes."

And made a dangerous promise she wasn't sure she could keep. Not only that, but she dreaded returning to Yirrie. She'd been gone all day, shirking her chores. Yirrie would likely have something to say about that. Trepidation rolled through her.

She stuffed the half-eaten bread back into her bag, then tossed the apple core to the waiting pixies who were watching her eat.

"And what were they?"

Though she had promised the sprite to tell her upon her return, now she wasn't so sure. Apprehension wafted through her as she thought of the strange wizard in his mysterious cabin.

"You promised," she said, reminding her.

"I did." Snow gave her a nod. "Did you keep your promise?"

"Yes!" she said, emphatic. She, too, sounded a bit out of breath. "I told no one, just like you asked."

Snow lifted her hand and allowed the sprite to land. She dropped and sat, drawing her knees to her chest.

"I found the dark wizard's cabin deep in the woods," she said.

Annilen stared up at her with rounded eyes full or shock. "You did?"

"Yes, and the wizard is...well, he's not exactly alive. But his spirit is," she said. "And he's tied to—" She pressed her lips together in a tight line.

"To what?" Annilen asked on a gasp.

Snow wasn't ready to give up her true identity. She worried if she told Annilen about Seraphina, she would then have to explain how she knew about the evil queen.

"To someone. Someone using his magic," she said.

"Do you know who?" the sprite asked.

"No," Snow said. Lying to her friend sent a wave of guilt through her but she had to do it to protect her from Seraphina's terrible darkness.

"Now, I really must go," Snow said. "The day is getting late and Yirrie will want to know where I've been."

Annilen got to her feet. "I'll come with you."

"No, you better not. I will likely be in some trouble when I return to the village."

Understanding dawned on her small features as she recalled their earlier conversation. "Good luck, Snow."

"Thanks. I'll need it."

Annilen fluttered off into the forest. Snow got to her feet, brushing away the dirt from her seat. She started to take a step, when Faradill's voice floated through her mind.

*You know who is using the dark wizard's magic. Don't you?*

She paused there, her heart ramming hard in her chest as she turned back to the tree. She pressed her palm against the roughened bark and closed her eyes, connecting with the ancient oak.

"I do," she whispered.

*And this person is dangerous.*

"Yes," she replied. "And I have to protect you, all of you, from her."

There was a long pause. Finally, he said, *Who are you really, Snow?*

Her eyes popped open. She craned her neck to look up at the leaves overhead and the branches swaying slightly in the breeze.

"I am no one," she said at last. "I release you."

She removed her hand from the tree and hurried through the forest.

It was dusk when she returned to the village, exhausted from the trek. Her feet ached from the constant walking. As she arrived, the village Elders were preparing for that night's festival. Yirrie and Elator placed small loaves of bread from the day's baking on each of the tables. Snow hoped to skitter around them unnoticed, but it was not to be.

Yirrie spotted her right away. Her face was pinched in fury as she glared at her from across the way. She halted what she was doing, handing Elator the loaf of bread she held, and then marched toward Snow with a purpose that told Snow she was about to be in terrible trouble.

"There you are! Just where have you been all day?"

Yirrie took a step back to look Snow up and down. Her face contorted into one of distaste as she realized Snow wore pants and a tunic instead of her normal gown attire. She noticed, too, the flask and the small bag she'd taken with the bread and apples.

"You've been hiking through the forest, haven't you?"

"I—"

"And don't lie to me, Snow."

Her mouth had gone dry. She swallowed hard, trying to come up with some viable excuse. The truth was, she had none, and she knew she would face Yirrie's wrath for leaving the safety of the village.

"Yes," she said at last, defeated.

Furious, Yirrie took her by the elbow and dragged her away from the others. She dropped her voice to a roughened whisper. "How can you expect the Elders to protect you if you refuse to stay within the borders of the village? If they find out—"

"They won't," Snow said.

"How do you know?" Yirrie snapped. "Did anyone see you leave?"

"No one saw me leave this morning. It was early before anyone was about," Snow said.

She wanted to tell her about the dark wizard, the cabin, Seraphina, and the missing mirrors. But Yirrie would not understand. There was only one person in the entire village who would and she doubted Yirrie would let her out of her sight to visit Master Harwin.

Yirrie continued to drag her through the village to their house. "You are going home, Snow. You're going to stay put in your room even if I have to tie you down to keep you there."

"I'm sorry, Yirrie—"

"Sorry isn't enough," she snapped. "Elator and I were worried sick about you all day. He had to help me with the baking. It's not something he likes to do or is good at, either."

Snow almost snickered at that, but managed to keep it at bay. Yirrie was angry and she had a right to be after Snow's disappearing act all day.

At their door, Yirrie pushed it open. She didn't release her until she was at her bedroom.

"You'll stay here tonight while we're at festival. No sneaking out any more." She gave a nod toward her room.

Snow turned to see her window was boarded up from the outside. She stared at it in abject horror with the awful realization her connection to the outside world was forever closed. She would never see the sunrise again from her window.

"You boarded up the window?"

"I had Elator do it to keep him from burning more of the bread," Yirrie said. "I also have someone watching the front of the house. If you leave again, I will know."

"So, I'm to be a prisoner here in my own home?" she asked.

"It's for your own good." Yirrie softened then, releasing her elbow. Shimmering tears stood in her eyes, the worry lines deep around her mouth. "It's the only way to keep you safe. If the Elders know you were out of the village..." Her words trailed off.

"I understand," Snow said.

The underlying meaning was there. If they knew, they would want her gone. She would be banished from the village. Just as she had been banished from her true home. The home Seraphina stole from her.

"Good night, Yirrie."

Snow stepped inside her room and closed the door. For a long moment, there was silence and then Yirrie's footsteps. The front door opened and closed, leaving Snow alone in the house.

She stumbled to the bed and collapsed, exhausted and defeated.

# Chapter 14

When the mysterious woman who commissioned the enchanted blade left his forge, Roderick consulted a map. He quickly made the calculations that it would take him nearly four days to ride from Bridgefort to the queen's castle in the far north of the Mystic Vale. The quickest way was to go through the Wyldwood Forest, something he was not too keen to do. There were stories the forest was enchanted or haunted or both.

Thinking of that, he snickered. Here he was worried about an enchanted forest, when he would have an enchanted blade at his side. He needn't worry about the forest.

If he was going to personally hand deliver the queen's dagger, he needed to start right away. He closed his forge, shuttering the front of it. He took his horse and rode to the edge of town, where there was a copse of trees. It was here he discovered the willow tree with the lustrous, rainbowlike bark. He had never seen anything like it before.

He dismounted outside the thicket, patting the horse's neck. The willow tree stood tall in the center, the top of it just visible over the other trees. He ducked and stepped under the willow's elongated branches with their pale green leaves and paused there. The other trees blocked out the afternoon light to the willow tree, but even so, the iridescence of the bark was visible.

He placed his palm on the smooth trunk of the tree and closed his eyes.

"Mystical forces that dwell," he said, "grant me your favor for the forging of this spell."

Through his connection with the tree, he sensed it come alive.

"Allow me to create this enchanted blade," he continued, "from the tree where dreams and rainbows cascade."

The tree's branches shuddered, rippling around him.

*I grant you the favor to forge this blade, through whispered secrets here in the shade.*

The tree said this in his mind, granting him the permission to once more the use its bark to forge the blade.

*Tell me, dear one,* it said in its mellifluous, soft voice. *Who will wield this blade?*

Whenever he decided to forge an enchanted blade, he received consent from the tree. It wanted to know who would be the one to wield the blade.

"I'm to take it to the queen of the Mystic Vale," he replied.

Silence descended. He didn't know much about the tree. He had stumbled upon the copse of trees by accident. The foliage around the willow formed a circle and stood like tall sentries, hiding it from any passing visitor who would only give it but a glance.

But Roderick, with his connection to the elements, sensed there was something different about these particular trees. He'd stepped through them and found the willow, its long branches swaying slightly in the breeze.

When he connected with the willow, he had sensed the presence of something ancient and magical deep within it. It was willing to share its magical properties. Why it chose him, he wasn't sure. He used bits of the bark when he forged the steel, as well as using his own bit of magic to infuse within it. He didn't really understand how it worked, only that it did.

He'd made three blades. One for himself, one for the king, and one for an elven noble passing through town. He said it was a gift for his son and he wanted it to give him strength, courage, and confidence. Roderick hadn't heard from the elven noble since then, but he hoped the blade had done just that for his son.

Now, the willow's branches swished.

*The Queen of the Mystic Vale is not the rightful ruler,* it said.

"How do you know this?" he asked.

*There is unrest throughout nature, especially in the Wyldwood Forest. Unrest I do not understand.*

Roderick remained where he was, his hand against the trunk as he considered the tree's words.

"Should I not enchant the blade?"

Another pause, then, *You should, but chose your recipient wisely, dear one, for all is not what it seems.*

Cryptic words from the ancient willow. His brows drew together in question.

"What does that mean?"

*You will have your answer when the time comes. Now, go forth and forge your blade.*

"Thank you, ancient one," he said.

He took the dagger, which he'd strapped to his side, and scraped a bit of the bark from the trunk, placing the shards in a small wood container to keep it safe. He bid farewell to the willow tree and returned to his forge where he began to work.

Roderick spent long hours in his forge working on the blade. He mixed the bark shavings within the steel when he placed it in the fire, heating it up and then placing it on the anvil to hammer it into the shape of the long, straight blade of the dagger. Since the queen's messenger didn't specify what type of dagger, he decided to make it into one best used for thrusting and stabbing.

When he finished the blade, it shimmered with the rainbowlike steel mimicking that of the bark from the willow tree. When the light caught it, it had a sort of iridescent glow. He finished the handle in a barrel shape, making it rounded and perfect for the palm. Now that the blade was complete, it was time to pack his saddle bags for the long journey north.

# Chapter 15

Snow spent most of the days and nights locked in her room. By choice.

Yirrie was determined to keep her safe and out of the forest. But what the elven woman didn't know was that she was beginning to lose her strength from not being part of nature. Connecting with the forest gave her the strength, fueled her energy. Without it was like living without food and water.

She had grown weaker and weaker as the days passed. Her mood plummeted without seeing the sun light her window.

Yirrie tried on more than one occasion to coax her out of her room. Tried to get her to return to festival for the remaining nights. But Snow wasn't having it. She was not interested in joining any of the festivities. Even Elator tried to persuade her to return to festival by suggesting Ardan had been asking about her. She did not want to see Ardan and his adoring looks again.

Finally, only when festival was all over, all of the couples made their intentions known, and things returned to normal did Snow crack open her bedroom door and peer out.

Yirrie and Elator had retired for the night. The house was silent and dark. And though the moon was no longer full, Snow needed to slip into the forest where she would find solace and strength and renewed life.

Of course, it would be difficult to sneak away from the house with someone watching the door as Yirrie had mentioned. But perhaps that was over now that she was sequestered for days on end. She'd proven to Yirrie she wasn't leaving.

She crept from her bedroom, pulling the door closed behind her. She made her bed look as though she were sleeping buried under the blankets. The window was still boarded up, so it kept the room plunged in total darkness. If Yirrie or Elator looked inside, all they would see was a rounded shape on the bed and nothing more.

It was her one chance to slip out unnoticed. Now that festival was over, she would have a better chance at that.

But first, before she returned to the forest, she had a stop to make.

Rather than dress in one of her usual gowns, she opted for the pants, tunic, and vest combination. Her hair was pulled back and tied with a leather thong. She carried her boots so as not to make any unusual noise as she tiptoed to the front door in her stocking feet.

At the front door, with her heart ramming against her chest, she twisted the knob. Holding her breath, she pulled open the door thankful for the silent hinges and stepped into the night.

She stood a moment on the stoop and her head tipped upward into the slight evening breeze, inhaling the damp scents of the world around her. It had rained recently somewhere deep within the world. She sensed the wild earthy smell on the wind and smiled.

But she didn't want to linger. She pulled the door closed, then paused to step into her boots. Then she hurried to Master Harwin's home, her heart in her throat as she made her way across the village.

She sensed the presence before she saw him. The hooded figure came out of the shadows, stepping in her path. The scream rose into her throat but she stifled it, pressing a hand against her pounding heart. The man shoved off his hood.

"Ardan!" She said his name on a gasp. "You scared me."

A sheepish look came over his face as he dropped his head and looked down at his feet.

"What are you doing here?" she demanded.

"Yirrie asked me to watch for you to make sure you didn't leave the village."

First shock then anger pounded through her. She clenched her fists into a tight ball.

"I'm not leaving the village," she said. "I'm going to see Master Harwin."

His head snapped up. "Master Harwin? Why?"

She huffed out a breath and shoved passed him. "I have to talk to him about something."

"I'll come with you."

Spinning around, she placed both her hands on his chest and gave him a shove. "No, you will not."

"But—"

"I can take care of myself."

"But Yirrie said—"

"I don't care what Yirrie said."

Turning on her heel, she stalked off once again toward Master Harwin's house.

"If you let me come with you, I won't tell her," he called.

Snow halted. So, it was to be blackmail then. Disappointment flooded through her that Ardan was willing to stoop to that level. She cut him a glance over her shoulder.

"Fine, then. Come on. But say nothing."

At Master Harwin's door, she pushed it open and paused in the little foyer with the desk. Ardan stood next to her. Knowing Harwin rarely slept, she marched to the door on the right and knocked. Moments later, a squinting, sleepy-eyed Master Harwin opened the door and poked his head out.

"Snow?" His gaze landed on Ardan. "And who's this?"

"This is Ardan," she replied. And then something occurred to her. "He has the enchanted blade."

Harwin's brows flew upward. "The enchanted blade?"

"And..." Pausing, she cut Ardan a glance. "I have answers."

Excitement lit his eyes as he waved them inside his home and to the table where they had shared tea once before. She perched on the edge of the stool, Ardan on the one next to her, and waited while Harwin started to brew a pot of tea.

Ardan leaned toward her, his voice low. "You told him about the enchanted blade?"

She nodded, remaining silent. When the kettle whistled, he brought it and cups over to the table, placing it in the middle. He poured two cups and slid one to Snow and one to Ardan, then poured one for himself.

"Well?" he prompted. "Let me see this enchanted blade."

Ardan remained statue still in his seat. Snow nudged him with her elbow.

"Show him," she urged.

Reluctantly, Ardan unsheathed the blade and placed it in the middle of the table. Harwin leaned forward, his brows drawn together, to get a good look at it. He reached for it, gave Ardan a questioning look.

"May I?" he asked.

The boy nodded.

Harwin picked it up, turning it this way and that, letting the light glint off the shiny, wavy blade. He *hmmed* deep in his throat.

In the lamplight of the room, there was a rainbow iridescent glow to the steel.

"What do you think now?" Snow asked.

"This was made by someone with a love of the craft. I have never seen a more perfect blade," Harwin said. "It's magnificent."

He handed it back to Ardan.

"Thank you," the boy said.

"It was definitely made by an Artificer," Harwin said.

"What's an Artificer?" Ardan asked.

"A master craftsman that can wield the elements," Snow answered.

"You mean with magic?" Ardan asked.

"Yes," Harwin and Snow said in unison.

Ardan sheathed the dagger once again, then reached for this tea. Harwin looked at Snow then.

"You said you had answers," Harwin said.

She nodded, then cut a glance at Ardan. "I do, but he doesn't know anything about..." She pressed her lips together.

Harwin grinned as he sat back in his chair, holding his cup. "I understand." He gave Ardan a look of earnest. "Would you mind waiting outside then?"

Ardan's eyes flew wide. "Me? But I'm supposed to keep an eye on Snow."

"I assure you she won't leave my sight," Harwin said with a grin.

Ardan glanced from her to Harwin, disdain clearly on his face. He took one last sip of tea, then rose from the table and shuffled out, closing the door with a snap behind him.

"You're not allowed to leave the village, are you?" he asked.

She shook her head, staring down into the tawny brew.

"But you did anyway, didn't you?"

She lifted her gaze to his finally. "I went to the wizard's cabin."

Awe was written all over his face. "You did?"

"Yes," she said. "And I found him."

"You found *him*?" His brows knit in confusion. "He was there?"

"Well, a version of him, I guess you could say."

"What does that mean?" he asked.

"There was something of his essence there," she said. "His name is Govan."

She quickly told him about the wizard helping a young peasant woman rise to her position of queen—Seraphina. And how that queen murdered the king, intending to take the throne for herself. She did not tell him about the young princess the evil queen sent into the forest to fend for herself and instead ended up living with the elves. Nor did she mention the king was her father.

Then she told him about the spell book Seraphina stole and how she acquired all three of the mirrors from the elves by using a portal.

"Queen Seraphina has the Magic Mirror," she said. "Govan told me she used the Magic Mirror to curse him and steal his magic. All that's left of him is in the cabin, which is what's feeding her magic and keeping her powerful. The only way to release him from his captivity and destroy her is by destroying the Magic Mirror."

Harwin sat back in the chair, his forefinger tapping on the table. "Interesting. I have never heard of such magic. How did she know we had the mirrors?"

"Govan knew. He was still connected to them even after you took them and hid them. He told her."

He remained silent for a long moment, his mind working as he considered all Snow told him. "This Queen Seraphina has no rule over us elves, but the Magic Mirror she possesses is quite dangerous."

"Yes," Snow agreed.

They stared at each other in uncomfortable silence. He was right in that the queen had nothing to do with the elves. The elves had no royal ruler, but were instead led by the group of Elders. He ran a hand over his smooth chin, still peering at her with contemplation.

"Perhaps you should be the one to destroy the Magic Mirror."

"Me?" The word squeaked out of her. "Why me?"

"You are human," he said as if he were speaking of the everyday weather. "You would have a higher chance of getting into the castle than any of us." He waved his hands to encompass that of the elves.

Something about his statement hit her hard, her gut clenching at the thought of returning to the castle. Even Govan suggested she return to destroy the Magic Mirror and release him from his captivity.

If she were to return, would Seraphina try to destroy her then? Snow was a threat to her throne as it was hers by birthright. She doubted the queen would merely step aside and allow her to have it now that she had come of age. Nor would she allow her into the castle to destroy the mirror.

The way Master Harwin looked at her, though, made her wonder if he knew her true identity. But that was impossible. Even when she stumbled into the forest as a child, she never told anyone who she was.

She resisted the urge to reach up and touch the pendant around her neck.

Still, Harwin continued to look at her with curiosity deep in his eyes.

"I seem to recall a story long ago about a princess who had gone missing and was presumed dead."

"Oh?" She reached for her tea cup and took a sip, not meeting his intense gaze.

"We don't get much news through the Wyldwood," he continued, "but sometimes travelers passed by the village seeking refuge for the night. They have tales of the outside world."

Snow dropped her hand into her lap, clenching it tight to keep it from shaking.

The outside world to the elves was the other kingdoms which surrounded the Wyldwood Forest. The Mystic Vale to the north, the Feywood to the south. Each had their own ruler.

He leaned forward. "Why were you so interested in the dark wizard and the mirrors?"

"I wasn't," she said, too quickly. "It was just that I wanted to help you find out what happened to them."

He lifted a brow, as though he didn't quite believe her.

"Where are you from, Snow?"

Startled, the question pounded through her, leaving her momentarily speechless.

"You came to us ten years ago, yes?" he asked.

"Yes," she said and managed a weak smile as if the subject didn't bother her one bit.

"And ten years ago, we heard the stories of the missing princess. The princess who was exiled by a tyrannical queen." He tilted his head to the side, looking her over. "Are you that princess?"

She pressed her lips together, recalling the day she had stumbled into the forest alone and frightened. She had managed to make it all the way from the castle without being spotted by any villagers. It had taken her days to traverse the kingdom. She hid in barns, stealing food to survive along the way. She recalled how hurt she was none of the servants came looking for her. Now that she was older, she understood it was probably Seraphina's doing. If they left to search for her, they would tempt her wrath.

Finally, she said, "What if I am?"

He sat back in his chair, his gaze never leaving her face. "Hair black as ebony. Lips red as the rose. Skin white as snow."

A prickling sensation when over her. "Where did you hear that?"

"That's you. Isn't it?" he asked, ignoring her question.

She shook her head. "I don't know how it could be."

The pendant felt heavy around her neck. The one that proved she was Princess of the Mystic Vale, heir to the throne. The one with the rose and crown embossed on it.

His eyes glinted with knowledge and a smile crossed his face at her denial. "I rarely leave my archives, but I am not so sheltered I don't hear the stories from others."

Finally, Snow leaned forward, reaching a hand toward him. He grasped hers, his hand warm on hers.

In a low voice, she said, "I am that princess."

"I knew it!"

"But," she said quickly and squeezed his hand to press her point. "You cannot tell anyone. No one knows. Not Yirrie or Elator. Promise me."

Harwin didn't move for a long moment as she gripped his hand.

"Why do you not wish for anyone to know? You are a princess and—"

"Seraphina cannot know I'm here."

Even as she said it, she realized the truth of it. Seraphina likely already knew she was there. That was why the Shadow came for her and tried to kill her.

Finally, Harwin said, "I promise."

She released his hand and sat back in the chair. "Thank you."

"But, Snow, why do you stay here? You are of age now. You can return and take back your throne." He paused, a knowing smile coming over his face. "And destroy the Magic Mirror."

It was a valid question. "How can I fight her? She has the Magic Mirror and castle guards and soldiers at her disposal. I am one person."

"Perhaps the Elders can help—"

"No," she said, cutting him off with a slash of her hand. Then she shoved her chair back, the legs scraping along the floor. "I must go. Poor Ardan has waited long enough."

Harwin also rose. He came around the table and reached for her, gripping her by the shoulders. "Consider it, Snow. The Mystic Vale is yours by birthright. If you destroy the mirror, then you destroy Queen Seraphina and her magic."

And the dark wizard, but she didn't say it.

If she left the Wyldwood, she'd leave Yirrie and Elator behind. How would they take the news she was the missing princess and she decided to return home to reclaim her throne? She wondered if they would even believe her. The only proof she had of her identity was the pendant around her neck.

She gave him a nod. "I'll consider it."

"Thank you for telling me about the dark wizard and the mirrors. Now, I must decide how to share that information with the Elders." A sort of sadness crossed his face.

"I think you tell them you were unable to prevent their theft. After all, she used a portal to steal them," she said. Then she bent and kissed his cheek. "Good night, Master Harwin."

His eyes lit with a spark of joy. He pressed his hand against his cheek as she turned to the door and left.

# CHAPTER 16

S now exited Harwin's. Ardan leaned against the desk in the center of the room, his ankles crossed, staring at the ceiling. He came to an abrupt upright position when he saw her. Snow marched toward the door without giving him a wayward glance. He followed, right on her heels as she exited the building.

The evening breeze rolled over her. She paused a moment, closed her eyes, and inhaled the scent of the night air. It was redolent with the earthy, woodsy aroma of the surrounding forest. She sensed Ardan's presence next to her as he shifted nervously.

"You can go home now." She cracked an eye and looked at him.

"I don't think I should." His hand rested on the dagger hilt, as though he were prepared to pull it at any moment.

"I think you should."

Without waiting for a reply, she started off through the village heading to the edge where it met the forest.

"Where are you going? What did you talk to Master Harwin about? Why did I have to leave?" He was out of breath as he fired off his questions, trying to keep up with her accelerated pace.

"Where I'm going you can't come," she said. "My conversation with Master Harwin was confidential and that's why you had to leave." She never broke stride as she spoke. The closer she got to the edge of the forest, the stronger, more energetic she felt.

"But, Snow—"

"Listen, Ardan." She halted, turning to him and putting a hand on his chest. "I know you mean well and you're trying to do what Yirrie wanted you to do but there's something I have to do. Alone. You can't come with me."

Question flickered through his eyes. "Why not?"

She huffed, frustrated, and dropped her hand. "You won't understand."

"I might." There was a twinge of hurt in his voice. "If you'll give me a chance."

And suddenly guilt swept through her. She understood what he was trying to do, truly, but she didn't want him with her when she stepped foot in the forest to recharge. It was something she did alone. Only Annilen and the other forest creatures understood.

He reached for her hand, grasping it in his. "I like you, Snow."

Oh, dear. That wasn't good.

"I didn't choose anyone at festival," he added.

And that was even worse.

"Ardan—"

"Allow me to escort you."

She blew out a heated breath. The last thing she wanted was for Ardan to have feelings for her. The fact he chose no one at festival was a terrible sign he was more interested in her than she was of him.

What harm could it do to have him with her in the forest? She reasoned if anything else happened, if there was another Shadow, then he would be there to help her. Finally, she relented and nodded.

"All right. I need your word you will tell no one."

He squeezed her hand. "You have my word."

She released him and continued on, aware of the many promises the elves made to her. Harwin keeping who she truly was to himself. Now Ardan will see her elemental magic at work. Even though Yirrie and Elator knew of it, they didn't understand how connected she was to the world around her.

When she stepped out of the protective circle of the village and into the forest, she halted and closed her eyes to attune to the world around her. Ardan's shuffling feet alerted her to his presence next to her. He didn't possess the stealth she did and it annoyed her.

"Be still," she snapped.

He stiffened but no longer moved. "What are you doing?"

"Shhh."

With her eyes still closed, she sensed Faradill deep in the forest standing as a sentry among the other oaks keeping watch over the domain. The leaves rustled in the breeze. Annilen and her fellow sprites were preparing to sleep as they buzzed around their small homes, some of them within the trunks of trees. That is, if the trees allowed it. Crickets chirped. An owl hooted. Rustling underbrush indicated a nocturnal animal foraging for a late-night snack. The sound of the stream rushing over rocks inhabited by water sprites. The bray of a unicorn.

And, deep in the woods, the clop of hooves.

She opened her eyes, still attuned to the sound of the hooves and started forward at a furious pace. Hunters tended to come through the forest at night searching for their prey. She made it her mission to run off these pesky hunters. They weren't wanted here.

Ardan stomped through the forest, his noisy steps scaring off any animals. Snow wasn't used to all the noise of snapping sticks and crunching leaves. Her steps were stealthier and placed with purpose. Irritation clawed through her that he insisted on following her.

Up ahead was the clearing where she had rescued the unicorn not so long ago. There was no unicorn or hunter there tonight.

"Shouldn't we have a torch or something?" As he said it, he stumbled over a fallen log.

"I can see fine."

Indeed, her eyes adjusted to the nighttime shadows with ease. Because she was so much a part of this world, she was at home. With no moon, though, it was quite dark. She suppressed a snicker at the thought of Ardan having trouble seeing. Likely why he continued to make so much noise.

Faradill was past the clearing, but the horse's hooves she heard came from the south. She stopped there and waited, stretching her senses to attune to the world around her. It was definitely a horse. Not a unicorn.

Ardan stopped next to her, looking from the clearing to her and back again.

"What is it?" he whispered.

"Someone is coming."

"How do you know?"

"I can sense it."

Again, his gaze swiveled from her to the clearing and back again. "You can?"

"Yes. Now shh."

She waited there, her hands clenched at her side in preparation to use whatever means necessary to stop the intruder.

The horse came into view then at a slow walk. The man on his back was nothing but a silhouette against the backdrop of the forest night. He held the reins loosely in one hand as though he were on an evening ride without a care in the world. He rode through the clearing northward. When he was closer, she stepped into his line of sight, spooking the horse. It whinnied its distress.

The man, startled, pulled the horse to a stop. "Whoa, girl."

"Who are you and what are you doing in these woods?" Snow demanded.

He sat tall and still in the saddle. Shadows concealed his face. "I'm passing through, my lady. That's all."

"Passing through? No one passes through these woods."

Even as she said it, she recalled Master Harwin's words of travelers who once came through these woods looking for respite. Was this man one of those?

"Well, I am." There was a distinct smile in his voice.

"At this time of night?" she asked.

Ardan stepped up next to her, his shimmering blade in his hand. She hadn't heard him move, nor did she realize he had unsheathed the dagger. The stranger remained still in the saddle for a long moment.

"Yes, my lady. I was hoping to find a place to stop and rest the horse and myself for the night."

"There is no place to stop here," she said, her voice hard and unforgiving. "You should turn back."

He gave a small laugh. "I'm afraid I can't do that." He inched the horse closer to the two of them. "You have an interesting blade there, my lord."

"I am no lord," Ardan said. "And this is an enchanted blade."

"Indeed?" The man sounded intrigued. Then he dismounted the horse, coming around the front and holding onto the reins. He walked toward the two of them. "May I see it?"

"No," Snow answered. "You may not."

The stranger paused within a few feet of them and now she was able to make out his features. He was tall, broad-shouldered, wearing a hooded cloak. His face was still shrouded in shadows but she was able to see his pale blue-green eyes and square chin with a dimple in the center. His face was covered in stubble, as though he had been traveling for a few days.

Her heart skipped as she peered at him. Her magic reached out to him, tingling and sizzling. She sensed something earthy about him. Something that told her he was like her. He had a crisp, clean scent that reminded her of a spruce tree, but underneath that was the heady scent of wood smoke. He was earth and fire. He was wind and sun.

He was an elemental.

He cleared his throat. "My lady, you're staring."

"More like gaping," Ardan added, his tone flat with a tinge of jealousy.

She jerked herself out of her thoughts and tried to look away from him but found she could not. She was drawn to him in a way she had never been drawn to anyone.

"Show him the blade, Ardan," she heard herself say.

He gave her a look as though she'd lost her mind. Perhaps she had but said nothing. He handed the blade over to the stranger, who took it and examined it with a critical eye. He twisted and turned the dagger. Since there was no moonlight, it was hard to see the wavy steel. Even so, it still shimmered with its iridescent glow.

"This is a fine weapon," the stranger said. He lifted his gaze back to Ardan and gave him a magnificent smile. "And I should know. I forged it."

"You're the master blacksmith?" Ardan asked.

Snow continued to gape, her heart doing double time her chest. *He* was an Artificer. What had Master Harwin said? They knew how to manipulate fire, air, and the iron deep within the earth.

"I've been called that," he said with a nod, sounding humble. He returned the dagger to Ardan.

"My father visited your forge. You made this for me," Ardan said.

The stranger stepped closer to look Ardan up and down, then stepped back. "Your father was the elven lord who commissioned it?"

"He was," Ardan said sounding proud.

The stranger's gaze turned to her then. "But you are not an elf."

"I am not," she agreed. "I'm human."

One dark brow raised, his expression curious and interested. "I've heard stories this forest is enchanted. I see the stories are true."

She flushed, her cheeks burning.

"If you're truly passing through, then we should let you continue on your way," Ardan said, clearly ready to be done with the stranger.

"I am passing through," he said. "I mean no harm to anyone."

"That's good. Because I am the protector of this forest. I do not take kindly to hunters who try to hurt those who inhabit this place."

She didn't know what made her say it. Ardan's head snapped in her direction and she could feel his stare boring into the side of her head. But she kept her gaze locked on the handsome stranger with the blue-green eyes standing in front of her.

"I assure you, I am no hunter." He granted her a knee-melting smile. "I'll be on my way then."

He headed around the horse, who had stood patiently waiting for him to return to the saddle.

"If you're looking for a water source for your horse," she said, "there is a stream that runs east to west just north of here. You can rest there for the night, too."

A faint light of wonder twinkled in the depths of his eyes. The beginning of a smile tipped the corners of his mouth. Despite the shadowy darkness, she saw it.

"Thank you, my lady. I am grateful for the information."

He stuck his foot into the stirrup and hoisted back into the saddle, taking the reins in his weathered hands. He continued his path to the north. Snow remained where she was watching him leave until he was well out of sight. Her heart sang with delight and, for the first time, joy bubbled through her.

"We should return to the village now," Ardan said.

But she didn't want to. She wanted to stand there with the vague hope the stranger with the blue-green eyes would return.

"Snow?" he queried.

She exhaled a deep sigh of contentment. "Yes, I suppose you're right."

He reached for her hand, tucking it into the crook of his elbow. He was talking, but she wasn't listening. Instead, she was thinking about the stranger. The stranger, she realized, she would likely never see again.

# Chapter 17

Roderick awoke the following morning when his horse nudged him with her nose, then snorted at him. The stars were gone, replaced by the morning sun. Birds sang their happy tunes high atop the trees and the stream the lady mentioned rippled over rocks in a soothing trickle that sent him right to sleep.

Smiling, he patted the horse's nose.

"All right, old girl. I'm awake. And you're right. We should be going."

He had a difficult time not thinking about the girl in the forest. There was something special about her, something that told him that though she was human, she was not all she appeared to be. It was difficult to ignore the earthy scent of magic emanating from her. He wondered if she realized how intoxicating that was.

In all his years, he had never met another elemental, though he certainly knew there were others like him. His parents, may they rest in peace, did not possess the magic as he did.

But the girl did. The moment he stepped down from the saddle and approached her, he sensed it. She had a fire deep within her. When she said she was the protector of the forest, he believed her.

What baffled him the most was that she was with the elven boy who she called Ardan. He had his enchanted blade. How had the two of them come to be in each other's presence? They didn't seem as though they were a couple. In fact, she seemed more irritated with him than anything. Ardan, other the other hand, was enamored with her.

Even without his magical senses, Roderick saw that about the elf.

She was lovely with red lips and moonlight pale skin. It was difficult to see in the darkness, but he guessed her hair was black as a raven. She had high cheekbones and a heart-shaped face with a chin that came to a point. He admired how she clenched her long, slender fingers into a fist, as though she meant to do him harm if he stepped out of line. The thought made him smile. He regretted not getting the girl's name.

The horse nudged him again, breaking him free of his ruminations. He patted her nose again and then went to the saddle bag, reaching in for an apple.

"I know we should be going," he said as the horse munched away. "But I can't stop thinking about that girl."

A snorted response, which made him chuckle. He took up the reins and led her away from the stream, heading north and to Seraphina's castle to deliver the queen's dagger.

It was a long ride through the Mystic Vale northward. He passed through several small villages, all of which seemed to have no joy about them. The tension was high in each of them. He stopped at a local inn in the village of Westfall for a midday meal and was welcomed by the innkeeper. From him, Roderick learned why there appeared to be no happiness in these villages. Seraphina's rule was one of suppression. She taxed them to the point of poverty.

The innkeeper told him the story of the missing princess. That she mysteriously disappeared after the king died under suspicious circumstances and Seraphina proclaimed herself queen.

"What happened to the princess?" he asked.

The innkeeper shrugged. "No one knows."

After he finished his meal and threw some gold coins on the table, he continued his journey.

He did not arrive at the castle until the sun had long set. Rather than ride up to the castle gates, he dismounted and walked the rest of the way, leading his horse by the reins. There were guards posted outside the door, which he expected. He did not expect the guards standing along the wall pointing arrows at him ready to shoot him if he made a wrong move. He gave them a cursory glance as he approached the outer wall, then fixed his gaze on the two flanking the open portcullis.

One guard stepped forward, holding out a hand to stop him from advancing further.

"State your name and your business here," the guard said.

"Roderick of Bridgefort. I come at the behest of your queen to hand deliver the item she requested."

"What is this requested item?" the guard asked.

"She commissioned a special blade from me. I'm a blacksmith," he replied. He preferred not to say, but then he decided he wouldn't get very far if he didn't.

"Wait here," the guard said.

He disappeared through the portcullis, leaving Roderick standing there in the breezy night air with his horse and the other guard staring him down. Above him, the rest of them kept their arrows nocked against their bows, ready to fire.

Finally, the guard returned with another man who was taller. He wore a red and white cloak over his armor with the sigil of a rose and crown along the back.

"I am Erick, Captain of the Guard. Give me the weapon and I will deliver it to the queen." He held out his hand and waited.

Roderick glanced from the man's open hand up to his face, giving him a faint smile. "I'm afraid I can't do that. I was asked to personally deliver it to the queen."

"Asked by whom?" demanded the captain.

"The messenger she sent to me to commission the blade a week ago."

The captain stared at him as though he had grown a second head. "I know of no such messenger."

"Then perhaps you should ask your queen about that," Roderick said, refusing to back down.

"Perhaps I will." He dropped his hand. "Come with me. We will stable your horse while you meet with the queen." He gave a nod to the other guard, who reached for the reins.

Before he led the horse away, Roderick reached into the saddle bag and brought out the dagger which was sheathed in a leather scabbard and wrapped in a thick cloth. The captain of the guard eyed the weapon with interest.

"Don't worry," Roderick said. "This is the weapon she commissioned."

Erick said nothing as he motioned for Roderick to follow him. He led him through the portcullis and across the bailey. They entered the main keep, where the captain led him to a large room hosting one throne. Torches lined the walls every few feet. Large braziers burned bright in each corner, giving the room a warm glow. Even so, the room was less than inviting.

"Wait here," he ordered.

Then he was gone, leaving Roderick to stand there alone in the middle of the room feeling awkward. It wasn't long before he returned, a woman following him.

When she came into view, he recognized her immediately. This was the messenger who came to his forge and commissioned the enchanted blade. She gave him a broad smile as she passed by him and headed right for the throne, her black gown trailing after her and the heady scent of peonies. The captain remained standing behind him, his feet shoulder-width apart and his hands clasped in front of him.

She perched on the edge of the throne, leaning on one of the arm rests. There was a deep glint of something wicked in her eyes that gave Roderick a feeling of unease.

"Master blacksmith," she said, her voice ringing out in the cavernous room. She waved him closer. "Please approach and show me the dagger you forged."

He remained where he was. "Where is the queen?"

The laugh bubbled up her throat. "I am the queen."

He stared at her, long and hard and realized what a fool he'd been. The messenger who came to him in this forge *was* the queen.

"Your majesty, he claims a messenger commissioned the blade from him a week ago," the captain said.

"A messenger did," she confirmed. "That messenger was me. Come, master blacksmith, and show me this weapon."

With a cautious glance over his shoulder to the captain of the guard, he unwrapped the dagger in the leather sheath. Erick rested his hand on the pommel of his sword, ready to wield it should he make any threatening moves.

Roderick stepped closer to the queen and handed it over. She took it, unsheathing it with a flourish and holding it up into the flickering light. Rainbow iridescence flickered up and down the steel, giving it that ethereal glow of enchantment. Excitement lit her eyes as she gazed at it, moving it to and fro with the flick of her wrist.

"This is a magnificent blade," she said, her voice full of admiration.

"Thank you, your majesty."

"You delivered as promised. We must toast this momentous occasion."

With a wave of her free hand, a table appeared next to her. On the table, was a silver ewer and two silver goblets. She poured from the ewer a pale liquid he assumed was mead. She picked up one of the goblets and extended it to him. He eyed the dagger still in her other hand and hesitated.

She chuckled. "I see the fear in your eyes. Do not worry, sir, for I do not intend to stab you with your own blade. I merely wish to offer a toast."

He stepped forward and took the goblet. She replaced the blade back into its sheath, then picked up the second goblet. She tapped hers against his and then drank. Though he was still unsure, he drank. It was sweet, leaving a strange after taste on his tongue.

She grinned, taking the goblet away from him and placed it back on the table.

"How do you like my apple cider?" she asked. "It's an old family recipe I brewed myself."

He didn't answer as she waved her hand, making the ewer and cups disappear. Then she motioned to Erick behind him. He stepped forward with a heavy purse in his hands and walked it to the queen. She took it from him and placed it in her lap. The captain remained by the queen's side. Roderick eyed the purse heavy with coin.

"I promised you five thousand gold coins." She rested her hand on the purse in a protective gesture.

"You did, your majesty."

"And I will give it to you when you do something else for me."

Unease flickered through him. "That was not part of the deal. The deal was I forge the blade, which I did, and hand deliver it to you, which I also did."

"Yes, and a fine job of it you did." She gave him a vicious smile. "But there is something else I require. A certain task. If you agree, then you will receive this," she patted the round purse of coins in her lap, "and an additional five thousand gold."

His mind went blank, a whirlwind of confusion swirling inside him as he tried to make sense of her request and her offer.

"What sort of task?" he asked.

She extended the sheathed blade to the captain, who took it. He remained where he was, holding it as though waiting for her command. A flicker of fear went through Roderick as he watched the captain, wondering if he was about to be stabbed with his own dagger.

But surely not. She said she wanted him to perform a task. Her wicked smile widened.

"There is a woman living in the Wyldwood Forest. Hair black as ebony. Lips red as the rose. Skin white as snow." Even as she said it, she rolled her eyes at the description, as though it pained her to speak the words aloud. "Her name is Snow White."

With the description, the image of the girl he met in the forest immediately sprang to mind. He was certain she was the one he met the previous night as he traversed the forest. He stood ramrod straight, his nerves jangling and his heart pounding a wild beat.

"She is my sworn enemy," the queen continued, "and a threat to the crown. *My* crown. She must be dealt with."

Again, Roderick eyed the dagger as the captain turned it over in his hand, the hilt toward him. Understanding struck him. If the queen wanted him to deal with Snow White, there was only one outcome. But he waited patiently for her to continue with her request.

"I want you to kill her. Cut out her heart with this dagger," she waved toward it in the captain's hands, "and bring it to me."

Then she placed her hand palm upward. A flicker of red smoke plumed in her palm and then was replaced with a wood box. The emblem on the top was that of a rose and crown, the royal sigil of the Mystic Vale.

"Place her heart in this box. It's enchanted and will tell me if the heart you bring me belongs to Snow White."

Erick reached for the box, holding it in one hand and the dagger in the other. He walked to Roderick and extended both to him. Roderick eyed them with disbelief. How was he supposed to kill the beautiful girl in the forest by cutting out her heart? And what sort of callous queen was this Seraphina? What had Snow White done to deserve such a fate?

"Do you agree?" she asked.

"If I refuse?"

She chuckled, a malevolent laugh deep in her throat. "If you refuse, then you will be placed in my dungeon for the rest of your days." She rose from the throne then, unfolding her long, slender body in a fluid motion, and walked toward him. "I should tell you the cider you drank was poison. A slow-acting poison. If you fail to kill Snow White, if you betray me in any way, you will fall into a long, eternal slumber."

Questions arose in his mind. Like how the queen would know if he betrayed her.

As if hearing his thoughts, she added, "And I *will* know. Bring me her heart, and I will give you the antidote. Fail, and the sleeping curse will take you. You have a fortnight to accomplish this task. A fortnight before the poison takes hold and plunges you into a deep, everlasting sleeping curse."

She must have spies within the forest itself. That or she intended to use her wicked magic to make sure he carried out her demand.

"So, what's it to be, blacksmith? Do you agree to do this task for me?"

If he refused, he would never leave this castle. If he agreed, he would have to destroy a beautiful young woman. His choice was clear. He reached for the box and the dagger.

"I agree, your majesty."

# CHAPTER 18

Ardan hardly let her out of his sight. In fact, it drove her mad that he was her constant shadow, no matter where she went or what she did.

Mostly, she spent long hours in her room, staring at the boarded window. A few times, she had the impulse to march around to the back of the house and rip off the wood. But explaining to Yirrie and Elator why would be difficult.

As much as they taught her about nature, connecting with nature, they did not understand how deep her magic went. She missed her friends, Annilen and Faradill. She worried there were hunters in the woods looking for unicorns.

On the night of the full moon, she was curled on her bed gazing at the covered window wishing she was in the forest, talking to Faradill and Annilen. Listening to the hoot of the night owl and the chirp of the crickets. The rustle of underbrush as a nocturnal animal foraged for food. How she missed it all.

She held the pendant between her thumb and forefinger, thinking about Master Harwin and the dark wizard. Both of them urged her to return home and reclaim her throne.

But how? She had no army. It wasn't likely the elves would back her. Tasnia would be happy to see her go.

A knock on her door brought her out of her thoughts. Odd, this time of night.

"Yes?" she called.

The door opened a crack and Elator stuck his head inside. He gave her a mischievous grin. "Yirrie is sleeping."

He said this as if this was the best news.

Snow sat on the edge of the bed, her bare feet on the floor. "Is she?"

Elator pushed the door wider and whispered, "Come with me."

Then he disappeared into the shadows of the house. Snow, uncertain what he was up to, grinned. She reached for her dressing gown and pulled it on over her shift. In truth, she had been about to crawl under the covers and try to sleep but now she was curious to see what Elator was up to.

She hurried through the house and found him standing at the front door. He put a finger to his lips to indicate silence and she nodded, her heart pounding with excitement.

Elator pulled open the door and waved her through it. She saw there was a small fire and two chairs on either side of it. Grinning, she stepped outside into the night. Behind her, Elator closed the door, then waved her to one of the chairs.

"What's all this?" she asked.

"You've been stuck inside for days," he said. "I know what it means to you to be out in the evening air when there's a full moon."

Surprise flickered through her. "You do?"

He nodded as he lowered down into one of the chairs. Snow did the same.

"Yirrie doesn't understand, but I do. You are connected to nature more deeply than any of us are. I sensed that when we found you at the foot of that tree ten years ago. I sense it even now," he said.

Words failed her as she looked at the man who had raised her for all these long years. She hadn't given him enough credit for understanding her. He reached for a long stick by his chair and handed it to her. There was a fat marshmallow stuck on the end.

When she was a girl and had first come to the village, she and Elator spent hours outside late into the night roasting marshmallows. He told her fantastical stories of when the elves were under the rule of the High King, when the landscape of their kingdom was different. When dragons roamed the skies.

Of course, she never believed these stories, but she loved hearing them.

She took the stick from him.

"You understand me," she said, wonder in her voice.

"I do. I am not so unlike you." He stuck the marshmallow in the fire, turning it slowly to roast it evenly.

She watched the fire flicker for a long moment, then said, "This means a lot to me."

"I know you are human," he said. "But you're special. We've always known you were special since the moment we saw you sleeping at the foot of the tree. That seems like only yesterday."

"But you've never treated me as if I were different."

She thought about the past and how they had raised her, loved her, kept her safe. And all she'd done was run off to the forest, breaking through the magical barrier Tasnia placed to keep her safe from more dark magic. She'd broken her promise she would stay within the boundaries of the village.

"We tried not to," he said, still turning his stick. "But we both understood that someday you may want to return to where you came from."

Hot pinpricks went over her skin as she cut him a glance. "Why are you telling me this?"

"Because I want you to know that I understand if you have to leave it. You're a young woman now. Perhaps you want to return to your parents—"

"No," she said, cutting him off. Her gut clenched. "My parents are dead."

But there was something to return to—her throne. Rule of the Mystic Vale kingdom which did not include the Wyldwood Forest.

"Ardan told me about the stranger in the forest," Elator said.

Snow's head snapped over to him as cold pinpricks went through her. "He shouldn't have done that."

Elator cut her a glance, but there was no anger in his eyes. "He said the man was human, like you, and that you seemed to make a connection with him."

She stared at him. She tried to think of a response, but her mind was blank. He shifted in his chair, still slowly turning the stick with the nearly charred marshmallow on the end.

"I think what I'm trying to say, Snow, is that if you wish to return to your world, then you should."

"But...What about Yirrie? Won't she be upset?"

"I'll handle Yirrie." He gave her a small smile.

"You think because I made a connection with another human that I want to be among them. Is that it?"

His shoulders slumped as he nodded. "Don't you?"

Snow sat back in the chair, the stick dangling from her hand as she thought about his words. He was, essentially, releasing her from their village. Though not in a way that appeared to be pushing her out. He wanted only the best for her and, it seemed, he felt as though the best was for her to return to her own world, leaving the isolated world of the elves behind.

Did she? She had no place to go, no place to live. No place among humans. How would she survive among them once again?

"I don't know," she said, her voice hollow. Then, "I'm sorry I broke my promise to stay within the village protective magic."

He made a derisive sound. "Snow, what Yirrie doesn't understand is how connected you are to the energy of the surrounding nature. I do. I understand there is nothing that will keep you within the confines of this village." He paused, pulling his stick out of fire and frowning at the burned gooey substance on the end. "I regret boarding up your window, but Yirrie made me do it."

It meant a lot to Snow to hear him say it. For a moment, she didn't feel so isolated with the elves.

"I brought you out here tonight because I thought it would help."

How kind of him to think of her when all Yirrie wanted was to keep her locked up inside the house.

"Thank you," she said on a whisper. "It does help."

Even though she wasn't in the forest itself, being in the night with the full moon overhead seemed to help recharge her. She was grateful for the time and for Elator.

She also understood he brought her out here to talk to her about meeting the stranger, something Ardan should have kept to himself. He promised not to tell anyone and yet he'd told Elator.

The stranger with the blue-green eyes was on her mind a lot lately. In fact, she hadn't stopped thinking about him since the moment she met him. When he rode away, she wondered what it would be like to call out to him and beg him to take her with him. Would he have refused or agreed?

Ardan was right. There was some kind of connection between them that surfaced almost the moment they came face to face. She suspected it was because they were both elementals. That alone seemed to connect them to each other. It didn't mean they were destined to fall in love, though.

Did it?

It was silly to think about, so she shoved the thoughts away.

Elator tossed away the stick with the burned marshmallow and then rose, stretching his arms over his head.

"Well, I think I'll leave you here to enjoy the peace and the fire."

She glanced up at him. "What about—"

"Don't worry about anything." He granted her a smile. "Good night, Snow."

"Good night."

She watched him return to the house, the door closing softly behind him. Elator was right. It was difficult for her to remain within the confines of the village, when the forest beckoned. She rose from the chair and gave a glance back at the closed door of the house.

Her heart rammed hard in her chest. She knew she was going to do it before she took her first step. Gathering her dressing gown in her hands, she hurried toward the forest.

# CHAPTER 19

The light of the full moon was a blue-white veil that descended on the forest washing it in an otherworldly glow. It was almost as though every leaf of every plant sparkled under the shaft of moonlight. With her heart light and her emotions running high, she headed out of the village. Her destination was her favorite spot at the foot of Faradill.

Snow glanced back a few times to check to see if she was followed, but there was no sign of Ardan. Perhaps Elator had called him off for the night, giving her the opportunity to spend her evening under the moon and the stars. It was a gift. One for which she was eternally thankful. Elator understood her, something she had not realized until they sat by the fire together.

As she headed through the forest, her senses attuned to the faint sound of horse's hooves. She halted near the clearing where she'd first met the stranger, where she'd saved the unicorn from the hunter and paused to listen.

She expected to see another hunter and waited at the edge of the clearing as the distinct sound of hooves came closer and closer.

Until at last the stranger came into view. She stiffened, her heart ramming hard in her chest.

He pulled the horse to a halt, then jumped down from the saddle, gripping the reins in one hand as he moved closer. He came into view, the glow of the moon bathing his face in light. She stifled the gasp as their eyes met.

The stranger had returned. How could this be?

When the thought slipped through her mind, she stiffened. She clenched her hand into a fist, ready to call upon all the forces of nature around her to protect herself. They stared at each other in a long beat of silence. There was only the sound of the crickets.

"You again," she said at last, her voice strong and sure.

"I confess it is a strange thing to meet you once again in the same place." There was a smile in his voice. A smile she didn't like.

Who was he and why was he here? It had been days since they met. She had thought of him often and wondered if they would see each other again. She never expected it to happen so soon, if at all.

"What do you want?" Her words were hard and full of suspicion.

"My name is Roderick. I'm a master blacksmith in the town of Bridgefort. I make armor for King Alfred."

She lifted a brow. "That did not answer my question. Why are you in my woods once again, sir?"

"It is a fair question," he said. "Are you the one they call Snow White?"

She went very still as she peered at him, her hand still clenched. Regret for leaving the confines of the village slashed through her. She was no longer within the safety of the Elders magic and tonight, it might cost her. Her senses stretched outward, touching on the vines and the brambles and the nocturnal creatures. A rustling nearby startled him. His head swiveled from side to side as he listened.

She ignored his question. Never had an outsider come into these woods with her name upon their lips. It unnerved her.

"Again, I ask. What do you want?"

He took a tentative step toward her. Without thinking, Snow lifted her hand, still clenched. Several vines sprang upward, reaching for him. Sensing them before he saw them, his hands flew up. The vines stopped mid-reach. Their magic clashed against one other, the vines shuddering.

"You are an elemental," he said.

"As are you," she replied. "Your presence in these woods is unwanted."

"I understand your unease. Especially since I come at the behest of Queen Seraphina."

She doubled her efforts to attack him but his magic held strong. If he was a messenger for Seraphina, then her instincts were right in that he was trouble.

"I mean you no harm," he said. He twisted his hands palm up in surrender.

"How do I know you're telling the truth?"

"I suppose you'll have to trust me."

His magic pushed back against hers. She felt the ripple of it through her clenched fist, her wrist and then up her arm. If she released him, would he attack her?

"You and I are a lot alike," he said. "I want to help you."

"Help me how?" Her eyes narrowed to slits.

"Release your magic. I'll release mine. Then we can discuss. You have my word I will not harm you," he said.

She regarded him coolly, not budging.

"I never go back on my word," he added.

With reluctance, she released her magic. He released his. The vines fell away, back into their normal place. They stared at each other a long, silent moment. When it was clear he wasn't going to attack her, she relaxed a little.

"All right, Roderick. Why did the queen send you?"

He kept his hands visible. "She told me you are her enemy. That you are a threat to her throne."

Snow laughed, but said nothing. Yes, indeed, she was the queen's enemy. She was a threat to her very existence.

"Why is that?" he asked.

She considered his question, trying to decide how to answer. He was a stranger, so telling him the truth about who she really was didn't seem like a sensible thing to do. But then, how to answer him without telling him the truth?

"Who are you to her?" he asked before she could come up with an answer.

She sucked in a breath, then exhaled it. "I am no one to her."

He shook his head. "I disagree. If you were no one to her, she would not be so determined to do away with you."

That caught her off guard. "Do away with me?" she repeated.

"She wants you dead."

An interesting choice of words, almost as though he already knew who she was.

Of course, Seraphina wanted her dead. She used her dark magic to force Annilen to tell her Snow was living in the elven village. She sent the Shadow to kill her. Snow regarded Roderick and understood why, then, he had returned. He had come to kill her.

"You speak as though you already know who I am when I have not given my name."

"Seraphina told me there was a woman living in the forest with hair as black as ebony, lips red as the rose and skin white as snow. There is only one person in this forest that matches that description. You. You are Snow White," he said.

She lifted her chin and looked down her nose at him. "Are you going to kill me then?"

"As I said, I intend to help you."

He had avoided her question altogether. Irritation swept through her. Did he think she would accept this as an answer? She scoffed. "Do what?"

He considered her for a long moment. There was a thoughtfulness in his eyes as he chose his next words.

"When I traveled through the villages from here to the queen's castle, I stopped along the way in Westfall to take shelter and have a meal at one of the inns. The innkeeper there was a jolly man who liked to tell stories," he said.

"What does this have to do with Snow White?" she asked, still in denial of giving him her true name.

Roderick ignored her question and continued. "He told me the story of Queen Seraphina and how she came to power when the king died. The kingdom, it seems, was to pass to the king's only daughter but she had mysteriously disappeared. No one knew where she went or even if she still lived. He said her name was Snow White."

The blood roared in her ears as she stared at him, her heart a raging beat. Around her, the flora and fauna shuddered, as though they sensed the terror shifting through her.

"The princess disappeared ten years ago," he said. "Judging by your age, my guess is you have come of age and are the rightful ruler of the Mystic Vale. Not Seraphina." As he said this, he eyed the pendant around her neck.

It was then she realized it was no longer under her gown. It rested against the material and glinted in the moonlight. He moved closer, closing the distance between them and halted mere inches from her. Her gut clenched with his nearness.

"The royal sigil of the Mystic Vale is the rose and crown."

He reached for the necklace, picking it up between his thumb and forefinger. "The rose and crown that looks just like this." He ran his thumb over the sigil. "Tell me. Are you Snow White?"

Her eyes met his. And in those depths, she saw a man who was determined to find out the truth about her. There seemed to be no malicious intent behind those eyes. Nothing that would indicate to her he wanted to kill her. Even so, she wasn't sure she fully trusted him.

"Yes," she said at last, the word a hiss of ice between her teeth. "I am Snow White."

# CHAPTER 20

A sense of triumph went through Roderick when she confirmed she was, in fact, Snow White. They stared at each other. Then she slapped his hand away. She spun away from him, her hair flying around her head and her body rigid with her anger.

He saw the sigil when he was in Queen Seraphina's castle.

Even though the innkeeper never spoke of Snow White by name, when the man told him about the princess who disappeared years ago, he put the pieces together. He had a feeling that if Snow White reappeared after years of being in isolation, the people would rally behind her and help her get her throne back. They'd had enough of Seraphina's high taxes.

Snow White put distance between the two of them, then spun back to face him. Her cheeks were flushed. There were deep lines between her brows.

"Well? Are you going to kill me?"

How could he kill a woman as lovely and magical as her? He thought of the wooden box in which he was supposed to place her heart and pushed away a shudder.

The enchanted blade he forged for the queen was hidden in his saddle bag. The one he had forged for himself was belted to his side. But she hadn't noticed that.

"I'm going to show you something."

She huffed, clearly annoyed he had refused to answer her question once again. He walked over to the saddle bag and pulled out the enchanted blade. He'd carved the handle himself from rosewood and inlaid it with intricate gold spirals. The grip was solid against his palm when he tested it. Now, the blade was encased within a leather sheath.

Holding it in his hands, he walked back to Snow White and paused in front of her within arm's reach. Her gaze was leery as she eyed the dagger in his hands.

"Sometimes I accept commissions. This was one of them." He extended the dagger to her. When she hesitated, he said, "Take it."

She reached for it. He noticed her hands shook slightly as she removed the weapon from his hands and held it.

"Wield it," he said.

Curiosity replaced her leeriness as she pulled the dagger from the sheath. She stifled a little gasp as the moonlight caught along the iridescent edge of the blade, making the rainbow light dance up and down the perfect steel. Eyes lit with wonder, she turned the blade back and forth watching the flickering light. She shoved it back into the sheath and handed it back to him.

Reluctantly, he took it.

"Don't you want to know who commissioned it?" he asked.

"No but I suppose you're going to tell me."

"Queen Seraphina came to my forge and asked me to make her an enchanted blade." He held it up. "I did. Then she asked me to hand deliver it to her in her castle in the Mystic Vale."

Snow White looked utterly unimpressed. "And?"

"I took her the blade, but she decided she no longer wanted it for herself. She wanted someone to use it on her behalf."

"This is a fascinating story," Snow said. "Perhaps you'd like to get to the point?"

"She told me she wanted the heart of her enemy cut out and brought to her in a wooden box."

Her face paled. She understood what he meant and eyed the dagger once again.

"This dagger...this enchanted dagger was meant to kill you."

"She sent you here to kill me, then," she said. "Because I am a threat to her and her throne."

"Yes," he agreed. "But I'm not here to kill you."

"Then why are you here?"

He dropped to one knee and held the dagger up to her. "I'm here to bequeath this enchanted blade to you so that you may defeat the queen and regain your throne."

She froze, gaping at him in disbelief. Her eyes met his, glittering with skepticism she no doubt felt.

"How am I supposed to defeat the queen with nothing more than a dagger?" she demanded.

"I will help you."

She huffed out a breath, then pushed her fingers through her long, tangled locks. "Get up."

"You are the rightful ruler of the Mystic Vale—"

"I know who I am. Get *up*, please." Frustration edged her voice.

He stood, unable to stop the flood of disappointment. She had refused the dagger. Was she also refusing the call to reclaim her throne?

"There is much you don't know," she said. "Much you don't understand."

"Then tell me. I wish to understand. To know. I *want* to help you."

"You don't even know me," she snapped.

"That's true. But I know what the people want. I heard it throughout the villages as I traveled to the castle. They want Seraphina gone. And they long to have their rightful ruler back on the throne," he said. "They aren't sure if you're dead or alive. They hope you're alive."

"All of this is too much."

She turned away and started through the forest, her bare feet near silent along the bracken. He marveled at that a long moment before he was spurred into action. It was then he noticed she wore a shift and a dressing gown over it. She had fled her house in the middle of the night and hadn't bothered to dress. Something about that endeared her to him.

Still holding the dagger, he followed her as she made her way through the woods with a clear path in mind.

"You don't understand anything about me or who I am," she said.

Her pace was quick. She wasn't even winded as she made her way through the trees, holding up the edge of her gown to keep from tripping.

"Returning to reclaim my throne is not as simple as everyone seems to think."

"Everyone like who?"

"You, Master Harwin, the dark wizard." Realizing what she said, she snapped her mouth closed, pressing her lips into a thin line.

"Who is Master Harwin?" he asked, still following her. His booted feet crunched over the bracken.

She halted, turned to him in a huff. "You walk too loud."

Then she picked up her skirt and ran. He was so shocked by what she said, he didn't think to follow her. He stood there, watching her long wavy hair bounce up and down her back as she made her way through the trees, her white nightgown a beacon in the night.

Finally, he spurred his feet into motion and ran after her.

He found her kneeling at the foot of a large oak tree, one palm flat on the trunk and her eyes closed. He halted. She seemed to be in some sort of meditation. After a long, quiet moment, she opened her eyes and fixed her gaze on him.

"Faradill says I should trust you, though I don't know why."

"Faradill?"

She glanced upward at the treetop. He understood then. Faradill was the oak tree. She waved him toward her with her free hand. He approached. When he was close enough, she reached for his free hand and pulled him down to the ground. A small smile played upon her lips. She pressed his palm against the trunk next to hers.

The deep, ancient voice boomed inside his head.

*Hello, Roderick, master of the forge.*

"He knows my name," he said.

"Of course, he does. I told him. Faradill is the oldest, wisest oak in the forest."

*You are an elemental, like Snow. You are also an Artificer.*

"He called me an Artificer." A shudder of confusion went through him. He had never heard the term before.

"I can hear him, too, you know," she said. "And yes. You're an Artificer."

"What is that?"

"Tell him, Faradill," she said.

*You have an ancient power none now possess. You have the ability to manipulate fire, air, and earth.*

"Is he wrong?" she asked.

He swallowed hard, his throat dry. "No."

"Good." She took a deep breath, expelled it. "No one knows the story I'm about to tell you. Not even Faradill. Not even the elves."

"Elves?"

"Shh," she said. "I am also an elemental. I am one with nature, as you are, but not as powerful as you are. I can speak to all manner of creatures. The elves helped me hone that ability from the time I was a child. And yes, it's true. I am the missing princess. I am Snow White, heir to the throne of the Mystic Vale."

# Chapter 21

As soon as she'd said it, a sense of relief pounded through her. She had never admitted it to anyone. Master Harwin had guessed, but she had never said she was the missing princess. She had never acknowledged that he was right.

It was as though saying it aloud would conjure Seraphina's dark magic. She knew the queen had the Magic Mirror, but not knowing how it worked, she wasn't sure if she was able to see her at this very moment with Roderick. She assumed that was the case. And if it was, then telling Roderick the truth—her truth—would be no surprise to Seraphina.

Still, she needed to be careful and choose her words.

Roderick waited patiently for her to tell her story. He had one hand pressed against the tree trunk, the other still clutched the sheathed dagger.

"My mother died when I was quite young," she said. "I don't remember her. My father remarried when I was six because he was certain I needed a mother in my life. He married Seraphina. When I was eight, my father died. Seraphina killed him because she wanted to rule the Mystic Vale. What she did not know was that my father's title passed to me. She would not rule as regent. She had no power there.

"To gain control, she told me everyone in the castle hated me. She told me I was nothing but a useless child and the best thing for me was to leave and never return. That if I returned, she would make sure I would live out my remaining days in the dungeons under the castle."

"And you believe her?" Roderick asked.

"I was eight. Of course, I believed her. I ran away. I ended up here in the Wyldwood. As soon as I stepped foot into the forest, I understood it. And it understood me. I was connected to nature in a way I had never been connected before. Eventually, I found my way to the foot of Faradill. The elves found me the following morning and took me in as one of their own. They raised me. I've lived in the eleven village for ten years."

"Do they know who you are?" he asked.

"They do not." She sighed. "I suppose I will have to tell them in time."

"Why don't you?"

"Yirrie, my surrogate mother, would be devastated if I left. Elator is her husband. He understands me more than she does," Snow said.

"You mentioned a Master Harwin and a dark wizard. Who are they?"

"I'm getting to that."

She told him about the first night of festival and how the Shadow tried to kill her, how she heard the woman's voice in her head telling her she was coming for her. She understood now that voice was Seraphina's, that the queen controlled the Shadow. That she intended to kill her that night.

"Ardan's enchanted blade saved me from the Shadow," she said. "*Your* enchanted blade."

"It can cut through dark magic?" he asked, a hint of wonder in his voice. "I had no idea."

"Neither did Ardan until he did it. After that, I decided to visit the Master of Archives, Master Harwin. I wanted to find out more about the enchanted blade."

She told him of visiting the archives and finding the three mirrors missing and about the dark wizard. How he had helped Seraphina gain access to the kingdom and rise to power from a peasant to the queen she was now. How the dark queen turned on him and used his magic and his knowledge to steal the mirrors from the elven archives. How she was sustaining his presence deep within the woods in his cabin through a Magic Mirror curse. How the Magic Mirror must be destroyed to eradicate the queen's magic, release him from his imprisonment and allow him to rest at long last.

Roderick did not reply for a long moment as he sat there, his hand still against the trunk of the tree. He released the dagger, letting it fall into his lap.

"That's quite a story," he said.

She thought she heard a twinge of doubt in his words. "It's all true."

Skepticism crossed his features. "You expect me to believe a dark wizard lived in these woods?"

Before she could answer, Faradill's voice floated through her mind.

*The dark wizard gave us life.*

Startled, his head snapped toward the tree, then he glanced upward at the leaves rustling in the faint breeze.

"What does that mean?" he asked.

"It means the dark wizard used his magic to enchant the forest. He brought the pixies and the sprites and all manner of magical creatures here. That's why the elves drove him out. He was using the nature around him to try conquer the forest," she said.

"He was an elemental," Roderick said.

She nodded. "Like us."

As she said it, she saw the flickering light of iridescent wings and smiled. Annilen had joined them. She held out her hand to allow the sprite to land. When she did, she looked Roderick up and down with a critical eye.

"Who's this?" he asked, leaning closer to get a better look at her.

"This is Annilen. She's a forest sprite."

"Who are *you*?" Annilen asked. "And what are you doing in our forest?"

Roderick's brows rose. Snow giggled.

"She's rather protective of the forest," Snow said. "Annilen, this is Roderick. He's come from the village of Bridgefort."

The little sprite put her fisted hands on her hips. "If he's come to do you harm, my lady…"

"Not at all," Roderick said. "I've come to help her reclaim her throne."

"Throne?" Annilen's little face upturned to her, question written all over it. "What does he mean by that?"

Snow bit her bottom lip. There was no sense in trying to hide it now. Faradill heard the story. Likely it was moving through the rest of the forest. By morning, all creatures within, even the plants, would know her true self.

"She doesn't know?" Roderick asked.

"Know what?" Annilen tilted her head to one side, peering up at Snow with her brows knit together.

"No one knew until tonight," Snow said. "I am the heir to the throne of the Mystic Vale."

Annilen's eyes went wide with shock. "You're a…princess?"

"Rightful queen," Roderick corrected.

Annilen curtsied low. "Your majesty."

"Don't call me that," Snow snapped. "I'm not."

"You are," Roderick said.

*Indeed, you are,* Faradill agreed.

Snow sighed. "I know, but it feels strange to say it out loud. For the last ten years, I have denied my true identity. I kept it buried deep down. I did not expect to ever return to the castle. I was content to live here among the forest and the elves."

"Then Seraphina wins," he said. "Seraphina has won long enough. It's time to dethrone her."

"How? I have no army and only a dagger as a weapon." She nodded to the dagger still in his lap.

"An enchanted dagger," he reminded her, a glint of humor in his eyes. "We can raise an army."

She lifted a brow. "You're mad to think that."

"We can," he insisted.

"How?" she demanded.

"We visit every village between here and the castle. Once they know you're alive and ready to take back the throne, I have no doubt they will follow you."

"All those who live in the forest will follow you, too, your majesty," Annilen said.

*And you have all the power of nature behind you*, Faradill added.

A tingling sensation went up her spine as she glanced from the little sprite to the old tree. It meant a lot to her Annilen was willing to stand with her. If she knew her friend, then Snow knew Annilen would tell everyone.

Faradill was right. She *did* have the power of nature behind her. She glanced at Roderick, who waited for her to respond to his suggestion. He was an Artificer. He had even more power than she did. He was a blacksmith. Perhaps he would be willing to help make weapons for those who would follow her into battle against the queen.

She immediately shoved all those thoughts aside. It was nothing but a dream.

"You have doubts," he said. "I see it in your eyes."

"Of course, I do," she agreed.

"You have the power of nature, as Faradill said, and all those in the forest. The villagers, too. And I would bet the elves would help," he said.

She scoffed, thinking of Tasnia and her snooty ways. "The elves have no interest in human affairs. They are content to remain in their forest village hidden away from the rest of the realm."

Aside from that, the last person she wanted to tell was Yirrie. Snow gave a silent blessing to Faradill, then dropped her hand from his trunk. It suddenly occurred to her she wore nothing but her shift and dressing gown. She got to her feet.

"Where are you going?" Roderick asked.

"I must return before I'm missed."

Annilen stifled yawn. "Me, too. Good night, Snow." She fluttered off, leaving a trail of pixie dust shimmering in her wake.

"What about—"

"There will be no more talk about reclaiming the throne. You should return to Bridgefort," Snow said.

"You're not even going to try?" He clutched the dagger within its sheath.

"I'm afraid it would be a fruitless effort. Good night, Roderick, and farewell."

With that, she picked up the edge of her gown and headed home.

Roderick watched her walk away, leaving him there at the foot of Faradill. He knew without a doubt he could not return to Bridgefort. He also knew that if he didn't do as the queen bid within the fortnight, then he would fall into the sleeping curse. The queen was not generous enough to disclose how to break the curse. Already two days had passed while he journeyed to the forest, so time was of the essence.

Perhaps the curse could be broken by shattering the Magic Mirror. Snow said it would break the curse on the dark wizard, releasing him and ripping away the queen's magic.

*You must convince the princess. The evil queen's reign must end.*

It was Faradill's voice that floated through his mind. "How do I do that?"

*Go to the elven village in the morn. Find her there.*

"I don't think she wants me to do that," Roderick said with a shake of his head.

*It is the only way,* the tree said.

Roderick leaned back against the oak, stretched his legs in front of him, and crossed his ankles. He still held the sheathed dagger, the one with which he was supposed to kill Snow White.

Faradill was right. He had to convince her before the sleeping curse took hold of him. He was running out of time.

How he would convince her, he did not know. In the morning, he would find her in the village and try.

Snow made her way back to the village, her senses on high alert and her ears attuned to every sound within the forest. Roderick's words weighed heavily on her mind. Though he was sent to kill her with the enchanted blade, she decided he was no threat. He had many opportunities to do it and hadn't. Instead, he had offered her the weapon.

She hadn't seen Seraphina in a decade. Likely the queen hoped she had perished within the forest, never to be seen again. Now, it seemed, rumors circulated about the missing princess in the villages. She had no proof that Roderick told the truth, but she did wonder how the villagers remembered her.

Her father, though, had always taken her with him when he visited the villages. Before he'd married Seraphina. Before she murdered him for his throne. Perhaps the villagers remembered her from those few visits, even though she was a child. She, herself, barely had the memories. They were nothing but fragments at the edge of her mind.

She slipped back into the village and hurried home, unnoticed by anyone since the village was sleeping. At the door, she paused, her heart in her throat and her hand shaking as it hovered over the knob. The fire pit was nothing more than embers now. Taking a deep breath, she twisted the knob and pushed open the door to darkness.

She paused in the doorway, waiting for Yirrie to chastise her. When there was silence, she breathed out a sigh of relief and closed the door, then hurried to her room. In her room, she pressed her back against the door. A gasp escaped her.

The board over the window was gone, allowing shafts of moonlight through the dirty panes. She smiled, hot tears springing to her eyes as she hurried over. The window opened and closed with ease.

Elator did this. He removed the board to give her back nature and moonlight. She pressed her forehead against the cool glass, smiling.

"Thank you, Elator," she whispered.

Then she shed her dressing gown and slipped into bed. It wasn't long before she was fast asleep.

# CHAPTER 22

Morning light brightened her window, pressing against her closed eyes. As she lay curled on her side, she smiled, stretched, and opened her eyes. It had been weeks since she'd seen morning light gracing her window. It made her happy to see it once again.

Snow bounced from the bed and dressed in a simple gown. She didn't know what Yirrie had planned for today, but decided to see if there were any chores with which she could help. As a peace offering. They hadn't been speaking much since Elator boarded the window. She brushed her long, black hair, tying it back.

When she opened her bedroom door, she smelled spice tea and baking bread. Her stomach rumbled. She made her way to the kitchen to see Elator at the table with his morning tea and Yirrie busy making more bread.

"Good morning," she said, announcing her presence.

Yirrie halted what she was doing to peer up at her in shock. Elator sipped his tea with a faint smile and gave her a nod. Snow walked over to him, bent, and kissed his cheek.

"What was that for?" he asked.

She grinned. "Nothing special." Then she bustled into the kitchen and washed her hands. "Can I help you with anything, Yirrie?"

She gaped a long moment and then finally nodded. "One of the Elders is ill. I'm taking a care package to him and his family. You can help me with the baking."

As Snow threw herself into her work, she hummed a faint tune. Despite everything that happened last night, her heart was light. She decided she was not going to worry about the dark wizard, Seraphina, or Roderick today. She was going to enjoy the day. Perhaps she would even ask Ardan to walk with her in the woods.

Even as she resolved to push all those thoughts to the back of her mind, she sensed a ripple of energy entering the village. She halted her kneading for a moment, letting the feeling wash over her. The tingling sensation shuddered through her with such force, her hands halted in the dough. For a moment, she tapped into the feeling, trying to understand what it was. It was nothing like when the Shadow creature came to her on the first night of festival. No, this was something different. It was not dark magic.

The feeling faded and she went back to her kneading, though it was hard to shake that sense that something wasn't quite right. When she finished with the dough, she placed it in a bowl and covered it with a towel to let it rise.

Yirrie gave her the broom to sweep the kitchen floor. As she started on her next task, there was an abrupt knock on the door.

Her gaze flew to it, her heart suddenly in her throat. She froze, the broom in hand. Yirrie went about the business of making another batch of dough while Elator unfolded his long body from the chair and lumbered to the door.

When he opened it, Tasnia stood on the other side with a fierce look about her. Angry lines creased her forehead.

"Tasnia?"

Yirrie dropped what she was doing, her head snapping up. She reached for a dish towel, wiping her hands and hurrying over.

"There is a stranger in the village," Tasnia said. Then her gaze cut to Snow. "A *human* stranger."

That rippling sensation shuddered through Snow once again as she clutched the broom until her hands ached.

*Roderick.*

"A human stranger?" Yirrie repeated. "Who is it?"

"A man," Tasnia said, her gaze still focused on Snow. "He's asking for Snow White."

Elator and Yirrie both turned their gazes to her. Yirrie's was one of apprehension while Elator's was curiosity.

"Do you know this man?" Yirrie asked.

Snow pressed her lips together, trying to decide how to answer. "I—"

"He called her *Princess* Snow White," Tasnia said.

Elator and Yirrie both gaped at her. Her heart clogged in her throat as she continued to clutch the broom handle. How could he have followed her to the village? She wanted him to return to Bridgefort and forget this nonsense about her reclaiming her throne.

"Snow?" Yirrie asked. "Why would he call you princess?"

She sucked in a deep breath, held it, and then expelled it. "I don't know what to say."

"Perhaps you should come speak to the stranger," Tasnia said in a way that sounded like more than a suggestion.

"I forbid it," Yirrie snapped. She clutched the dish towel in her hands until her knuckles were white.

Elator reached for her, placing a consoling hand on her shoulder. "Yirrie, we knew this day might come."

"If her family has come for her, then they can just go away," she said with such vehemence it surprised Snow. "She belongs here. With us."

"Yirrie—" Elator began.

"He's not my family," Snow interrupted. "But he *has* come for me."

Yirrie sniffed. Her eyes filled with tears as she looked at Snow. "What does that mean?"

"It means he wants me to return to the Mystic Vale and reclaim the throne that is mine by birthright."

Silence descended between them. Tasnia remained in the door, standing rigid, her eyes hard and unforgiving. Yirrie twisted the towel in her hands. Elator dropped his hand from her shoulder and gave Snow his full attention. But when he spoke, he spoke to Tasnia.

"Bring him here, Tasnia."

"No!" Yirrie said on a gasp. She wrapped her hand around his upper arm. "You cannot—"

"Yes, Yirrie. We have much to discuss with him and Snow."

"Very well," Tasnia said without emotion and was off before Yirrie could protest again.

Snow went back to sweeping, trying to occupy her hands and her mind and not think about Roderick or how furious she was with him for coming to the village when she told him to return home. Now, things were altered between her, Yirrie, and Elator. The air had shifted around them.

She should have known something was wrong when she felt the shift in energy. She wondered, then, if that was when Roderick broke the magical barrier and entered the village. He was a stranger, after all, and the Elders would immediately sense a stranger within the borders of their village. Most of the elves were reclusive by nature.

Moments later, Tasnia returned with Roderick following her. She paused at the doorway and made a hand motion for him to enter. Snow caught his eye but did her best to act normal. She replaced the broom in the nearby closet. Yirrie bustled into the kitchen to put the kettle on to boil. Elator greeted Roderick with a broad smile, though Snow was aware it was forced.

"I leave him with you, then," Tasnia said. She closed the door behind her with a snap.

Roderick stood ramrod straight, glancing between the three of them. Snow busied herself at the table, cleaning up the remains of breakfast Elator left behind.

"Snow?" Elator asked. "Are you going to introduce us to your friend?"

She dropped the dishes in the sink and turned to him, her gaze on Elator. Her fury was so great, she refused to look at Roderick. "He's not my friend."

At least not yet. At the moment, he was her sworn enemy by coming into the village.

"My name is Roderick," he said. "I'm a master blacksmith from the village of Bridgefort in the Feywood Kingdom. I've come with a gift for the princess—"

"Do *not* call me that," she snapped, her voice hard with a hint of warning.

But Roderick was impervious to the heated glare she pinned on him. "Is that not what you are? Princess and heir to the throne of the Mystic Vale?"

Her hands trembled with rage as she clenched them into tight, white-knuckled fists. Her nails dug into her palms, a physical manifestation of the boiling anger consuming her.

Elator and Yirrie both gaped at her. It was Elator who spoke, his tone even and quiet.

"You are the heir apparent?"

"I am nothing!" Snow slashed a hand through the air in her fury.

Roderick stepped toward her. "You are not nothing. The people in the villages of the Mystic Vale love you and want you to be their queen."

"Oh, what do you care?" she snapped. "Why do you even have an interest in the Mystic Vale when you are from the Feywood?"

"Snow!" Yirrie said her name on a gasp. "Whatever else he is, Mr. Roderick is our guest."

Just then the tea kettle whistled. She bustled to the stove as Snow continued to glower at him.

"Forgive us. We have been inhospitable," Elator said then. He waved to one of the dining chairs. "Please, sit and enjoy a cup of tea and some apple bread my wife made."

Watching Roderick take his seat at the table, Snow concealed her anger. She wanted to shout at Elator for allowing him a seat at their table. With a confident demeanor, he swung his long leg over the chair and lowered himself down, all while maintaining eye contact with her. Yirrie brought over the kettle, four cups, and sliced bread on a tray. She placed it in the middle of the table and took her seat as Elator sat across from her.

They all glanced her way, but Snow refused to move.

"Snow, please sit," Elator said.

She wanted to refuse. Everything inside her told her to remain where she stood. But when she looked at Elator, saw the expectant look on his face, she forced her feet to move. She lowered herself into the chair opposite Roderick. Yirrie poured tea, handing him a cup.

"Now," Elator said, "perhaps you begin at the beginning. What brings you here to our village?"

# CHAPTER 23

Roderick watched Snow from across the table, heart pounding a wild beat. Her cheeks were flushed and pink. Clearly, she was unhappy with him. She hadn't wanted him to come to the village to see her here, and yet, here he was.

Tasnia told him Elator and Yirrie were the ones who raised her from the time she arrived when she was eight. He didn't know much beyond that, only that it was clear the woman didn't care for the situation. She said it with a look of distaste on her face.

He reached for the enchanted blade which he had carried in with him. No one had noticed. Not even Tasnia. He placed it on the table in front of him. Snow's eyes narrowed to slits as they darted to the sheathed blade, widening with her annoyance and her suspicion. Tension radiated from her like a coiled snake ready to strike.

"What is that?" Yirrie asked.

"That is an enchanted blade," Roderick said, never taking his eyes off her. "I forged it."

"I prefer not to have weapons on my table," Yirrie said with a sniff of derision.

But Elator looked as though he were awestruck. "May I?"

"Of course." Roderick pushed the blade toward him.

Snow huffed. "This is ridiculous."

As she said it, Elator removed the blade. Both he and Yirrie gasped with their admiration and appreciation of a fine weapon. Snow tried hard not to look at it, but it was difficult. It truly was a magnificent dagger.

"I have never seen the likes," he said.

"There are only four of them in the entire realm," Roderick said. He gave Snow a pointed look.

She knew Ardan had one.

He pulled his own dagger out of the sheath by his side. He placed it on the table next to the empty sheath.

"I forged them all," he said. "One belongs to a young elven boy."

"Ardan?" Elator asked.

"Yes, I believe that's his name." Still, Roderick's gaze never left her face.

"Ardan was the one who used his enchanted blade to save Snow from dark magic," Elator said. He replaced the blade into its sheath and handed it back to Roderick. "It's a remarkable weapon. However, we still do not know who you are or why you're here."

"I'm here to give Snow this blade so that she may kill the queen who usurped her throne and take it back."

Snow huffed out a breath as Elator and Yirrie both looked at her with surprise and question in their eyes. She sat back in the chair and crossed her arms over her chest showing her frustration and annoyance.

"That is *not* going to happen," she said.

Roderick forged on. "I was sent here by the queen to kill Snow White and bring back her heart in a wooden box."

Both of them gasped with their shock. Roderick continued.

"But I have no intention of doing that."

Elator leaned forward. "What are your intentions, then?"

"I intend to help her regain her throne as she is the rightful ruler of the Mystic Vale."

"And how do you intend to do that?" Elator asked.

Which only served to infuriate Snow even more. "Do not encourage him, Elator."

"I intend to take her into the villages north of here so that she can meet her people and know that she is loved and that they want her on the throne. So that she can see what Seraphina's power has done to them and the people of her kingdom. So that she will know she is the only one who can free them from the queen's tyranny," he said.

Snow snorted derision. "With what army?"

"With the people of the kingdom. They will answer your call to arms," Roderick continued.

Elator and Yirrie both glanced between Roderick and Snow.

Elator said, "So, it's true then. You are the heir to the throne of the Mystic Vale?"

Snow remained silent in her defiance. Roderick leaned forward. "Tell them, Snow."

She pinned him with a heated glare as he sat back in the chair, taking the steaming cup of tea and sipping. A smug sense of triumph shifted through him. He was getting to her, at last, and forcing her to tell them the truth. Her truth.

"Yes, Snow. Tell us," Elator urged.

She inhaled a deep breath, exhaled it. Then she began the tale once again about her banishment.

"She told me I was nothing more than a nuisance and I wasn't wanted there. I ran away. I made my way through the villages southward to the forest."

She paused, remembering that day as clearly as though it were yesterday. She dragged her lower lip through her teeth.

"I found my way into the forest. It wasn't long after that you and Yirrie found me." She unfolded her arms and reached both hands out to them. One to Elator and one to Yirrie. They each clasped her offered hand. "But that doesn't mean I have to leave here. I'm happy here with you and the other elves."

Elator's face softened. "Snow, I think we all know what a falsehood that is. You say you're happy here, yet you leave the village to go into the forest every chance you get."

He wasn't wrong and she hated that he knew it. She released both their hands and sat back into the chair once again.

"I don't mean to," she said at last. "It's just that the forest calls to me and I must answer."

"What does that mean?" Up until now, Yirrie had been silent as she listened to them.

"It means I draw strength from nature," Snow said. "It means without it, I grow weak."

"It's why I removed the board from her window," Elator said.

"You—"

"We will discuss later," he said, cutting off his wife.

Snow almost smiled at that. "What Roderick has told you is true. I am the heir to the throne. I am the rightful ruler of the Mystic Vale."

"Why have you never told us this?" Elator asked. He didn't hide the disappointment on his face.

Seeing that sent a dagger right to Snow's heart. Heat pounded through her cheeks. She shook her head. "At the time, I was a child. I was afraid if you knew my true identity, you wouldn't like me anymore. Or you would send me back to her."

"Oh, Snow." Yirrie pressed her shaking fingertips to her lips. Tears danced in her eyes once again. "It didn't matter to us who you were. Only that you were here with us and safe."

"You could have told us the truth," Elator said. "And we would have protected you no matter what."

"But you can't protect me. Seraphina found me here in the village."

"And she will again," Roderick said. "That's why you have to leave."

Frustration edged through her. "But I have no army and the elves won't fight for me if Tasnia has anything to say about it." Snow was aware of how the Elder felt about her.

"You don't know until you ask," Elator said.

Snow shook her head. "We all know she and the others want me gone. That I don't belong here. And besides, the elves have no interest in affairs outside the forest *or* this village."

"Let me talk to her," Elator said.

"What good will it do?" Snow asked.

"At least let me try."

"Elator, Snow is right. Tasnia and the other Elders will never agree to fight for Snow or the Mystic Vale. The elves fighting days are long over," Yirrie said. She reached across the table and grasped Snow's hand. "You don't have to leave. You can stay here with us."

Snow appreciated the gesture. A small smile played at the corners of her mouth. If only it were that simple. If only she could forget Seraphina wanted her heart in a wooden box.

"But, Snow, if you stay here, you're risking—" Roderick began.

She slammed her hand down on the table, rattling the dishes. "That's enough. I know what I risk. Whether I go or stay is my decision, no one else's."

With that, she fled the dining area and hurried to her room, slamming the door behind her. She pressed her palms against her hot cheeks. She was tired of everyone trying to get her to do what they wanted her to do. Roderick wanted her to return to the Mystic Vale and reclaim her throne. The dark wizard wanted her to destroy the Magic Mirror and release him from his curse. Yirrie wanted her to stay in the village with them and live out the rest of her days. Even Master Harwin suggested she return to the Mystic Vale to confront the queen.

No one seemed to care or think about what she wanted. All she wanted to do was live in peace within nature. She didn't want to think about the throne or the Mystic Vale or Seraphina. Did that mean she remained here with the elves? She didn't know anymore.

She eyed the window across the room. The forest beckoned. The impulse to climb out the window and run to sit at the foot of Faradill was almost too much for her to resist.

Running into the forest would solve nothing, though. Roderick was right. If she remained here, the chances Seraphina would return to find her were great. Despite the Elder's magic around the village, there was still a chance the queen's dark magic could pierce through it.

She slid down the length of the door, resting her back against it and drawing up her knees, encircling them with her arms. She had a decision to make. She just didn't know what that decision was going to be yet.

A soft knock sounded on the door.

"Go away," she said.

"I just want to talk." It was Roderick.

"You've talked enough," she snapped.

There was a long pause, then he said, "Snow, I'm sorry. It was Faradill's idea for me to come here but I should have stayed away."

Faradill? Her brows drew together in question. She recalled something he said to her not long ago. That darkness had crept back into the forest and that it will return. Chills skittered up her spine then and now as she recalled the words of the oak.

She pulled herself to her feet, then flung open the door, but Roderick was gone. She rushed into the kitchen to see the enchanted blade was still on the table where he left it. Yirrie was in the kitchen washing dishes. Elator was nowhere to be found.

"Where is Roderick?" she asked.

Yirrie glanced over her shoulder at her. "He's leaving. Elator is escorting him out of the forest."

On impulse, Snow snatched the dagger off the table and hurried out to find them.

# CHAPTER 24

"Magic Mirror on the wall, tell me, who is the fairest of them all?"

Seraphina brushed her long, black hair with an ivory comb, content in the knowledge Snow White was dead.

The mirror came alive. "With dreams that sparkle and passions that enthrall, in your heart, you're the fairest one of all."

She stopped brushing to glare at the featureless face in the mirror. "The princess is not yet dead?"

"No, my queen. She lives."

In a fit of rage, she threw the comb across the room. It clattered against the stone floor. "I knew I couldn't trust that blacksmith to do it."

He heart pounded like a war drum as she stormed back and forth across the room, each footfall echoing with her fury. Then she halted, staring into the mirror.

"Where is the blacksmith?" she demanded.

A long pause before the mirror responded. "In the village with elves so fair, where moonlight weaves a silken air, beneath the boughs of ancient trees, a forest where magic flows with ease."

"Is he with Snow White?" she asked.

"Indeed, he is, my queen."

She opened her palms, watching as purple fire danced between her fingers. "Then let them both feel my wrath."

Snow hurried through the village looking for Roderick. She found him along with Elator and Ardan on the edge of the village just inside the Elder's protective magic. She should have been surprised to see him talking to Ardan about his enchanted dagger, but she wasn't. Roderick pulled out his own blade and showed it to the young elf.

It was a simple thing. Almost as though they were sharing a love of enchanted weapons. Or perhaps merely a love of weapons. Even Elator was impressed with the craftsmanship of the daggers. She halted there, watching them as they compared blades, their voices hushed. She was unable to hear what they said. Their comradery, though, made her smile.

As she took a step toward them, the air shifted. A bitter breeze blew through the trees, which was odd in the middle of summer. Her senses suddenly went on high alert as she stood there, gazing around the treetops, watching the leaves dancing in the late afternoon sunshine.

But something was wrong.

A quick glance at Roderick told her he sensed the same thing. His face had paled. Their eyes met. His brows drew together in concern. Instead of sheathing his blade, he clutched it in his fist, as though ready to do battle.

A flash of light at the edge of the village exploded followed by an odd shattering. It occurred to her the magic barriers the Elders constructed were broken. Her heart rammed against her chest. She clutched her skirts, ready to run. But Roderick was already moving toward her.

Wraith-like creatures invaded the village, sweeping around the trees. In an instant, Roderick was at her side, his hand wrapping around her upper arm.

"We have to get you out of here," he said.

"What is it?" She watched in horror.

"Snow?" Yirrie called from the front door.

"Get back inside and stay there!" Roderick shouted.

The slamming of the door was evidence enough Yirrie had obeyed.

Snow's gaze was fixed on the creatures floating through the village. One seemed to fixate on her and sped toward her. She stumbled backward, despite Roderick's hand on her arm. As it neared, she realized it was more of a black mist in the shape of a wraith, faceless yet terrifying.

A puff of purple smoke billowed upward from the ground. Once it cleared, Seraphina appeared. The wraiths skittered behind her, hovering there waiting for her next instructions. Roderick shoved Snow behind him, holding his enchanted blade at the ready. Her gaze flickered from him to Snow and back again. A tense silence settled over the village.

Snow was aware of the other elves witnessing the arrival of the queen. She was also aware Ardan was taking long, slow steps toward them. She cut him a glance and gave him a quick shake of her head. He halted where he was.

"Well, well," Seraphina said, her voice ringing out across the village. "Snow White still lives. A pity you did not perish years ago."

Snow pressed her lips together into a thin line.

A commotion caught her attention. Tasnia and the other Elders had arrived. Even Master Harwin was with them, which was a surprise. Seraphina flung out a hand, pushing them back.

"Who are you?" Tasnia demanded. "What do you want here?"

"I am the queen of the Mystic Vale," Seraphina said, her voice strong and sure. Her gaze flickered back to Roderick. "He knows what I want."

"The stranger?" Tasnia asked.

The Elder didn't understand what was happening, but Snow did. Perhaps if she gave herself to the queen, she would leave the village.

"Yes, the stranger," Seraphina snapped, her words venom. She pinned Tasnia with her lethal glare. "I have broken through your magical barrier, elf. You have harbored this individual long enough. Now, it is time for her to return with me. As my prisoner."

Ardan moved to stand between the queen and Roderick and Snow. "You can't have her."

"Ardan," Snow gasped.

He did not realize the danger he'd put himself in by standing up to the queen.

"Step aside, young elf. My quarrel is not with you, but with the princess."

This time it was Elator who spoke. "She belongs here with us."

Hot pinpricks of fear skipped up her spine, tingling the back of her neck. Elator moved to stand next to Ardan, making her cringe. She appreciated they wanted to protect her, but she feared what would happen to them if they tempted Seraphina's fury.

"You have to stop them," she whispered to Roderick. "*Do* something."

"Stand aside, you pathetic weaklings, and give me what I've come for. *Her*." She pointed at Snow. "If you do not stand aside, then I will be forced to take drastic measures."

A glint of a blade in Ardan's hand caught Snow's attention. She realized then he wielded his enchanted blade. He charged the queen. Snow shouted something incoherent—intending to tell him to stop but it came out as nothing more than a shout.

Seraphina sensed the attack before it came and spun, using a punch of magic to shove him away from her. He went flying across the village and somehow managed to hold onto the hilt of his blade. She seethed, her hands balled into fists as she pinned the young elf with her death glare.

Snow wanted to run to him, to see if he was all right, but Roderick spun and pushed her back, holding her in place.

"I have to help him," she said, desperation lancing through her voice.

"She means to kill him," Roderick said, his voice low.

As the queen advanced on him, she realized she intended to do just that. She raised her arms over her head, ready to strike once again with her magic.

Snow wasn't going to allow her to hurt Ardan. She shoved Roderick off her and stepped back, raising her own arms level with the ground. The vines and the leaves and the trees answered her call. The vines struck first, wrapping their long tendrils around the queen's raised arms, tightening with every struggle she made to get free. A shriek of frustration exploded from her.

"Release me!" she demanded.

"Never." Snow stepped around Roderick and faced the queen, no longer afraid. "You will leave this place and never return."

A long beat of silence passed between them as the wraiths hovered behind the queen, desperate for their next order. Then Seraphina emitted a long, low laugh.

"You silly girl. You think you can defeat me?" She shook her head, still smiling. Then she used a bright flash of magic to singe the vines and release her bonds. "You will never defeat me. Attack her."

The wraiths charged Snow White.

But Roderick was ready for them. He lunged as one whipped overhead, stabbing with the enchanted blade. The wraith emitted a high-pitched screech and then dissipated into mist. Ardan joined the fray with his blade, destroying another one.

With shaking hands, Snow wielded the one Roderick left on the table, killing another one as it tried to attack her. Seraphina emitted a cry of frustration and sent three more wraiths to attack. Snow, Ardan, and Roderick all stabbed them with their enchanted blades, killing them.

"You traitor!" Seraphina shrieked. "Instead of killing her with that blade, you *gave it to her*!"

Her wrath was directed at Roderick. She flung her hands toward him, a stream of magic pulsing from her fingertips. It looked like lightning. When it hit Roderick, he flew backward, landing against a tree. Snow gasped, watching as he fell to the ground, unconscious.

"I should have killed you myself when I had the chance," she said, advancing on Snow. The lightning danced between her fingers as she lifted her hands to attack.

Suddenly, she cried out in pain, her back bowing and the light disappearing from her fingers. She spun to face the attacker. Ardan yanked his dagger from her shoulder. As soon as it cut her, there was a hiss and smoke rose from the wound. She shrieked out of pain and frustration and anger.

Snow sucked in a sharp breath. "Ardan!"

"You!" the queen seethed.

Rage creased the queen's face as she turned to the young elf. Snow clutched her dagger, torn between helping Roderick and defending Ardan. Just as she decided to sprint to the elf's side, Seraphina flung her lightning hands toward him.

A flash of light blinded Snow for a brief moment. When it cleared, she saw Ardan on the ground with a smoking hole in his chest.

"No!"

She ran to him, dropping to her knees beside him. His eyes were glassy as he looked into nothingness. He was dead. Tears flooded Snow's eyes as she reached for his hand, clutching it in hers.

Tasnia was finally spurred into action. She and the other Elders joined hands in a semi-circle around Seraphina. Too late did she realize what was happening to stop it. The Elders chanted something in elvish and light swarmed around them, moving in a shimmering cloud toward the queen. Seraphina backed up but there were others behind her doing the same thing. She was surrounded.

With clenched fists and a scowl etched deep on her face, she let out an exasperated cry before vanishing into thin air, leaving behind a swirling cloud of angry purple mist.

But the damage was done. Ardan was dead. The village would never be the same.

# CHAPTER 25

The moment the queen disappeared, the Elders stopped chanting and dropped their hands. They turned their attention to Snow, who still sat on the ground beside Ardan's lifeless body, her face tear-streaked. Tasnia moved to tower over the two of them, her eyes ablaze with seething rage that threatened to consume everything in her path.

"Move away from him," Tasnia ordered.

Shivering with fear, Snow got to her feet and slowly stepped back. The Elders formed a circle around his lifeless body, once again holding hands as they edged her out. They began to sing.

A lament for the loss of the young elf. The others joined in, moving behind the circle. Even Elator and Master Harwin. Snow backed away from them and headed to where Roderick still lay on the ground. He was coming to, shaking his head and trying to understand what was happening. She reached a hand down to him. He took it and allowed her to help him to his feet.

His keen eyes took in the scene. He turned to her, question on his face.

"What happened?"

"Ardan stabbed Seraphina. Then she killed him for it."

Roderick wrapped an arm around her shoulders, pulling her close. She allowed him to comfort her for the moment, but she couldn't help but think this was his fault. If he hadn't come to the village, Ardan would still be alive. It was almost more than she could bear.

When the melancholy song ended, all but the Elders moved away. A shriek from the other side of the village as Ardan's mother shoved aside those in her way. When she saw her son, her hands went to her blanched face. She fell to her knees next to him, bowing over his body as she sobbed.

Tasnia turned to Snow and Roderick.

"You are the cause of this. Both of you," she said.

Roderick stepped forward. "This isn't Snow's fault. It's mine."

"Yes," Tasnia agreed. "Yours for coming here. You drew the dark magic. And now this queen knows of our existence." Her gaze landed on Snow. "She pierced through the perimeter magic with ease. Our village is no longer safe. I cannot allow our people to be in danger because of one human."

Snow lifted her chin, looking down her nose at the Elder. "Then what will you have me do, Tasnia?"

"Leave this place. Never return."

Roderick said, "You're banishing Snow White from the only home she's ever had?"

Her glittering gaze flickered to him. "Yes."

"Tasnia—" Elator began.

"I will not hear any objections. My word is final," she snapped. "Nor will we support the girl's claim as the rightful ruler of the Mystic Vale. Human affairs do not interest us."

Word, it seemed, traveled quickly. Tasnia went to console Ardan's mother. Elator approached then, a strange look of apology and sorrow on his face.

"Snow—"

"There is nothing left to say," she said. "Ardan's death is my fault."

"It's not," Roderick said. "It's mine. I should have never come here."

"No, you shouldn't," she snapped, unable to hide her ire. "You should have returned home."

"Snow, we don't want you to leave," Elator said.

"You don't. But Tasnia does. The other Elder's will agree with her."

"I don't," Master Harwin said as he approached. "We witnessed history here today."

She almost smiled. "No doubt you'll record it in your archives."

"Indeed," he said. "Ardan's name will be forever linked to the dark magic attack on the village. He defended us and you. He gave his life to save yours."

Snow didn't see it that way but she appreciated the thought. She merely nodded.

Movement caught her eye. Tasnia was speaking in low tones with the other Elders, glancing over her shoulder at Snow. She was conversing with the others to convince them of her decision.

"They will vote to remove me from the village," Snow said. "And I will go. Willingly."

"But—" Elator began.

"I *must*," she said. "If Seraphina found me here once, she will find me here again. Roderick is right. She'll return. And next time, she may kill more."

Tasnia returned to her with the others trailing behind her. Her features were hard, unforgiving, as she looked at Snow.

"We have decided," she said. "The Elders vote was unanimous. Snow White, you are hereby banished from our village forever."

Despite already knowing the outcome, her heart dropped into her churning gut. "Allow me to gather my things and bid farewell to Yirrie?"

Elator turned pleading eyes on the Elder. "Yirrie will be devastated if she leaves without saying goodbye."

"Very well. You have but a few moments. Then, you must go." She turned her lethal gaze on Roderick. "Both of you."

With a nod, Snow returned to her home for the last time. Elator was right. Yirrie would be devastated in so many ways. But Snow could no longer stay here.

She didn't know where she would go. She certainly didn't want to go with Roderick. Perhaps she could flee into the forest and live the rest of her days there near Faradill.

Her heart heavy, she opened the door and stepped inside. Yirrie was busy pacing the length of the kitchen as she wrung her hands. Worry lines were between her eyes. She halted as they entered. Her relief was short-lived.

"What is it? What happened? I heard a commotion but I was too afraid to open the door and look out."

Elator went to her, took her by the elbow and led her to the dining chair. "I think you should sit down."

"Why?" she demanded.

Snow remained where she was, just inside the door of the small house. Roderick didn't enter at all. That was wise of him. He decided to wait outside and closed the door behind her. They were sealed in silence.

"What's happening?" Yirrie said, glancing from Elator to Snow and back again.

"Queen Seraphina arrived," Snow said. "She attacked. Ardan tried to defend me. He stabbed her."

A bright smile showed on her face. "He did?"

"Seraphina retaliated. He's dead," Snow said, her voice flat.

Elator reached for Yirrie when she let out a sharp cry of despair. He wrapped his hand around hers, holding it tight.

"There's more," he said.

"Tasnia blames me for the attack on the village. She's right. It is my fault. I'm banished."

"No!" Yirrie practically shrieked. "That can't be. Elator, talk to her."

"Tasnia's decision, along with the other Elders, is final. I cannot change her mind," he said. Sorrow tinged his voice.

"I'm going to pack."

Snow walked through the house toward her bedroom with purpose. She refused to look into Yirrie's eyes, for if she saw the pain and the hurt there, then she would fall apart. She didn't have time for that. She had to pack and get out as quickly as possible.

But Yirrie jumped up from the table and stepped into her path. When she refused to move, she reached for Snow, wrapped her into a fierce hug and held her there for a long moment. When she pulled back, she held her at arm's length.

"What will you do? Where will you go?" she asked.

Snow shook her head. "I don't know."

"Will you go with Roderick?" she pressed.

Again, she said, "I don't know."

"Will you reclaim your throne?"

"I don't know!" Snow shook her off. Agitated, she stepped around her and hurried to her bedroom.

She slammed the door, then leaned against it, forcing away the tears that wanted to erupt. Then she opened her eyes, and took one last look at the room that was hers for the last ten years. She didn't even know what to pack. Then she spied the silver circlet Elator had given her on the first night of festival. With her heart in her throat, she stepped to her dressing table and picked it up. Eyeing herself in the mirror, she placed it on her head.

*Fit for a princess.*

Perhaps Elator wasn't wrong in his assessment. She grabbed a bag and shoved an extra dress inside it. She packed her pants and tunic she liked to hike in. Then she whisked the cloak out of her wardrobe. She shouldered the bag. With her head held high, she opened her bedroom door. She went to Yirrie, hugged her tight, kissed her cheek.

"Farwell, Yirrie. Thank you for everything you did for me. I will love and miss you always."

It was more than the woman could bear. Her breath hitched with a sob. She ran to her bedroom, closing the door behind her. Snow turned to Elator. She hugged him next. When she pulled away, he eyed the circlet on her head, a small smile playing at the corners of his mouth.

"Perhaps you will wear it when you sit the throne and rule the Mystic Vale. In remembrance of us."

Hearing those words was like a dagger to the heart. She didn't know what to say to that, so she nodded.

"Farewell, Elator. I will love and miss you, too."

He kissed her cheek. "Farewell, Snow. May you find the peace and happiness you seek." He gave her one last smile. "I better check on Yirrie."

Then he was gone.

Taking a deep breath, Snow walked to the door and left the house, never looking back.

# CHAPTER 26

Roderick waited for her outside. Tasnia and a few of the other Elders stood guard, as though waiting for her to emerge from the house. The last person she wanted to see was Roderick.

Clutching the strap of the bag, she walked with purpose through the village, passing him by and never making eye contact. Even so, he fell in step behind her as did the Elders, as if making sure she made her final exit from the village.

"Why are you following me?" she demanded, knowing he was right behind her.

"Where are you going?" he countered.

She hadn't decided yet, but now was as good a time as any. "I'm going to Faradill. I'll make a place for myself there."

"Are you sure that's wise? Seraphina is still out there—"

She spun to face him, put a hand on his chest and shoved. "Please stop following me."

Then she turned and ran as fast as her legs would take her. She never looked back. She didn't want to look back. The day was waning and she wanted to be settled at the foot of Faradill by the time night fell.

She didn't stop running until she'd reached him. Then she fell to her knees, dropping the bag at her side. The circlet slid off her head and landed on the ground in front of her. She collapsed, putting her head in her hands and let the tears flow.

For the second time in her life, she'd lost her home and her family. A family she'd come to love as much as she loved her own mother and father. Seraphina had won once again.

*She hasn't won yet, little one.*

Faradill's voice floated through her mind. She looked up at the old oak, tears clouding her vision.

"Hasn't she?" she asked. "She destroyed my family. Now she's destroyed my life with the elves."

The flutter of Annilen's wings signaled her arrival. Snow held out her hand to allow the sprite to land.

"Snow? Are you all right?"

"Not really." She sniffed.

"What's happened?" Concern creased her little face.

Seeing her friend's concern made her smile. "It's a long story."

The sound of hooves echoed through the forest. Fury pierced through her as she got to her feet. Annilen fluttered next to her head, then finally alighted on her shoulder.

"What is it?" she asked.

The horse came into view then, with Roderick on its back. Snow stood rock still as she watched him approach and then dismount.

"Stay where you are," Snow demanded.

He held up one hand as if in surrender. "Snow, I came to apologize."

She folded her arms, defiant. "I do not want your apologies. I want you to leave."

"What happened?" Annilen whispered in her ear.

"He's responsible for me leaving the elven village," she said, glaring at him.

His gaze flickered to Annilen on her shoulder and back to her face. "Do you mean that? Truly?" He clutched a sheathed dagger in his free hand, while he continued to hold up the other. "Because if that's what you want, then I'll go. But I'll not return to Bridge-fort."

"Why did you leave the elven village?" the sprite asked.

But Snow ignored her. Despite her inner voice telling her not to ask, she asked, "Where will you go then?"

"North of the forest. To the villages of the Mystic Vale. To West-fall and Lighthill and Brookdale. To tell them about the coura-geous princess who was banished by the elves because she was attacked by their evil queen. To ask for their support in helping her get back the throne that is rightfully hers."

Annilen gasped. "The evil queen attacked you and you were banished? That hardly seems fair."

"It wasn't fair." He held up the dagger and said to Snow, "You forgot this."

He extended it to her, but she refused to move.

*The elves banished you,* Faradill said, but it wasn't a question.

"Yes, they did," Roderick answered, for he, too, heard the oak speak. "Because of me. Because I led Seraphina to the village and her. And because a young elven boy died."

Annilen fluttered off her shoulder, turning to look at her with her fingers pressed against her mouth. "Someone died?"

"She killed Ardan." As she said it, tears clotted her throat.

She swallowed hard as she stood there, trying to decide what to do or say next. A strange shudder went through the forest. Almost as though all of nature understood who and what she was and what had happened.

Finally, she said, "You would do that for me? Speak on my behalf to the villagers?"

"I would do that for you and more. I'd do whatever possible to see you defeat the queen and take back what is yours."

"Why?" she asked. "Your kingdom is the Feywood. What is your interest in the Mystic Vale?"

He took a step closer. "My interest is in you, your highness. From the moment we met, we had a connection. I've never felt that with anyone before. I've never met another elemental. I did not know you were the target of the queen's wrath until I took her the enchanted dagger she commissioned. Even at that moment, when I promised to kill you, I knew I could not. Because you're special."

*He is correct. You are special,* Faradill said. *There are very few elementals in this realm.*

"If I wanted to kill you," he said, "I would have already."

"I realize that. You had many opportunities," she said.

"Then I ask you to trust me. Come with me to the villages, so you can see for yourself," he urged. "They want the rightful ruler on the throne. Not this imposter."

*You must go,* Faradill said. *Her magic is strong. Her hatred for you grows even stronger. She must be defeated.*

Snow said nothing as Faradill's voice faded from her mind. She continued to stand there, staring at Roderick holding out the dagger to her as her mind worked to form a plan. Perhaps he was right in that she would find support for her cause in the villages of the Mystic Vale. She had never ventured outside the Wyldwood since she arrived ten years ago. Would they even remember who she was? Would they believe she was the princess?

She thought of the pendant at her throat, hidden under her gown. Reaching up, she tugged it out from under her dress and let the pendant rest in her palm, gazing down at it. She swiped her thumb over the rose and crown, the royal sigil of her family line.

"If I go with you," she said, choosing her words slowly, "and we gain supporters, will you fight with me?"

"I will be by your side until the very end." He moved closer, closing the gap between them. "I swear this to you."

He glanced down at the pendant resting in her hand, then reached up and closed her fingers around it. It was as though he sensed her apprehension.

"They will know you by your pendant," he said. "They will support you and your cause."

"Are you certain?" She lifted her gaze and met his. It made her heart turn over.

There was an inherent strength in his eyes as well as determination and sincerity. With his hand on hers, she sensed the elemental magic swirling within him. It buzzed through her, connecting them together. As though they were meant to be.

"Yes," he said at last. "I'm certain."

He reached for her free hand and placed the dagger in it. She stared down at it as her gut clenched.

"The dagger?"

"It's yours," he said. "Your weapon to fight Seraphina."

Faradill's voice filtered through her mind. *You have the power within you to defeat her. If you have need of us, call and we will answer.*

She glanced up at the ancient oak, the leaves fluttering in the breeze.

"He's right, you know," Roderick said, his voice soft. "You have the power."

She took a deep breath, expelled it. "Then perhaps the time has come for me to fight for what's mine."

# CHAPTER 27

I t was almost nightfall. After the events of the day, exhaustion had set in, leaving her body fatigued. She placed the dagger on the ground next to her and pretended it didn't exist. All she thought about, though, was what happened to Seraphina when Ardan stabbed her with his. The way her skin seemed to sizzle. She wondered if that would happen to her should she be stabbed with it. She shoved away those thoughts.

"We will camp here tonight," she said. "In the morning, we will begin our trek to the villages to see if your claim about me is true."

She gave him a pointed look as she settled down at the foot of Faradill, still trying to come to terms with her emotions. Grief over the death of Ardan. Anger at Roderick for coming to her village. Yes, Ardan defended her and the village from Seraphina's attack, but none of that would have happened if it hadn't been for Roderick.

Annilen curled up next to her on a bed of leaves making her body as small as possible to keep warm. Snow rested her back on the trunk of Faradill, spreading her cloak over her as a makeshift blanket. She used one corner of it to cover Annilen. The sprite looked up at her with sleepy eyes and gave her a grin, then yawned and pillowed her head on her arms.

Roderick pulled a bedroll from his saddle bags, then unfolded it on the ground opposite Snow, then laid down on his back, his hands under his head as he looked up at the sky.

"I am sorry, Snow," Roderick said, his voice quiet in the gloaming. "I never meant for any of that to happen."

She wanted to tell him it was all right, that it didn't matter. But it wasn't all right and it did matter. Ardan's life mattered. The village mattered.

"I hope you'll accept my apology," he added.

"Perhaps I will."

"But not today." He didn't move to look at her, but she sensed his dejection.

She did not reply. She snuggled under the cloak, closed her eyes, and allowed sleep to take her.

The dream came almost instantly. Of Seraphina standing before one of the mirrors in a chamber somewhere deep within the castle. She understood that this was one of the mirrors stolen from the elves' archives.

It was a large, round mirror in an ornate gold frame. But the strangest thing of all was there was no reflection. It was simply a blank silver. Then a voice rang out.

"Magic Mirror on the wall. Who is the fairest of them all?"

It was Seraphina.

A featureless face flickered into the silver. "The fairest of them all, my queen, is the one who seeks wisdom and kindness, befriends those in nature, for true beauty lies within the heart."

Seraphina clenched her hands into tight fists as she spun from the mirror. Rage etched her face, making the lines go deeper and deeper.

"I am no longer the fairest in the land," she said.

"No, my queen. It is Snow White you seek who is the fairest in the land."

She snarled with her anger. "She must come to me, then, since the blacksmith cannot kill her. I will destroy all she holds dear if she does not present herself to me. Snow White must die."

Snow startled awake, jerking upright with her heart beating a rapid rhythm. The forest was still cloaked in darkness. Roderick still slept across from her, though he had turned on his side sometime during the night. She glanced down at Annilen who was still curled on her side and fast sleep.

*You sense something, don't you?* Faradill asked.

"It was only a dream," she whispered so as not to disturb the others.

*A dream that is not so far from reality,* he warned.

"I understand. On the morrow, I will begin my new journey."

She settled back down against the trunk of the old oak.

*You must forgive Roderick,* he said then. *For he is the only one who can protect you from what is to come.*

"From the queen?" she asked.

*The queen and her dark magic.*

"I will consider it," she promised.

She tried to sleep, but as night turned to morning, she hadn't. She was still sitting against the tree when Roderick yawned, stretched, and sat up on one elbow.

"You're awake early," he said.

She merely smiled. "I am. We should be on our way."

As she picked up the cloak, Annilen stirred and came awake. She fluttered upward to face Snow. "Are you leaving now?"

"Yes," Snow said.

"Can I come with you?"

She shook her head. "It's far too dangerous for a sprite."

Her expression fell into one of sadness. "Will I see you again, Snow?"

That sent a pang to her heart. She granted her a smile. "Of course, you will! I will return and when I do, I will make sure that all those in this forest are safe forever."

"Do you promise?"

"With all my heart," she said.

Annilen flew closer, her iridescent wings brushing against her cheek. Snow understood this was a gesture of affection. Then the sprite was off, disappearing into the morning light. Roderick rolled up his bedroll, then tucked it under his arm as he stood. Snow draped the cloak over her arm and got to her feet. Glancing down, she eyed the dagger still in its leather sheath.

She bent and picked it up, acknowledging the slight weight of it in her hand. The circlet Elator gave her was still on the ground, too. She picked it up and held it a moment, thinking of him. She placed it back on her head.

"What's our first stop?" she asked.

"The village of Westfall," he said. "A small but vibrant village with boisterous people who are not shy about telling you their opinion about anything." He grinned.

"Are they?" She was amused by the thought of this. "I can't wait to meet them all."

He reached a hand out to her. "We can ride together."

She wasn't sure about that and eyed his hand with suspicion.

"I can put your cloak and your bag in my saddle bags. And give you a way to wear the dagger on your hip." He nodded to the weapon still resting in her hand.

"Oh, that's not necessary—"

"You may have a need for it," he said. "Allow me?"

At last, she nodded and handed over her bag and cloak. He eyed the circlet still on her head. She tilted her head back, a bit defiant.

"I'm wearing it," she said. "It was a gift from Elator."

"Wear what you wish, princess." He reached for her, then, hooking his finger under the chain around her neck and flicking the pendant out from under her clothes. "But let them see this. The sigil of your royal house. Then they will know you are the true princess and rightful heir to the throne."

She started to object when she realized he was right. She nodded agreement, but it was difficult for her to keep the pendant out where it was to be seen. For the last ten years, she'd kept it hidden under her clothes at all times.

Roderick packed her things in the saddle bags.

"Come, princess. Let us break our fast in Westfall, for there is a tavern there that serves the beast oat cakes you've ever had." He held his hand out to her.

He was hard to resist. She took his hand and followed him to the horse. He mounted first, then helped her up behind him. They rode away and for the first time since she was a child, she left the Wyldwood Forest.

# CHAPTER 28

They rode into Westfall into the center of the bustling village where there was a lively market square. Snow was used to the calm, quietness of the elven village deep with the forest, so she wasn't sure where to look first. The smells of the market made her stomach rumble. Everything from freshly baked bread, which reminded her of Yirrie, to succulent roasted meats and fresh meats that included fish, fowl, and pork.

On one corner was a fruit and vegetable cart, the vendor a jolly man with a wide smile and a thick mustache under a bulbous nose. He greeted every passerby with a jovial wave and a hearty good morrow.

Another merchant had a cart piled high with furs. Next to that, bolts of what appeared to be expensive fabrics he was more than happy to peddle to anyone who took an interest. Next to him, a woman with woven baskets. Beyond that, Snow heard the clang of a smith. There was a candlemaker, a butcher, a carpenter, an apothecary, and more.

The villagers were dressed in vibrant colors—red, green, blue, yellow. In the center of town, there was a large fountain with a dancing waterfall that caught her attention. No one seemed to notice them as they rode into town and paused in front of the tavern.

Roderick dismounted first, then reached up to help her down. He tied up the horse, then took her by the hand and led her inside.

A large fireplace dominated one corner, but it was dark. Since it was still warm outside, there was no need for a roaring fire. Long tables lined the room as well as a few smaller ones scattered about. A bar on the other end of the tavern hosted a bartender who, even at this early hour, was offering up ale and mead to anyone who wanted it.

They took a table toward the back of the room, near the fireplace.

Snow looked around, her eyes pausing on the happy people who seemed to be perfectly at ease. They talked and laughed with one another with such raw emotion. She had never seen anything like that in the reserved, quiet elven village. Certainly, they exhibited emotion, too, but nothing as merry as these folks.

"Snow, you're staring," he said.

She snapped her gaze to the table in front of her, examining the scarred wooden top as if it was the most interesting thing in the world. "I didn't mean to."

"They are a cheery lot." He chuckled. "Good humored mostly. This is the largest of the three villages we'll be visiting."

"The others are smaller?" she asked, meeting his gaze.

"Yes. Westfall is further away from the castle and Seraphina's reach, so she isn't as interested in it. The others she likes to torment since they're closer."

"What does that mean?"

A tavern maid bustled up to the table with a bright smile and a twinkle in her deep brown eyes.

"Good morrow, my friends. What can I get ye?" she asked.

"Oat cakes, porridge, and waffles, if you please," Roderick said. "For the both of us. And a strong pot of tea with cream and sugar."

She dipped a curtsy and gave a nod before she hurried away.

"What are waffles?" Snow asked. The word felt foreign on her tongue.

"Ah, you're in for a treat." He gave a broad smile. "To answer your question, though, from what I gathered in the other villages, Seraphina has raised taxes on them several times to the point of putting them into poverty. She takes the food they grow and harvest for herself, barely leaving any for the villagers themselves. They're poor and starving."

Horror struck through her. "That's terrible."

"Here, though, Westfall thrives. I understand there is a significant underground movement to help the other villages when they can. But if they get caught…" His voice trailed off as he shook his head.

"What?" she asked, leaning forward.

"Well, you can imagine Seraphina's reaction to that."

She sat back in her chair, chewing on her bottom lip. "She would punish them, I'm sure."

He nodded.

The tavern maid returned with a tray holding a teapot, two cups, creamer and sugar bowl. She plopped it down on the table without a word and then scurried away to handle the next customer who arrived at the table next to Snow and Roderick.

He poured the tea, first her cup then his. He pushed the cup toward her.

"Cream or sugar?" he asked.

She shook her head.

Hearing about the other villages sent a pang of worry through her. If the people were taxed to that extreme, how did they manage to live?

Roderick poured a dollop of cream in his tea followed by a small teaspoon of sugar, then stirred.

"How will they know I am..." she paused and leaned forward, dropping her voice. "You know."

"The princess?" he asked.

She sucked in a sharp breath and sat straight, glancing around to see if anyone heard. No one had. They all continued about their business as if she were a normal patron on a normal morning in Westfall.

"They will in time." He gave a smile as he lifted the cup and sipped.

"You have a plan, don't you?"

"I do."

"Are you going to share that plan with me?"

"Should I?"

"It would be nice," she said, agitation clawing through her. She gripped her tea cup in one hand, the warmth pulsing through her palm as her hand cramped.

"If I do, and you don't approve, then I cannot move forward with that plan."

She clenched her jaw. "Why? Are you planning to stand on the chair and announce my existence to the entire tavern?"

He flushed hot, then laughed as he dropped his cup on the table. "Actually, I was."

She gaped at him, mortification shifting through her. "You can't."

"Why not? Is it not the truth?"

"It is, but—"

He shot to his feet so fast, the chair scraped against the floor with a squeak. He clapped his hands to get the attention of the patrons.

"My lords, my ladies, I have an announcement you will all want to hear," he said, his voice loud and sure and strong.

Snow wanted to crawl into a deep hole and hide. She sat, paralyzed, as she stared at him as heat pounded through her, willing him to return to his seat and be quiet. But he did not.

All eyes focused on Roderick. And then he did exactly as she had suggested. He stepped into the chair to elevate himself above all the others.

"Well? What is this big announcement?" a gruff patron at the bar demanded.

He was a burly man with a thick head of hair that tumbled to his shoulders and a belly that hung over his belt. He leaned back against the bar on his elbows holding a large tankard in one hand of what she assumed was ale.

"The princess and heir to the throne is not dead," Roderick said. "Nay, she lives. And she sits right here." He motioned to her.

All eyes turned to her, boring into her. But she kept her gaze focused solely on Roderick who stood tall in the chair, his gaze flickering around the room asking anyone to defy him.

Then someone laughed and rose from his seat near the front of the room. "How do we know you're telling the truth? That she is who you say she is? The princess disappeared years ago."

"I tell you true, good sir," Roderick said. "She lives and she is ready to reclaim her throne from the evil queen."

A tingling sensation went through her as she stared at him, her mouth suddenly dry. Her hands shook. What if these people thought she was an imposter? And then she recalled the pendant around her neck. The one that would show the world she was the princess. With her heart pounding a wicked beat, she placed her palms flat on the table and pushed up from the chair.

"Roderick speaks true," she said, trying to make her voice strong. "I bear the sigil of the royal house. The rose and the crown. It was a gift from my father before the queen murdered him in his sleep."

Surprised, he glanced down at her. Then a smile pulled up the corner of his mouth. He jumped down from the chair and moved to stand next to her.

"My good friends," he said, motioning to her, "your princess and heir to the throne."

A deafening silence descended around them. The large man at the bar pushed off his stool, still holding his tankard of ale. He moved toward her, his steps slow and sure and his gaze narrow. He paused in front of her.

"If you are indeed the princess, then let's see the sigil," he demanded.

She held the pendant in her palm and extended it as far as the chain would allow. The man squinted at her with his suspicion, then leaned down to examine the pendant resting against her hand. It gleamed in the half light of the tavern, the rose and crown winking up at him. He lifted his gaze to hers, then dropped to one knee, bowing to her.

"Your majesty," he said, his voice rough.

Others crowded around then, determined to get a look at the pendant she held. She refused to slip it off her head for fear someone would take it from her and she would never see it again. Every person who saw the sigil on the pendant dropped to a knee or curtsied to show their respect.

"You told us true, good sir," the large man said to Roderick. Then to Snow, "We are honored by your presence. But tell us, why have you been gone so long?"

She cut a glance to Roderick, who still stood next to her. He gave her an encouraging nod.

"When I was eight, the queen banished me from the castle. She told me I wasn't old enough to rule and that everyone hated me anyway. I ran into the forest—"

"The Wyldwood?" a woman in the back asked on a gasp.

"Yes," she said.

"But that forest is haunted," a man said.

"It is not," she said. "It is inhabited by elves who protect it with their light magic. Seraphina managed to invade that light magic with her darkness. She attacked me there and nearly killed me."

"That's why we need your help," Roderick said, taking up the story. "We intend to return to the castle and get back her throne, but we cannot do it alone."

"You want us to fight for you," the large man said, his gaze pinpointing on Snow.

It wasn't a question but she nodded anyway.

"It is the only way to stop the queen from raising taxes even more and starving you out of your own kingdom," Roderick said.

A man from the back of the tavern dressed as a ranger moved forward. He had his hand on the hilt of his sword. Roderick wrapped his fingers around the dagger at his waist and stiffened eyeing the man as he approached. He shoved off his hood and dropped to a knee in front of Snow and bowed his head.

"I will protect you with my life and my sword, my queen," the ranger said. "You only need to tell me when the fight."

Her heart skipped a beat. Next to her, she sensed Roderick relax and release his hand on the hilt of his dagger.

"I will fight for you, too, princess," the man with the tankard announced.

"As will I!" Another next to him stood up.

More volunteers shouted their support until finally a host of cheers went up in the tavern. Roderick took over, then, telling them the strategy for the planned attack. It was something they hadn't discussed yet. She watched as he worked the room, telling them to meet in the field of the castle in less than a week's time.

She wondered, then, if that would be enough time to gather more forces from the other villages. But Roderick seemed to know what he was doing. She was grateful, but also feeling a bit left out.

As she sat watching him, the dream returned to her, haunting her. It was as though someone watched her and she wondered then if Seraphina saw her through the Magic Mirror. Was it truly a dream or a premonition?

The tavern wench bustled up to the table and dropped a heaping plate of food in front of her and then on the other side where Roderick was sitting. She flashed a bright smile.

"On the house, your majesty!" She dipped a curtsy and hurried away.

Snow peered down at the plate of food with a large round golden-brown pastry that had a grid-like surface impression. Despite her rumbling stomach, she had lost her appetite. She couldn't shake the sense of foreboding hanging over her.

# CHAPTER 29

Roderick returned to the table moments later, a broad smile on his face as he sat in front of his heaping plate of food. He held up the grid-like pastry.

"Waffles!" he announced. "They're delicious. Trust me."

She peered down at it as though it were a foreign object. "I seem to have lost my appetite."

That made him stop buttering his waffle and look at her. "Why?"

"Something feels...off," she said. "I can't explain it."

He glanced around the tavern looking for an imminent threat. "We're safe here."

Her gaze flickered up to his. "Are we?"

He dropped his fork and reached for her hand across the table. "What's wrong? I thought you would be happy we managed to recruit the first soldiers to help us in the fight against Seraphina."

"I am happy about that."

She glanced around the tavern as the people went about their business as though nothing had changed. The large man at the bar continued to drink his ale. The ranger returned to his seat at the back, hood up, smoking a pipe, as though he hadn't pledged his life to protect hers.

"But?" Roderick asked, his voice gentle.

She inhaled a deep breath, expelled it. "It's just that I can't shake the feeling she's watching through her mirror."

"If she is, then she knows we are coming for her." He released her hand and went back to buttering his waffle, then poured a heaping portion of honey on top of it.

"Doesn't that ruin the element of surprise?" she asked.

He sliced a corner of the waffle and stabbed it with his fork. "She has to know we're coming for her."

"We?" Snow lifted a brow.

He dropped his voice. "She sent me to kill you. I didn't. She knows that. She's also intelligent enough to realize that if you're not dead, you're still a threat to her."

Her stomach twisted into a knot as a sick feeling erupted through her. "I think this was a mistake."

He dropped his fork and pinned her with his bright gaze. "No, Snow. You're doing the right thing."

"But—"

"Sometimes the right thing is the hardest thing," he said, his voice soft and gentle. "When we finish breakfast, we will ride out to the next village."

"Which one is that?" she asked.

"Lighthill. But I must warn you. Things are much different there than here."

She pushed food around on her plate, watching as he dove into his with alacrity. "How different?"

He stuck a bit of waffle in his mouth, chewed, swallowed. "Different," was his only response.

She didn't like the sound of that one bit. As she poked her waffle with a fork, the door to the tavern burst open with a loud thud.

"The Wyldwood Forest is on fire!" a man shouted.

Her heart leapt to her throat as she jumped up from her seat, her chair scraping along the wood floor and then tipping over. Patrons spilled out of the tavern into the street, but Snow was faster. She moved past them all. As soon as she was outside, she saw the dark plume of smoke in the distance curling upward into the bright blue sky.

She sucked in a shuddering breath, as she thought of the elven village, Faradill and Annilen, and all the other creatures inhabiting the forest. She closed her eyes and opened her senses to nature, reaching out to the forest.

The fire was large and raging, burning through trees. She cried out with the pain she felt from them. Her mind raced to find Faradill. Thankfully, he still stood and was out of the fire's path. However, the elven village did not fare so well.

"Snow?" Roderick's tentative voice at her side broke through her thoughts.

"The elven village." Her breath hitched, then her eyes flew open as she spun to face him, gripping him by the arm. "You have to do something!"

"Me?" He blinked.

"You are an Artificer. You have the power of all the elements. The power of water."

Understanding dawned. "But I've never used the power of water."

"Me, either, so we'll have to try together." She gripped his hand in hers and closed her eyes again. "The Sea of Mara is the closest water source. Envision it. Close your eyes."

"I've never been there—"

"The coastline is rocky," she interrupted. "With pale blue sand. The waves crash against the rocks. When the sand is wet from the undulating surf, it turns a deep blue. Can you see it?"

She peeked through her lashes to see his eyes closed. "Yes, I see it."

"Good. Keep that in your mind. Think of the water. The waves. The wind. The surf breaking on the rocks."

She released his hand and dropped to her knees, placing her palms flat on the ground. The earth was cool and sandy beneath her fingers. Once again, she closed her eyes, connecting with the nature around her, around them, and thinking of the rocks on the shoreline. The ground rumbled and came to life.

*Help us!*

The panicked voices of the creatures from the forest flickered through her mind. Was she too late? Was the village destroyed? The forest? Leaving one hand flat on the ground, she reached up for Roderick. It was risky, but she had to do it and she prayed the elves were out of the burning village. She thought of Elator and Yirrie and even the Elders, willing them to be safe.

"Take my hand."

He did, his fingers lacing with hers.

"*Where the rhythm of the tide softly beats, draw the water from the depths of the Mara Sea.*" She paused, her eyes opening as she looked up at him. "Send the sea to the village, Roderick."

He sucked in a breath through his nose, his hand tightening on hers. A droplet of sweat slipped down one side of his face. Still connected to the ground, she heard the crash of the tidal wave as it swelled and then flooded through the edge of the forest. Deep in her mind, she heard the sizzle as the fire snuffed out and the waters receded.

"You did it," she whispered.

Still clutching her hand, he opened his eyes and met her gaze. "*We* did it."

As she looked at him, she realized that while they were each powerful in their own right, together, they were formidable.

"What just happened?" someone asked. "The ground shook and then—"

"Shh! Listen!" someone interrupted.

Snow heard it then. The distant sound of water cascading over land. Her heart jammed into her throat as she realized their combined power managed to send a tidal wave all along the coastline, not just to the edge of the Wyldwood.

"Roderick!"

"I don't know how to stop it."

She released his hand and placed both on the ground, then bent forward. Her forehead touched the ground.

*"Water's wild and torrents flow. By these words I command, recede, retreat, reclaim the land."*

The villagers chattered around her, but she heard none of that as she focused on the sounds of the water flowing over the land. In her mind, she pushed the water back. It was as though the land inhaled a deep breath as it sucked the tide away. She didn't know how long she crouched there, but her back ached. Sweat trickled down the sides of her face. Her heart continued to palpitate a wild beat.

She reached out her senses looking for Faradill or Annilen or any of the forest creatures. Even though she was far away from the fire, she still smelled the acrid tang of smoke.

*You saved us, but we are damaged.* It was a collective voice deep in her mind. The voice of the forest. Hot tears pricked the back of her eyelids.

Roderick placed a hand on her shoulder. "Snow?"

Stiffly, she lifted her head. Every muscle and joint inside her ached. A breath shuddered out of her. She focused on her surroundings and saw the villagers returned to the tavern or their homes or shops. Only Roderick remained standing by her side, his hand on her shoulder.

"Where did everyone go?" She blinked away the tears and looked up at him.

"You spooked them a bit, I think," he said. "When the ground cracked and rumbled, they ran."

There were tiny fissures snaking along the ground around her, as though she was the epicenter. There was no more smoke in the distance. What did her nature magic look like to the villagers?

"But you didn't."

"I didn't," he agreed.

"It was the only way to stop the tsunami," she said.

"I know." His voice was quiet. He dropped to his knees in front of her, took her hands in his. "Snow, I may be an Artificer, as you said, but you...you have so much elemental magic deep within you. Did you know?"

She shook her head, the threat of tears still behind her eyes. "I couldn't save them all."

"But you *did* save some of them."

Her bottom lip trembled. "The village..."

He squeezed her hands. "We can't go back."

"Why not?" she demanded.

"Do you really want to see it burned to the ground?" he asked.

She considered this and finally shook her head. "But Elator and Yirrie..."

"We have to believe they are all right." He brought her hands up to his lips and kissed her fingertips. "We have to believe they got out."

His tenderness nearly made her come undone. She tugged her hands away from him and pushed from the ground, getting to her feet. He rose, too. She clenched her fists, staring toward the Wyldwood Forest.

"This is Seraphina's doing," she said. Her voice cracked a little when she said it.

"I thought so, too. She's trying to get to you, Snow. Don't let her."

He was right and she knew that. She whisked away the tears and took a deep breath, pushing back emotions that threatened to overtake her. She'd left behind the only real home she'd ever known. Left behind the two people who raised her these last ten years. When she left, she questioned if she made the right decision. She was certain she had now. Seraphina would destroy the forest no matter if she was in it or not.

"I'm not," she said, sounding strong and sure. Blistering determination seared through her. "Let's get my throne back."

He grinned. "As my princess commands."

# CHAPTER 30

Roderick was right. Lighthill was a much different village than Westfall. There was not the bustle of activity she had expected. Instead, there were only a few people out and about. Most of the shops were closed and boarded up. There were only a few street merchants. One sold fruits and vegetables. Another bread and pastries.

While those in Westfall had jovial smiles and boisterous laughter, the people of Lighthill were much more subdued. It was shortly after midday as they made their way through to the only tavern and inn with a dilapidated sign swaying in the faint breeze on creaking hinges. She glanced up at it, barely making out the faded letters that read *The Painted Owl.*

Roderick rode up to the inn and dismounted. "Wait here. I'll see if they can stable the horse."

"And if they can't?" she asked.

He looked thoughtful a long moment and glanced back out to the road, as though calculating the distance to the next village. "We will have to move on."

She hopped down from the saddle as he disappeared inside, uneasy with being left alone. Her hand landed on the hilt of the enchanted dagger. She glanced around the nearly deserted village, her heart breaking for these people who looked as though they had been worn down to the bone. Seraphina and her taxes must be taking a toll them.

"Yer a pretty thing."

The man's voice startled her. He approached, squinting at her in the waning afternoon sunlight. He had a scruff of beard on his cheeks and chin. His long hair was greasy and unkept. His clothes were worn, stained, and tattered.

"Where do ye hail from?" he asked.

Uncertainty flickered through her. How should she answer that question? If she told him she was from the castle, then he would resent her. Especially if he thought she was in league with the queen. If she told him she came from the Wyldwood Forest, he might think her mad.

"We traveled up from Westfall," she finally said.

"Westfall." He said it with contempt and then spat on the ground. "Nothing but troublemakers there."

Confusion flickered through her. Roderick said those in Westfall tried to help the other villages with an underground movement. Perhaps this man didn't realize that.

"Are ye here to steal from us, too?"

"Steal?" Shock rolled through her. "I don't understand."

"The way I see it, those from Westfall owe *us*." He thumbed at his chest as he eyed her, looking for any valuable she might have on her person. His gaze paused a little too long on her pendant.

She clutched the dagger tighter, ready to draw it should he make any sudden movement.

"Let her be, Caleb," another man said. He lumbered up behind the scraggly man and placed a hand on his shoulder. "Find someone else to hassle."

Caleb grunted, shot her a scowl, and trudged off.

The second man was younger than Caleb, but with a pronounced limp as he favored his left leg. His dark hair was shaggy, hanging down to his shoulders with a fall across his forehead. He had bright, intelligent eyes as he peered at her with an apologetic smile.

"You'll have to forgive him. He's a curmudgeon and suspicious of everyone."

"Is he? Why did he ask if we were here to steal from you?" she asked.

"Because that's what he thinks about Westfall. He doesn't want to believe what he sees. Those villagers do nothing but try to help us. It's Queen Seraphina that steals from us. I'm William, the innkeeper's son."

Snow was not surprised to hear about Seraphina stealing from the villagers. Roderick had told her as much. She looked to the door in which Roderick had disappeared into, wondering if he was still in there.

"Do you seek food and shelter?" he asked.

"And a stable for our horse," she said.

"We can accommodate you," he said. "We don't see many visitors like you."

"Like me?"

"Rich folk," he added. One corner of his mouth lifted in a grin.

She liked him right away. He was kind and reminded her a bit of Ardan, which sent a pang of grief through her.

Roderick burst from the inn, his face red with fury as he charged toward her. William stumbled back out of his way as he stuck his foot in the stirrup and settled into the saddle.

"We're leaving," he said, his voice gruff. He reached a hand down to her to help her up.

"Leaving?" Snow asked, remaining in place. "But I thought—"

"Innkeeper said there's no place for people like us at the inn and no room in the stable," Roderick replied.

"My father said that?" William asked, incredulous.

Roderick gave him a death glare. "Who are you?"

"Ah, this is William," Snow cut in. "The innkeeper's son."

Roderick glanced from her to him and back again, question and confusion written all over his face.

"William said there was plenty of room in the stable for our horse." She pinned him with her gaze. "Didn't you?"

He nodded so hard, a lock of his mop of brown hair fell over his forehead. "Give me a moment to speak to my father." And then he scurried into the inn, his limp a little more noticeable as he tried to hurry.

Roderick clutched the reins tighter in his hands. "Let's go, Snow. That man doesn't want us here."

"We will wait," she said, her tone patient. When he gave her a quizzical look, she added, "You said yourself we needed allies."

He started to object when William came out of the inn, a look of triumph on his youthful face. "Follow me." He waved them after him.

Snow gave him a glance and then followed the boy. Roderick hesitated a moment before nudging his horse into a walk. William led them to a stable behind the inn where there were several open stalls and a few horses already boarded. Once they were in the stable, he dismounted and relinquished the reins to William. He led it into the first open stall.

"I'll make sure your horse is brushed and fed," William said.

"What did you say to convince him?" Roderick asked.

William's cheeks flushed dark red as he suddenly turned shy, peering down at his feet. "I told him you would pay in gold."

Roderick shot her a surprised look. Snow's brows rose to her hairline.

"You lied," she said. "I never told you that."

"You didn't," he agreed, still staring at his feet.

She lifted her head a little higher. "However, we *can* pay in gold."

His head shot up as he stared at her, his eyes wide and his face now drained of color. Roderick lifted one brow at her and tilted his head to one side.

"We can?" he asked.

"We can't pay you today," Snow added, never taking her gaze off the boy. "But I promise to pay you and lift the taxes off the village once I regain control of the kingdom."

William stared at her as though she'd lost her mind. And perhaps she had. She wasn't going to get anywhere with her continued denial of her true identity. She slipped the pendant off her neck and approached him. Roderick watched with interest, his gaze firmly pinned on her. She ignored him.

"This was a gift from my father," she said, showing William the pendant. "It is the sigil of the Mystic Vale."

William stared down at it in wonder. "The rose and the crown."

"Yes," Snow said. "My name is Snow White and I'm the rightful heir to the throne. Seraphina is a usurper. She doesn't belong in power. I mean to see her dethroned."

William dropped to one knee and his head bent. "Your majesty."

"Get up," she said on a sigh. "All we seek tonight is a place to stay and a warm meal."

"And you shall have it. The tavern is next to the inn. I'll take you there now."

William started out of the stable trying his best to hide the limp. Roderick shot her a look that told her he was impressed as they followed the boy out.

"How did you get that limp?" she asked.

"Oh...it's an old injury. Nothing to be concerned about, your majesty."

"You don't have to call me that," she said.

"But you are." He gave her a winsome glance over his shoulder. "Aren't you?"

"I am but..."

"She's not quite used to that yet," Roderick put in.

"How about I call you my lady?" William suggested.

"How about just Snow?" she countered.

He grinned again and nodded.

# Chapter 31

Roderick was impressed. In Westfall, she was not ready to announce who she was to the crowd. Here in Lighthill, she seemed more than willing to tell them who she was and her intentions. They didn't accept her with open arms. It was more of a begrudging interest at best.

After telling William who she was and showing him the pendant, he led them into the inn which was connected to the only tavern in town. Inside, the patrons were not interested in anything but what she intended to do. She stood at the front of the room, her hands clasped in front of her and her head held high as she told them.

"I cannot do this alone. Those in Westfall have agreed to back me," she said.

"And ye expect us to do the same?" one man scoffed. "How do we know you're telling the truth?"

She clenched her fists, her body rigid as she stood facing them all. Roderick moved to stand next to her to give her strength and support.

"The princess speaks true. The queen commanded me to kill her because she's a threat to her throne."

Silence descended on the small crowd.

The barkeeper, a frowning man wiping the bar top with a damp rag, said, "But you didn't."

"When I learned who she was, I couldn't," Roderick said. "She's the only one who can end the suffering here and in Brookdale."

"The kingdom I want is one of prosperity," she said. "Not people starving because they're taxed and their crops are stolen."

"And you promise this?" another man said as he stepped forward.

"I do," she said with a nod.

"You'll keep your word?" he added.

"I will."

Her voice never wavered as she answered. Her hands relaxed and her shoulders drooped a little. She was losing hope again. Silence again. The man turned to the crowd, eyeing them all.

"Then I say we fight for her. Those in favor?"

When he said that, Snow blew out a shuddering breath. He would have never noticed it had he not been watching her as she looked at all the faces in the crowd as they considered. And then the barkeeper spoke first.

"Aye," he said. "I'm no good with a sword, but I'll fight for you, princess."

"As will I."

And so, it went and once they had all pledged, Roderick bought them all a round of ale and told the barkeeper to put it on his tab. Snow sat the table staring down in the frothy drink.

"You did it," he said as he joined her, holding his own tankard.

"I haven't done anything yet." She lifted her gaze to his. "Even with the men here, how many do we have? Two hundred? Three?" She shook her head. "It's not enough. Not against Seraphina and her forces."

"How many does she have?" Roderick asked.

"As many as she needs. She can conjure a dark army if she wants," Snow said.

He saw the desperation, the worry, the fear deep in her eyes. She was right. It wasn't enough. They would be slaughtered when they tried to approach the castle. He sat back in his seat, his mouth dry and his appetite for ale gone.

And he had yet to tell her about the sleeping curse placed on him. He was running out of time. He had to get them to the castle before the curse took hold of him.

An idea formed and he rose. "I'll be back."

"Where are you going?" she called after him.

But he was already stalking across the tavern and out the door. He headed to the inn, where he had words with the innkeeper earlier that day. They had since reconciled thanks to his son, William. The innkeeper, Jacob, lounged behind the desk. He shot Roderick a glare when he saw him.

"Come to make more empty promises of gold, my lord?" he snarled.

"No," Roderick said. "I need to send a message to King Alfred."

"King Alfred of the Feywood?" He snorted. "Why would he want a message from you?"

His incredulity raked on Roderick's nerves. "Are you going to help me or not?" he snapped.

The man snapped his mouth shut. "I don't have quill or paper. I can't read or write."

Roderick flushed with the innkeeper's reply. "Who does?"

"The chief magistrate," Jacob replied.

"Where would I find the chief magistrate?" he asked.

The innkeeper gave him a look as though he'd lost his mind. "Likely in the tavern. But be warned, he is not a friend to you or your King Alfred. He's loyal to the queen."

This posed a problem. If the chief magistrate was loyal to the queen, then Snow announcing her intentions and identity to the entire tavern was a terrible idea and would likely garner some type of retaliation from the evil queen. They needed to get out of Lighthill as soon as possible.

But he still needed to send that message. He needed someone else to help him. His mind raced as he tried to think of some other way to send a message to the king.

"Thanks for your help," he said.

He exited the inn, pausing there to look up and down the street. Most of the shops were closed for the night. His gaze alighted on each and every one, then paused on the apothecary. The man was closing up shop for the night.

A buzzing sound erupted somewhere in the distance. A flicking of iridescent wings in the deepening twilight caught his attention. He watched, fascinated, as the moving ball of light was headed right for him. On impulse, he held up his hand, palm out. The little sprite landed in the center of his hand. It was Annilen.

She bent over, her hands on her knees as she tried to catch her breath. Then she looked up at him, her tiny faced pinched with fear and concern.

"Annilen?"

"Where is Snow?"

"In the tavern," he nodded behind him. "What are you doing here?"

"The queen attacked the Wyldwood Forest," she said. "She set it on fire. Most of us managed to escape. Then there was this incredible wave of water that came. A wall of water!" She paused to gulp in a breath. "Was it Snow?"

He nodded.

She blew out a breath. "She saved us. But the elven village..."

"Was it destroyed?" he asked, his heart climbing to his throat.

"Only some," she said. "The Elders were able to protect most of it with their magic. But the forest..." Her breath hitched, causing her to emit a tiny squeak. "I've come to warn Snow the queen will be hunting her down. And I want to join her travels."

All the more reason to get out of Lighthill. It wasn't new information, either. He was aware the queen was looking to put an end to Snow White as quickly as possible. He was certain the Feywood king would help him, if only he could get a message to him.

And then an idea struck.

He walked away from the inn, Annilen still perched in his hand.

"Annilen, I'm sure Snow will want you to join her travels, but I have something more important for you to do."

She tipped her head to one side in question and suspicion. "What is that?"

"Snow needs reinforcements if she's going to defeat the queen. I think King Alfred can help us."

"The Feywood king?"

"Yes," he said. "I forged armor and weapons for him. He would come to her aid if I asked him...and told him Queen Seraphina plans to invade the Feywood and take over the kingdom for herself."

Her brows drew together. "Is she?"

Well, Roderick wasn't certain she was, but the queen was ambitious. It was only a matter of time before that were true. He nodded.

"Yes. You can get into the castle and find the king. Tell him you know me and that you are my messenger. Tell him the queen is mobilizing for an attack and to send forces north before she can march that way," he said.

"Will he believe me? How will he know I'm telling the truth?"

It was a good question. He had dealings with the king on numerous occasions. He'd made the king his own enchanted blade. The king had commissioned it and asked for something specific to be engraved in the handle—three initials representing his wife, his son, and his daughter. FJP for Filomena, his wife; James, his son; and Pippa, his daughter. He told this to Annilen.

"Can you do this for me?"

She was silent a long moment, then finally nodded. "If it will help Snow, then yes. I will do it."

Roderick grinned. He gave her directions to the castle and how to find the king. Then, the sprite fluttered away, carrying with her his hopes the king would bring his army.

# CHAPTER 32

Snow glanced around the tavern looking for Roderick. He hadn't said where he was going, and he hadn't returned. She shifted in her chair, feeling the dark eyes of a man across the room. He'd been staring at her since Roderick left her alone. She rested her hand on the dagger at her hip. Though she refused to make eye contact with the man, she knew he stared at her.

Finally, he rose from his chair and lumbered over to her. Her heart leapt as he approached, and her hand gripped the handle of the dagger as she prepared to draw it.

"Snow White." He drew out her name as he peered down at her.

She glanced up and met his sharp, assessing gaze. "Who are you?"

"The Chief Magistrate of this village." He gave her a toothy grin.

This wasn't good at all. Instinct took over as she whipped out the dagger and pointed it at him. "What do you want?"

He chuckled, clearly unaffected by the dagger pointing at him.

"The queen is looking for you," he said, ignoring her question. He made a motion with his head and then suddenly the table was surrounded by his men. "Might want to put down the dagger."

She clutched it tighter. Where was Roderick? She felt a prick on the back of her shoulder. She didn't have to turn around to know there was a sword at her back. The tavern fell silent as she sat there in a standoff with the Chief Magistrate who stared back at her.

"You're under arrest," he said.

One of his men plucked the dagger from her right hand with ease. Another on her left grabbed her by the upper arm and dragged her out of the chair. The man with her dagger fell in step on her other side. As the Chief Magistrate led her from the tavern, she realized her error in judgement. Announcing who she was to the entire tavern was a mistake. She scanned the faces of the crowd that stared back at her in silence. None of them made a move to help her.

The men led her from the tavern down the deserted street. She had no doubt they'd haul her into a wagon and take her to Seraphina.

Suddenly, the man on her right stumbled and fell. Her dagger he'd been holding tumbled from his hand and landed on the ground by his side. She eyed it, wishing there was a way to grab it. But then she noticed an arrow sticking out of his back. She sucked in a deep breath and glanced around, looking for Roderick. The man holding her by the arm jerked her toward him, then wrapped his arm around her. A blade pressed against her throat.

The Chief Magistrate seemed unflustered by events. He halted in the road and slowly turned to face her and his guard, his eyes scanning the area for the intruder who had dared to kill one of his men.

"Whoever you are, you will be arrested and taken to the queen, too," the Chief Magistrate said.

Still there was no one about. If Roderick was hiding, he was doing a great job of keeping himself invisible.

"Come out of the shadows and show yourself," he said.

Silence reigned as they all stood there waiting. She heard the whistle of the arrow through the air before she saw it heading right for her. She sucked in a sharp breath as the arrow found it's mark and landed in the head of the man holding her. His body went slack enough for her to jump away, the dagger falling to the ground as he died. She bent to pick it up and pointed it at the Chief Magistrate.

"Whoever you're working with will be punished," the man said, pinning her with his deep glare.

Those were his last words as an arrow landed in the center of his chest. He collapsed to the ground.

Snow remained where she was, her hand tightened on the dagger as she glanced around looking for her savior. William, the innkeeper's son, emerged from the shadows holding a bow.

"William! Do you realize what you've done?"

"Yes," he said, staring down at the dead men. "I saved you."

"You killed the Chief Magistrate and his men," she said on a breath. "You'll be hanged for that."

"I won't," he said. "We have lived too long under the man's tyranny."

Roderick rounded a building then at a dead run and came to an abrupt halt, his dagger in his hand. He quickly took in the carnage, the boy with the bow, and question lingering in his eyes.

"What happened here?"

"He was going to arrest Snow," William said. "I had to stop them."

"Gods," Roderick swore. "You've really done it now. Snow, we have to go."

She scooped up the enchanted dagger the guard took from her and holstered it. "And so does William."

"I'll be all right," he said. "But Roderick is correct in that you have to leave this place. The queen will send more men here when she discovers her Chief Magistrate is dead."

"But—" Snow began.

"You must go *now*," William said.

Still, Snow worried about the boy and what would happen to him should it be discovered he was the one who killed the men. And what of the dead men?

"I will dispose of the bodies while you escape," he said, as though he read her thoughts.

"Come, Snow. He's right. We have to leave." Roderick approached her, reaching for her hand.

She stepped away from him, though, and walked to William. She reached for him, placing her hands on his shoulders. "I will never forget what you did for me."

"I've saddled my horse for you as well as his. They are waiting in the stable." As he said it, he cut a glance to Roderick.

"I cannot take your—"

"I insist. A second horse will help you ride away quicker."

There was deep determination in his young eyes that told her she could not refuse. She understood, then, he wanted to make sure they escaped the village. She nodded, then gave him a quick kiss on the cheek.

"Thank you," she whispered.

She and Roderick hurried to the stable. The boy was right. He had, in fact, saddled the horses and made them ready to ride. They mounted and rode out into the late afternoon, leaving Lighthill behind.

"Do you think he'll be all right?" she asked. She cut Roderick a glance and noticed he had a grim expression.

"I hope so," he said.

But as his said it, she heard the note of worry in his voice. She understood, then, the sacrifice the boy made for their escape. And she would be forever grateful for that.

# CHAPTER 33

They rode away from Lighthill as darkness fell, blanketing the path in deep shadows. They headed north to the next village, Brookdale, which was close to the queen's castle. Snow was quiet as they traveled, thinking about the burned-out elven village, wondering if Elator and Yirrie survived. Wondering, too, if Annilen and her sprites made it away from the fire. She had no way to know. Only that she managed to save most of the forest from the devastation thanks to hers and Roderick's elemental magic.

And then she thought of William and hoped he was all right.

"We should stop for the night," Roderick suggested.

She took in their surroundings, but they were out in the open. No trees to hide them and there wasn't a suitable place to camp for the night. Not even a stream to water the horses.

"And where would that be?" she asked.

He cut her a glance. Though she couldn't see his expression in the darkness, she knew his gaze bored into her.

"You sound angry," he said.

"I am angry," she confirmed. "Angry Seraphina destroyed the village and the forest with fire. Angry she killed my father and took his throne and threw me out like garbage. Angry she killed Ardan."

"He sacrificed himself—"

"Angry I left the only true home I ever knew." She turned her head to meet his gaze, but his eyes were nothing more than black orbs in the shadows. "I realize he sacrificed himself to save me. I realize, too, there was nothing within my power to stop Seraphina from killing my father and taking over the kingdom. I was a child."

She looked away, peering into the deepening twilight. She was angry, too, Roderick pushed her into this journey. Though she understood why he did it, it didn't make her any less angry. In time, she would forgive him. But for now, she harbored that anger close to her heart because it seemed hopeless. She didn't have an army. All she had were villagers and farmers who were willing to fight for her and it wasn't enough.

"I'm sorry, Snow," he said, his voice low. There was genuine emotion on those three words.

Her eyes drifted closed as she rode on, clutching the reins in her hands until they ached. She heard herself say, "It's not your fault."

Though she wanted to place the blame squarely on him. It was no one's fault but Seraphina's she was now homeless and left to face an insurmountable task.

"I'm just...worried," she said finally. "I don't know how we will defeat her when she has so much more power. Dark power."

He was silent as they rode. So silent, in fact, she turned to look at him. In the shadows, she saw the pensive look on his face, the pinched expression.

"Perhaps I was wrong to push you into this," he said at last. "You weren't ready to leave the Wyldwood."

There were so many emotions at war within her. Guilt for leaving the forest. Worry for those she left behind. Fear facing her destiny. Perhaps he was right in that she wasn't ready to leave the forest, but then…would she ever be ready to leave? She knew the day would come. She just didn't know it would be because the queen sent Roderick to kill her.

"You were right to push me," she said. "I was hiding from who I was and from Seraphina. It's time I face her."

A deep, malicious laugh broke through the shadows and then a puff of smoke appeared in front of them. When the smoke cleared, Seraphina stood before them. They both pulled their horses to a halt.

"Yes, I agree. It's time you face me. I've been following your adventures with the help of my Magic Mirror. It's quite handy."

Snow's gut feeling the queen was watching them was correct. No matter where they went, they would not be able to hide from her.

The queen's eyes cut over to Roderick, then back to Snow. "Somehow, you managed to get into and out of Westfall without being detected by my soldiers. In Lighthill, you killed my Chief Magistrate. For that, you will pay."

Snow clutched the reins tighter in her hands as she peered down at Seraphina. Then she slid out of the saddle and moved around the horse to face her. She stood several feet away, her stance menacing. But Snow was not afraid.

"What are you doing?" Roderick said, his voice a roughened whisper.

"Doing what I need to do," she replied. Then to Seraphina, "Your reign is over."

"My reign is over when I'm dead." She lifted her arms.

"So be it," Snow said.

Seraphina struck then, sending a pulsing stream of magic directly at Snow. Roderick shouted something, but she ignored him. She was ready for that. She dropped to her knees, placing her palms flat on the ground and chanting under her breath, calling to the creatures of the world and the earth beneath her.

The ground rumbled. The horses whinnied with their fear. Her horse galloped away in to the night. Roderick was suddenly at her side, the enchanted dagger in his hand glowing.

"Since you cannot seem to carry out my orders," she said to Roderick, "I will kill the princess myself!"

She flung another bit of magic at her. Snow curled into a ball and rolled out of the way. Roderick jumped to one side to avoid the blast. His horse had also galloped away. Snow crouched once again on the ground, her hands flat in the grass. She whispered another chant and watched as the grass grew tall, winding around the evil queen's legs. She cried out in surprise and frustration before she managed to stumble away, stomping on the growing grass to get away from it and kill it.

Snow sensed roots deep within the ground under her hands. Seraphina pushed her palms outward facing Snow and called up another dark spell. She saw it coming but was trying to complete her chant before she moved. The spell smashed into her, shoving her to the ground and knocking the wind out of her. She laid on her back, looking up at the cold stars twinkling in the inky night sky. Were those the actual stars or was she seeing things?

Roderick shouted something. She felt his footsteps vibrate the ground as he charged. She wanted to cry out, tell him to stop, but she was too busy trying to catch her breath.

Around her, the sky brightened with more magic and she smelled the tinge of acrid smoke. Gulping in a deep breath, she managed to roll to her side. Roderick was crumpled on the ground at the queen's feet.

"You are beaten, little one. Give up this madness and I will let you live out the rest of your days in the dungeon," the queen said.

"Never," Snow said on a rasp.

Once again, she placed her palms on the ground. This time, she chanted quickly, bringing the roots deep within the earth to life. The ground split around the queen's feet. She glanced down, horror on her face, as she tried to stumble back. Her foot landed in one of the cracks, turning over her ankle and she fell. The roots erupted from the ground and wrapped around her, trapping her there.

Slowly, Snow climbed to her feet. Whatever dark magic hit her, it left her weak and bone tired. Or that could be from the effects of her own elemental magic. She made her way to Roderick's side. The enchanted blade was on the ground in front of him, no longer glowing. She pressed two fingers against his neck. A faint pulse beat there. Thankfully, he was still alive.

Seraphina struggled on the ground against the roots and vines that trapped her. She cried out in frustration, her agitation clear on her face.

Snow moved toward her, standing over her and looking down at her. She pitied the woman who had wanted to be something more than she was—a peasant girl. She'd managed to achieve so much, but at the cost of precious lives.

"It is *you*, Seraphina, who will live out the rest of your days in the dungeon of *my* castle. You will never again see the light of day," Snow said.

A brief flash of panic went over her face as she looked up at her and then she laughed, that deep guttural, menacing laugh.

"You think you have beaten me. You are wrong."

The queen's hands were still free. She managed to twist them and then disappeared into a puff of smoke, leaving behind the roots and vines resting limply against the cracked ground.

A groan behind her made her turn and drop to her knees next to Roderick. He came to, his eyes fluttering open. She helped him to a sitting position.

"What happened?"

"She got away."

His gaze landed on the destroyed ground. "You tried to capture her."

"Tried. Failed. I forgot about her magic." She helped him to his feet. "Are you all right?"

"I shouldn't have charged her," he said. "Her blast of magic was rather painful."

Whatever she did to him, it hit him harder than when the queen's magic hit her. "Let's find the horses and go."

He nodded, picking up the dagger and sheathing it. But as they searched for the horses, the ground rumbled. A different rumble than when Snow used her elemental magic to manipulate the earth. This was deeper and sounded more like a horde of animals. They both froze. She gripped his hand, moving closer to him.

"What is it?" Her voice was a whisper.

"I don't know, but I don't think it's over with the queen." He nodded to the distance.

There, she saw a black shadow rolling toward them. She sensed something sinister in that cloud of smoke, making all the hairs on her neck stand at attention. Roderick turned to her, gripping her by the shoulders.

"Run!"

They started to run away from the black cloud, but it was rolling in fast. She stole a glance over her shoulder and realized it was approaching at a rapid pace. They would never outrun it. And there was no place to hide on the flat plain. No trees. No nothing. A choked sob escaped her.

"Roderick—"

He reached for her, wrapping his arm around her just as the cloud overtook them. It was the last thing she remembered before darkness overtook her and then there was nothing at all.

Seraphina stood over the unconscious couple. Roderick's arm was still wrapped around Snow as though he tried to protect her. They lay sprawled in the middle of the throne room on the cold stone floor.

"Well, aren't they sweet," she said, her tone dripping with disdain. "I should have known he wouldn't be able to kill her. What a weakling."

She bent and snatched the enchanted blade from the sheath at his waist. The steel glistened in the flickering candlelight of the room. She examined it for a long moment before handing it off to her Captain of the Guard, Erick. Then she noticed a sheath at Snow's waist, which was similar to his. She removed the dagger. When she held it up, she realized it was the very one she had commissioned from the blacksmith to kill Snow White.

A spurt of rage went through her. She handed that one off to him as well.

"Do what you will with those," she said with a wave of her hand.

"And what do you want to do with the two of them?" he asked.

She tapped a finger against her chin. "What, indeed. I suppose I could kill them both now and get it over with. Or allow them to wake on their own and have a little fun with them."

"Fun, my queen?" He lifted a brow in question. "You mean torture."

She laughed, the sound deep in her throat. "I do. Won't that be delightful, Erick? Bring me two chairs and rope. Let's see if our little elemental enchantress still has powers when she's away from nature."

# CHAPTER 34

S now awoke to pain throughout her body. Her head hung between her shoulders, her chin on her chest. Her arms were in an awkward position, wrapped around something hard and unforgiving. She twisted her hands and felt the chaff of rough rope against her wrists. Then she realized then she was tied to a chair.

Without lifting her head, she tuned in her senses to her surroundings. The first thing she noticed was the empty sheath at her waist. She opened her eyes and saw stone flooring under her feet. There was silence around her except for the flicker of what sounded like candleflame. A warm glow shimmering across the floor and she suspected there were candelabras in the room.

She had no doubt she was in the castle in the Mystic Vale. The castle that was once her family home. The castle from which her father ruled the kingdom.

The castle that was hers by birthright.

She wanted to lift her head to see if Roderick was nearby, but she didn't want to alert Seraphina that she was finally conscious. Reaching out her senses, she listened to the sounds of the room and heard the soft breathing of someone else.

Tentatively, she lifted her head. Across from her, Roderick was also tied to a chair. His chin was on his chest. He wasn't awake yet. She tested her elemental senses to see if there was something—anything—she could use against Seraphina. She sensed no plants in her vicinity. Likely by design. Seraphina would know she had elemental power due to her previous display.

But Roderick's elemental magic was more powerful than hers.

"Roderick?" she whispered, her voice low and rough as she tried to wake him.

He didn't move.

She tried scooting her chair closer. The sound of the wood legs scraping along the stone was deafening in the silence. He stirred a bit, his head jerking to one side.

"Wake up," she said, this time louder in the hopes he heard her.

She pushed the chair forward once more. The noise exploded around them. This time, his head snapped up. He looked groggy, as though he just woke up from a long nap. He glanced around, confusion in his eyes as he tried to get his bearings. Then his gaze landed on her. His brows drew together in question.

"Where are we?"

"The Mystic Vale castle," she said.

"Are you certain?"

"It's the only place Seraphina would bring us."

Though she wasn't certain, it made sense Seraphina would bring her back to her childhood home to hand her the final death blow.

Why not kill her here, where her parents also perished? Where Seraphina took control and could enact her final revenge.

She got a good look at the room they were in. It was devoid of all furniture save for the chairs in which they were tied. There were large candelabras in each corner to give the room a warm glow. A wood door behind Roderick with iron hinges was the only exit.

"I'm sorry, Snow," he said, sounding dejected.

"For what?"

"For getting captured," he said.

"That's not your fault," she said.

She watched as he twisted his arms behind him, his face contorted in pain. "What are you doing?"

"Trying to get out of these ropes," he said.

"It's no use. The knots are too tight."

He grunted. "Still...trying." He sucked in a sharp breath, wincing in pain.

"Stubborn man," she scoffed.

"Yes, until I take my last breath."

Something about the way he said i made her chuckle long enough for him to pause and peer at her. "What's so funny?"

"That you freely admit you're stubborn. Have you been your entire life?"

"Just so." He gave a nod, a grin, and then went back to trying to free his wrists from the bonds. "I...almost have it."

He grunted, winced, and then he was free. He dropped the rope at his feet, but the damage was done. His wrists were red and raw and bleeding. He was out the chair and doing his best to untie her.

"Your wrists need a healer," she said.

"That's the least of our worries at the moment," he said. "We need to get out of here."

She felt the knot loosen and then she was free. "Not yet. Not until I destroy the Magic Mirror."

He walked around the chair and paused, peering at the door with the iron hinges. He walked to the door and gave it a tug, but it remained in place.

"It would stand to reason she wouldn't want us out of this room," Snow said.

She saw the contemplative look on his face and knew he was trying to figure a way out of the room.

"If you destroy the mirror," he said, slowly, "then she loses her power?"

"That's what the dark wizard told me," Snow said.

He took a deep breath, nodded. "Then let's find a way out of here."

But it was no use. The door was too strong to break through. Snow dropped to her knees and placed her hands on the stone flooring, reaching out with her senses. But there was nothing under the stone to help her. No bits of dirt or anything.

"There's nothing in here that can help," she said.

"Maybe not for your magic."

The way he said it made her pause and watch as he stood in front of the door. He placed his hand on circular door pull which she suspected was iron. He closed his eyes, no doubt tapping into his own elemental magic. Recalling that he was an Artificer, he had the power to harness more than just nature. She watched in rapt fascination.

The door pull began to glow. A pale yellow at first and then brighter and brighter until it was a molten red orange. She gasped as he tugged. The door clicked open with ease. He flashed her a triumphant grin.

"Is your hand not burned?" she asked.

He looked down at his hand, his fingers were slick with sweat and blood but appeared to be otherwise unscathed. "No."

She moved to stand beside him, taking his hand in hers and turning it over, running her fingers over his skin and marveling at how smooth and unburned it was.

"Incredible," she breathed.

"Now, let's find that mirror."

He stepped into the corridor and paused, looking left and right. He signaled all clear and then waved her to follow him. They paused outside the door, her heart ramming hard in her chest.

"Which way?" Roderick asked.

"I'm not sure where we are," she admitted. "The last time I was here, I was a child. My memories are not as clear of the castle as they once were."

Indeed, they had faded over time when she gave up hope of ever returning. Now, she stood in the very castle she was born in looking for a mirror with the ability to wield dark magic. Where would Seraphina keep that? No doubt someplace hidden and safe. Her bedchamber?

Yes, of course, that made sense. Her bedchamber, which used to be shared with her father. The residence bedchambers were in the north tower overlooking the lawn. Hers was down the hall from her parent's. She remembered that clearly, but how to get there?

Roderick waited patiently by her side while she chewed on her lower lip and tried to figure out which way to go. She was paralyzed by indecision. He must have sensed that for he gripped her by the shoulders, turning her to face him.

"Hey," he said and gave her a reassuring grin. "Don't second guess yourself. Listen to your gut."

She took a deep breath, nodded. "I think we should go this way."

She motioned down the hallway behind him. He took her by the hand and led her down the hall.

"My dagger is missing," she said.

"Mine, too. I'm sure Seraphina is happy to have both weapons at her disposal." His tone was laced with annoyance and agitation.

He didn't mention they were both enchanted blades. He didn't have to. One had been created for the sole purpose of cutting out her heart. She was aware the queen had obtained their greatest weapons.

Or had she? She and Roderick both had elemental magic. Perhaps there was a way to leverage it, though she wasn't sure how. Yet.

The corridor ended with only one way to go—right—so they followed that down to the next turn to the left. None of this seemed familiar to her and she wasn't sure where they were in the castle. It appeared to be a maze of twists and turns. There were no doors in the hallways. Only torches in brackets every few feet.

"Anything familiar?" he asked.

"Not yet," she said.

"It'll come to you." He sounded so certain she wanted to believe him.

Another turn and they found themselves in the great hall. A long wooden table that seated twenty was in the middle, chairs on either side. The enormous hearth on one end was dormant. Nothing but gray ashes.

Once there were tapestries along the walls and portraits high above in the gallery. All of that was gone now. Seraphina had them removed at some point. Her family history was removed, as though she had tried to erase them.

"You ok?" he asked.

She pointed toward the gallery. "There were family portraits there. Oil paintings of my parents and grandparents."

He looked upward to the area devoid of decoration. Then he gave her a sympathetic glance. "Perhaps she didn't destroy them."

It was almost as though he heard her thoughts. She shoved that away to deal with later.

"I think she'd hide the mirror in her bedchamber," she said. "Follow me."

Releasing his hand, she took off through the great hall, heading for the doorway. On the other side was a curved stone staircase leading upward to the north tower. As she hurried through the castle, a sense of foreboding filling her, she wondered where the servants and guards were. Surely, Seraphina would not leave the halls and corridors unguarded?

She would if she were planning a trap.

Snow's heart thundered in her chest as she exited the great hall. She paused only for a moment at the foot of the stone staircase, then, taking a deep breath, she ascended. Her legs burned with agony as she hurried up the narrow steps trying to keep her footfalls as quiet as possible. Roderick was right behind her, keeping close.

At the top of the stairs, with her chest heaving and her heart pounding, she paused a moment to catch her breath. Roderick moved to stand next to her, waiting for her to make her next move. He didn't question her or ask if she knew where she was going. He merely waited. She gave him a glance.

There was something in his eyes that told her he trusted her. That he believed in her. That he wanted her to succeed. And something else. Regret? Sorrow? She didn't know.

"It's this way," she pointed to the left.

As she started to go, he grasped her by the hand and pulled her to a stop. "Snow, there's something I need to tell you."

She turned back to him. "What is it?"

"When the queen summoned me here and demanded I kill you, she tricked me into drinking a slow-acting poison."

Snow gasped. "Poison?"

"If I failed to do her bidding—"

"You mean kill me," she interjected.

He nodded. "I would fall into an eternal slumber. She called it a sleeping curse."

"How can this curse be broken?" she demanded.

He shook his head. "I don't know. I only know I had a fortnight before it would take hold. Snow..." He took her hands in his, holding them tight and looking deep into her eyes. "Since we left Lighthill, I've been feeling strange. As though something is not right with me. I think it's the poison trying to take hold."

"Then we need to find a way to break this curse. We need the antidote."

"Only the queen has it," he said. "It's not likely she's willing to give it up." His mouth quirked a grin.

"Why didn't you tell me this before?" she wanted to know.

"Because I thought I'd have more time. *We'd* have more time. That we'd be able to destroy the queen and you would have your throne," he said.

"In a fortnight?" She almost laughed, but managed to hold it in.

"It was a hope and a dream and perhaps a wish." He squeezed her hands. "So, if something happens to me, promise me you'll go on. You'll fight her."

Her suddenly mouth went bone dry. Her stomach clenched with a distinctive fear. "*You* promised me you would be by my side the entire way."

He nodded before she finished. "I did and I'm sorry I didn't tell you then."

"I can't do this alone." Her breath hitched, a sob threatening to erupt. "I can't do this without you."

Something in his expression softened at those words. He cupped her face, then, gently tipping her head back. "You can. You will. I believe in you."

A breath shuddered out between her lips as he held her there, looking intently into her eyes. A sensuous light passed between them. His lips parted slightly and she understood then what he meant to do. She melted against him, wanting nothing more than his lips on hers, to feel his kiss, to know what it was like to taste him.

She wasn't exactly sure when her feelings had switched from anger with him to something more intimate. But shift it had. He had become a part of her that she was desperate to keep by her side. He'd traveled with her, told her story to the villagers in Westfall. Had he made mistakes? Yes, of course. Had she? Yes.

"Roderick?"

"Yes?"

"Are you going to kiss me?"

He tipped his head to one side, a smile tugging at the corner of his mouth. "Yes, I believe I am."

"Then get on with it."

He chuckled, a rumble deep in his chest. One hand brushed through her hair, cupping the nape of her neck, bending her back at just the right angle. Her eyes fluttered closed in sweet anticipation.

But before his lips met hers, there was a deep, malevolent laugh echoing through the hall.

"Aren't the two of you simply adorable?"

Seraphina's voice made them jump apart. Roderick pulled her close, then pushed her behind him as though protecting her from the queen.

"Just simply *adorable*. Alas, you both have to die. But not before I have a little fun with you."

A grin crinkled the corners of her eyes as she lifted her arms.

# CHAPTER 35

She flung a bolt of magic toward Roderick. Snow did the only thing she could think to do and shoved him out of the way while she dove in the opposite direction. He landed on the stone floor a few feet away. She managed to break her fall by throwing out her hands, which was a mistake. When she landed, the jarring sensation went through her palms all the way up her arms to her shoulders. She cringed and rolled to her side, before getting back to her feet.

Seraphina scowled and threw another bit of magic at Snow, this time wrapping her upper torso with tendrils of purple smoke that held fast.

"A binding spell," the queen said. "I was a fool not to use that on you both before."

As Snow struggled to get out of the bonds, Seraphina used the same spell on Roderick as he was climbing back to his feet. He'd taken the fall harder than she had.

"I thought to kill the two of you right away. But then I decided it would be much more fun to play with you for a while. My captain didn't tie your ropes tight enough, I see. For that, he will be punished. How you escaped the locked room, though, is a bit of a mystery."

She eyed Roderick with a wicked glint as she approached him, looking him over with disdain. "You have been nothing but a disappointment from the moment I met you. If you had complied with my request, I would have given you the antidote to the poison. Now, you will never get it."

"It's me you want, Seraphina. Give him the antidote and let him go," Snow said.

"How sweet," the queen said, her voice dripping disdain. "While I appreciate your sentiment, the answer is no."

"Please," she said. "I'll do what you want."

"Snow, don't," Roderick warned.

Seraphina angled her body toward her, intrigue written on her face. "Anything?"

Snow cut him a glance. He shook his head. She took a deep breath and returned her gaze back to the queen.

"Anything," she said.

The queen moved toward her with slow, methodical steps. "Will you abdicate your throne?"

Pain sliced through her. "Yes," she said, the word ice.

"No," Roderick said. "Don't do it, Snow."

The queen moved a step closer. "Will you recognize me as the true and rightful ruler of the Mystic Vale, willingly?"

Her mouth went dry as she met the queen's gaze. She lifted her chin a little higher. "Yes, I will."

"Snow!" Roderick shouted. There was desperation in his voice.

The queen smiled. "And will you announce this to the entire kingdom? That you are willingly stepping down?"

Her stomach churned as she stood there, looking deep into the queen's eyes and seeing nothing but greed, vanity, and pure evil. If she did this, her reign was over before it had a chance to begin. And likely her life would end. She would join her parents. Finally, she nodded.

"I will."

"Swear you will do this. Swear it by your royal blood."

She waved her hand to release the bond a bit and reached for Snow's hand. She brought it out, palm up, and held it in her icy one. The queen was cold through and through. The enchanted dagger materialized from thin air and landed in her other empty hand. She held it up, at the ready.

Roderick sucked in a sharp breath. "Don't do it, Snow. I beg you."

"Silence!" Seraphina said, snapping her heated glare in his direction. A gag appeared around his mouth.

The queen had learned the dark wizard's magic well.

"Swear it," she repeated.

Snow inhaled a deep breath, then let it shudder out. "I swear."

With that, the queen pressed the tip of the enchanted dagger into her palm, drawing a line until blood swelled. There was a hiss from the cut and then an image of steam formed in what appeared to be a leaf drifting upward from Snow's palm. Moments later it disappeared.

Seraphina used the tip of the blade to cut her own palm, then pressed it against hers. A heated sizzle went through her. Dark magic poured into her, suddenly at war with the light magic residing inside her. She had never felt it before. Not like that. It had always just been there. Snow cried out as the pain lanced through her. Her blood oath was complete.

Roderick made a muffled sound of agony behind the gag. Seraphina merely chuckled as she pulled her hand away. Then she turned to Roderick.

"You see how compliant she is?"

With a wave of magic, she healed the wound on her own hand but left the one on Snow's open and oozing.

Tears burst from Snow's eyes and trickled down her face. Her breath hitched on a sob. She hated herself for giving the queen what she wanted, for swearing a blood oath.

"Now give him the antidote and let him go," Snow said, her voice clotted with tears.

"Oh, no," Seraphina said. "I will do no such thing."

"But you—"

"I made no promises. You, however, promised me everything." A wicked grin erupted on her face. "For that, I thank you."

Fury erupted through her as she stared at the queen. Suddenly the corridor was swarming with guards. Two of them grabbed Roderick and started to lead him away. Snow glanced his way. Their eyes met. She saw the despair deep within the depths of his eyes and she knew in that moment she made a mistake. She should never have promised Seraphina she would abdicate her throne. Worse, she let down the people of Westfall and Lighthill. The people she promised she would take care of once she returned as the rightful ruler of the Mystic Vale.

The fight hadn't left her, yet, though. Despite the blood oath, despite her promise to abdicate, there was still a fierce devotion to the Mystic Vale deep inside her. She turned back to the queen, saw the smugness on her face as she watched them lead Roderick away. Something inside Snow snapped.

"Why do you hate me so much?" she asked, tears still in her eyes.

Seraphina looked momentarily taken aback by that. "Hate you?"

"You must. You've taken everything from me now," Snow said.

There was deep contemplation on the queen's face. "Because you are the fairest in the land. Because people love you more than they love me."

"You did all this because you're *jealous*?"

A dark fury creased her face. "I am not jealous. I wanted to elevate myself to someone of substance. I did. But you stood in the way of that."

"By murdering my parents and stealing my throne," Snow snapped. "Admit it. You wanted nothing more than power and glory. The people will *never* love you. You will *never* gain their loyalty."

"Be quiet!" She pressed a hand against her head, massaging her forehead. "I grow tired of you, girl. Captain, take her to the dungeon with the blacksmith."

The queen waved her hand and released her bonds as a man stepped up next to her. He took her by the arm and led her away.

"You may have my blood oath, Seraphina, but this is far from over," Snow said over her shoulder.

"You may think that," the queen said. "But you will never beat me. *Never.*"

Seraphina's anger-lined face was the last thing Snow saw before the captain led her away.

# CHAPTER 36

It was cold and dark in the dungeon cell. There was nothing but a pile of straw in one corner and a disgusting chamber pot in the other. It looked as though it hadn't been emptied since the last prisoner occupied the cell, whenever that was. Snow's stomach churned acid. She refused to look at either corner and preferred to hover near the bars.

Across from her, the guards deposited Roderick. But he hadn't made an appearance. He concealed himself deep in the shadows of the cell. Snow grasped the cold iron bars in her hands and peered through them across the way.

"Roderick?"

"She's won, Snow." His disembodied voice filtered across to her.

Snow refused to believe that. She gripped the bars tighter, took a deep breath, and tried again. "I was wrong to agree to her terms. But I thought she would give you the antidote and let you go."

"What would letting me go accomplish?" he demanded.

"You could go for help," she suggested. "Back to the villagers."

A long beat of silence passed. Then he said, "To what end?"

Frustration edged through her. "Did you forget all that we did while we were in Westfall? Those villagers are willing to fight for me."

"For the throne you no longer possess?" He sounded dejected.

She deserved that. He was right. She had relinquished it with ease and even swore a blood oath. But if there was one thing she learned from the elves, blood oaths were broken upon the death of one of the participants. Or, rather, the death of her magic. If the dark wizard told her true, destroying the Magic Mirror would remove Seraphina's powers because the dark wizard would die. Somehow, she had to convince Roderick to use his elemental magic on the iron bars like he had on the door.

"Listen to me," she said. "I know I am not your queen. But I *am* your friend. These bars are iron. You have the power within you to bend them and release us. I'm sure the Magic Mirror is in her bedchamber. If I can get there, then I can destroy it. Then Seraphina will lose her power."

Another beat of silence passed. She heard nothing but the flicker of the torches lining the walls outside the cells.

"Please, Roderick."

"Why? You gave up your throne."

That was a good question. Why did she give up her throne if she was now more determined than ever to get it back?

"I made a mistake," she said, her voice quiet in the shadowy darkness. She gripped the bars tighter, wishing she had half the power he did. "I'm sorry."

She heard movement in his cell. The shuffle of feet. The rustle of fabric. Then he appeared at the bars. He peered out at her, the torchlight flickering in his blue-green eyes.

"If you destroy this Magic Mirror, will your blood oath to her be released?" he asked.

"Yes," she said, though she wasn't sure if she was speaking the truth or not. If it convinced him to use his magic to release them, then so be it.

"How do we get to her bedchamber without her knowing?" he asked.

"I have a plan." That, at least, was the truth.

If memory served, there were several secret passageways within the castle. She wasn't certain, but she thought one led to the bedchamber occupied by Seraphina. A secret door was built into the wall to help the king and queen escape in case there was an uprising and they needed to flee to safety.

Roderick pressed his hand against the lock of the cell door and closed his eyes. She watched as he used his Artificer magic to heat it up like he had the door pull in their prison chamber. Moments later, it glowed with a bright yellow light. He gave a push. The door swung open on silent hinges. He stepped out of his cell and then used the same magic on hers. When the lock clicked free, he pulled open the door.

Grinning, Snow stepped out and, without thinking, she flung her arms around his neck and hugged him. He was startled for a moment and didn't react. Then, finally, he hugged her back. Snow pulled away, holding him at arm's length.

"Thank you! Now, let's find that mirror."

"And not get caught this time," he said.

She grinned. "Right. Follow me. I think I know a secret passageway."

They headed through the dank hallway lined with flickering torches to the exit. What they didn't account for were the men standing guard. Roderick motioned for her to stop as he crept up on the first one. He quickly knocked him out. The second one tried to give him some trouble, but he managed to incapacitate him. He swiped a sword.

"Just in case," he said.

She followed him up the stairs and out of the dungeon. As they exited, the captain of the guard intercepted them. Roderick held his sword aloft in defense.

The captain, though, appeared to have seen better days. His face was bruised and battered, as though he'd been in a tavern fight.

"You..." he said on a deep breath as he looked at Roderick. His gaze landed on Snow, then. "Both of you."

"Stand aside," Roderick said. "I don't want to hurt you."

The man's gaze danced between the two of them. Snow stepped around Roderick.

"What did she do to you?" she asked, referring to the queen.

"She didn't like the way I tied you up in the other room," he said. "And so, I came to release you from the dungeon but I see that's not necessary now."

Surprise flickered through Snow. "Why would you do that?"

"Because her tyranny must end. Come. I will lead you to safety," the captain said.

"Wait," Snow said. "There is a secret passage leading to her bedchamber. Can you take me there?"

He stared at her a long, quiet moment until he finally nodded. "If that's what you wish. But why?"

"She has a mirror there. A magic mirror," Snow said. "I need to destroy it."

His head tipped to one side. "What will that accomplish?"

"It will remove her magic and make her powerless," Roderick said.

The captain's hard gaze pierced through Snow. Then he gave her a nod. "Follow me."

# CHAPTER 37

The captain was adept at leading them through the passageways that were less populated. He knew the castle better than Snow, which made her a little sad. But then, it had been a decade since she stepped foot in her childhood home.

He led them to the north tower via a winding stone staircase that Snow scarcely remembered. Up and up they went until they finally came to the top where the captain turned to the right. He pushed open the first door he came to, then stood aside for them to enter. When they were inside, he closed the door.

The room was devoid of all furniture except for a large four-poster bed stripped bare. Seraphina was not one to encourage visitors. There was one candelabra in the corner of the room. The captain lit it, illuminating it in a warm yellow glow.

"The passage is behind that tapestry." He pointed to the length of material on the far wall behind the bed. "All the royal chambers are connected."

"I remember," Snow said with a nod.

She started to take a step toward the tapestry, but the captain grasped her arm to stop her.

"She's in there now," he said. "I will try to lure her away."

Snow considered this for a long moment, wondering if he was telling her the truth. Finally, she decided to trust him and gave a nod.

"Thank you."

But the captain hesitated another moment. "Are you certain destroying the mirror with take away her magic?"

Snow nodded.

Contemplation shifted through his eyes as he considered his next words. "The mirror is in a secret chamber behind a tapestry. One of the stones is a lever that will open the door to reveal the mirror."

"How do you know this?" Roderick demanded.

"When you spend as much time with the queen as I have, you learn things," he said.

"I appreciate your help," Snow said.

Her gave her a nod. "Good luck. Wait a few minutes before entering the chamber. I'll do my best to get her out."

Then he was gone, slipping through the door and closing it behind him with a soft snick.

"Can you trust him?" Roderick asked.

"I hope so," she replied.

She headed for the tapestry on the other side of the room behind the bed and pushed it aside. She immediately felt the draft from the cracks around the hidden stone door. She pushed, but nothing happened. She tried again in a lower spot on the wall. Still nothing.

"Can I try?" Roderick asked.

She stepped aside. He ran his hands over the stones from top to bottom, pausing every few inches, and then went back up again. His hand landed on one of the middle stones. He heaved against it with a mighty shove and pushed the door into the wall. It scraped along the floor.

As soon as the door was open, her nerves jingled. Taking a deep breath, she took the first step into the drafty corridor. Cobwebs hung from the corners. The floor was dusty from disuse. Perhaps Seraphina didn't realize the royal chambers were all connected with secrete passages that led out of the castle.

That gave her an advantage. She hoped.

She started down the hallway, but the only light was that from the chamber they left behind. It was faint at best. She glanced around the walls, looking for old torches in brackets. She found one a few feet away and pulled it from the bracket, but she had no way to light it.

"Let me try," he said.

She watched as he closed his eyes and placed his hand over the wick. A moment later, flame burst to life. She stared at him in awe.

"I didn't know you could do that."

"I didn't either," he said, looking perplexed. "I didn't think it would work."

"Well, I'm glad it did."

They started down the corridor, Snow leading the way with the flickering torch in hand.

"I feel different here," he said. "Like..." He paused.

"Like?"

"Like there is a tingling sensation deep inside me." He lurched suddenly, catching himself on the wall. His face paled.

She gripped his arm. "Are you all right?"

His eyes met hers. "It's the poison taking hold."

"Then we need to hurry."

"You go ahead. I'll catch up," he said.

"But—"

"I don't want to hold you up."

She hesitated, looking him over. Sweat dotted his forehead. Was it the poison affecting him? And if it was, did it have something to do with his sudden new elemental magic?

"I don't want to go without you," she said at last.

"I promise I'll catch up." He gave her a weak smile.

Before she did, she glanced around until she saw another torch. She lit it from hers and then handed it to him.

"Here. I don't want to leave you in the dark. Follow this until it dead ends, then turn left. The queen's chamber is the last door on the left. I'll leave it open for you."

Grateful, he took the torch and nodded.

"Snow, wait. There's something else I should tell you." She paused, gave him a quizzical look. "There's a certain tree with rainbow bark near Bridgefort that allowed me to forge the blade with a shaving of its wood. It's what gives the steel that shimmering glow. When I made the one for the queen, though, the tree told me to choose my recipient wisely, that she was not the rightful ruler."

Her brows drew together. "What are you saying, Roderick? She took the blade from me."

"Yes, but if you can get it away from her, don't hesitate to use it. That enchanted blade was meant for you," he said.

Hot pinpricks went through her. She wasn't sure what to say, so she merely nodded.

"Now, go. I'll be right behind you."

But something told her he wasn't going to make it.

She shoved the worry out of her mind and hurried down the corridor, turning left and then eyeing the secret door ahead. She stuck the torch in the bracket by the door and paused to listen. There were no voices inside the chamber. She took that as a good sign that the captain was able to get Seraphina out.

Taking a deep breath, she pulled open the door with a yank and was immediately faced with a tapestry. She paused there, listening for movement, but heard none. She peeked around the edge of the tapestry, glancing around quickly. Satisfied it was empty, she slipped out from behind it and paused to get her bearings.

The room was not as she remembered. Seraphina had no doubt taken it upon herself to redecorate once her father was dead.

The four-poster bed that dominated the middle of the room was still there, but there were different curtains surrounding it. An oversized bench was at the foot of it. On one side of the room was an elaborate wardrobe. A bureau and mirror next to that. The top was cluttered with hair pins, a comb, a brush, vials containing glittering liquids. A small, squatty bottle with a cork in the top was next to one vial full of pink liquid. Inside the small bottle, was what appeared to be pink shimmering sand. The balcony doors stood open to let the breeze in, the curtains at the doors fluttering in the wind.

And there, on the far wall, was a tapestry in muted colors of blue, green, purple, and garnet. She did not recall seeing this tapestry when she was a child, but then she didn't frequent this room, either.

She approached, her heart in her throat. There were no other tapestries in the room, so this had to be the one hiding the secret chamber with the Magic Mirror. She shoved it aside and examined the stones before her. They all looked the same. No one indicated it was a lever that would open the door.

There was only one thing to do. She started pressing on each and every stone starting at the top. Eventually, she would find the one that opened the door. Halfway down, a click and then stone scraped against stone as the door slid open revealing the reflective glass inside a large oval, opulent frame.

Frozen, she stood there gaping at it.

The mirror looked like any other ordinary mirror, but she knew without a doubt this was the one connected to both Seraphina and the dark wizard.

"Magic Mirror," she whispered.

If flickered to life, a featureless face appearing in the center of the oval with nothing but holes for eyes and a mouth. She jumped back a step and gasped. The face peered at her through the looking glass in silence.

"The fair maid has come, I see. Lips red as the rose. Hair black as ebony. Skin white as snow. It is you, Snow White."

Her heart pounded a wicked tattoo as she stared at the mirror. How did it know her? It had described her as Master Harwin did. A prickling sensation went over her as she peered into the mirror, wondering if Master Harwin had conversed with it before. He had been in possession of the Magic Mirror and the others, after all.

"I am Snow White," she said at last.

"The fairest in all the land. The one who has garnered the wrath of my queen. The one who will perish by her hand," the mirror said.

As he said it, a reflection flickered in the looking glass behind her. The glint of the enchanted blade winked in the candlelight.

# Chapter 38

Snow spun as the blade came down. She squeezed her eyes shut and put up her hands as if that would ward off the attack. The sharp pain sliced through one of her upturned palms. Blood welled at the shallow wound. A high-pitched screech rent the air followed by a thud on the stone flooring.

Dropping her arms to her side, she saw Seraphina sprawled out on the floor. Roderick climbed back to his feet as he stood over the queen, wobbly. Sweat dotted his forehead and trickled down the side of his face. His tunic was damp from it as well. His face was ashen.

"Roderick?"

"Destroy it, Snow," he said on a pant. "Before it's too late."

His legs gave out and he crashed to the ground in a heap. Snow hurried over to him, pushing him to his back. The blood from her palm smeared across his tunic. He was unconscious. Seraphina cackled her glee.

"The sleeping curse has finally taken hold. There is no one to save you now, dear girl."

Snow glanced up at Seraphina with all the rage burning through her. The enchanted blade was still on the stone floor past Seraphina. When she got to her feet, she failed to pick it up. Snow slowly pushed to her feet.

"I don't need saving," Snow said, her voice low and dangerous.

As fast as she was able, she dove for the enchanted blade. Seraphina realized too late what she was doing. Her hand landed on the hilt as the evil queen snatched her by the hair and jerked her upward. But Snow had the blade in her hand.

The queen pulled her head back, making her look up at her rage. Snow swiped the blade upward, her position awkward and uncomfortable, but she managed to put the sharp edge against the queen's throat.

"Release me," she demanded. "Give me the antidote to the sleeping curse."

"You think I'm afraid of a little dagger?"

She disappeared in a poof of smoke causing Snow to fall backward. She managed to catch herself with her free hand before she landed hard against the stone floor. She rolled to her side and got to her feet, still clutching the dagger in one hand. Seraphina stood in the doorway of the balcony, the breeze fluttering her gown and hair making her appear more menacing than she actually was.

They stared each other down for what felt like an eternity.

"You can't beat me," the queen said, swimming in her smugness.

With a wave of her hand, she conjured more magic to hurl at her. An illusion of a snake slithering toward Snow, hissing.

Snow almost laughed. She wasn't afraid of any creature, snakes or otherwise. She dropped to her knees, placing her hand on the cold stone floor. She used her nature power to call to it, to touch her mind to it, and to tell it she meant it no harm. The queen, however, intended to use it as a weapon.

The slithering voice inside her head hissed its irritation and turned on the queen. It slinked back toward her, hissing and uncoiling it's long, sleek body. Seraphina backed onto the balcony.

"You wench!" she shouted.

Snow stood. While the queen was occupied, she glanced around the chamber for something to use as a weapon to shatter the mirror. She hurried over to the bureau with all the glittering vials and decanters and wondered if one of them was the antidote to the poison that had put Roderick into a sleeping curse.

"Get away from there," the queen said, panic evident in her voice.

Remembering she had magic, the queen destroyed the snake with one swipe of her hand and then charged Snow. As she did, something crashed against the side of the castle making the walls tremble with a violent shudder.

It caught both of them off guard and they paused, staring at each other. The queen ran to the balcony. A frustrated shriek escaped her. She spun back to Snow, her face pinched with fury.

"You did this." Accusation laced her tone.

Snow had no idea what she was talking about. She was about to ask when something struck the side of the castle again, making the walls quake. Seraphina yelped her annoyance. She spun back to the balcony and stepped onto it. Whatever magic she used, made her glow into a bright white ball of flame.

Now was her chance. While she was occupied, Snow went back to searching for something with which to smash the mirror. Then she spied a brass candleholder. She snatched it, tossing the unlit candle the ground and hurrying back to the mirror. She clutched the enchanted blade in her hand slick with blood and sweat, and the brass candleholder in the other. She peered up at the distorted face with apprehension but knew it was what she had to do.

She swung the candleholder at the mirror. It connected with a crash but did nothing to damage it. Seraphina, however, emitted a high-pitched scream as though she were injured.

"What are you doing?" the mirror asked, panic lacing its tone.

Something smashed against the castle walls again. Snow assumed they were under some sort of attack. But who would be attacking the castle and why?

She didn't have time to puzzle it out as she smashed the candleholder against the mirror once again. Tiny cracks were evident in the glass.

"Stop!" the mirror shouted.

Snow hit it again. This time, an audible crack. Seraphina stumbled into the chamber from the balcony, her eyes wide with alarm.

Snow hit the mirror once more, this time with the base of the candleholder so it would do more damage. More splintering from the center. Another cry from Seraphina.

"Help! Help, my queen!" the mirror shouted.

She had to get it to stop talking.

A wild scream from the queen and the next thing she knew, Snow was grabbed from behind and dragged from the alcove with the mirror. Seraphina had her arm around her and then spun and shoved her to the ground. Snow landed hard, banging her elbow on the stone. Both the candleholder and the dagger flew from her hands and skittered across the floor.

Before she was able to right herself, Seraphina snatched her by the hair once again and dragged her to her feet.

Gripping her hard, she hauled her out to the balcony, shoving her against the railing.

"Look at them!" the queen shouted. "This is *your* doing."

Snow was shocked to see the lines of soldiers in the courtyard with not only a battering ram, but a trebuchet that continuously launched large boulders at the castle. She wasn't sure who the army was or where they came from, but she was grateful. On the edge, she saw a line of men and women, their hands clasped, and they were glowing.

The only thing it could be was elven magic.

She sucked in a sharp breath. How were the elves here?

Seraphina pushed her harder into the railing, shoving her over the edge.

"And you will die here in the same place you were born. How do you like that, *princess*?"

The queen grasped her by her tunic and shoved her upward, ready to push her over the railing. Snow saw the ivy climbing the walls of the castle and the edge of the balcony. She flattened her hands on the railing, reaching out with her senses and used her nature magic to call to the plants.

In one last fit of fury, Seraphina shoved Snow over the railing.

As she did, though, Snow called to the ivy. It sprang to life and immediately moved to intercept her, weaving to form a net to keep her from tumbling to her death. Then pushed her upward, helping her to step over the railing and back onto the balcony.

Seraphina gaped.

"It seems, oh wonderous queen, you forgot about the ivy," Snow said as she stepped down onto the balcony. "Now, shall we finish this?"

Another boulder crashed against the castle, as if punctuating her sentence. It bothered her a little they were destroying her castle, but she decided she didn't care much since she could always rebuild once she disposed of the queen.

The queen's momentary shock was replaced with her anger. She held her hands down, cupped them, and fire erupted inside her palms. She flung both fireballs at Snow. She ducked, crouching low on the ground as the fireballs flew over her head. She had to get inside and back to the mirror. It was the only way to remove Seraphina's magic. She hoped the dark wizard was right about that.

Closing her eyes, she lifted her hands, palm up. "Oh, creatures great and small, forest creatures, noble and free, I call upon you to heed the call, to protect where shadows fall."

"What are you doing?" Seraphina shrieked. "Stop! I command you to stop."

All Snow needed was a breath of fresh air to allow nature to recharge her. She sensed the awakening of the land around the castle, of the creatures—big and small, nocturnal and diurnal—coming to life and coming to her aid. The ivy crawled over the balcony railing, creeping along the floor toward the queen.

"I will never stop fighting for myself or my people," Snow said, her voice strong and sure. "Your reign, Seraphina, is over."

The queen stumbled backward trying to get away from the now quickly moving ivy. She wasn't fast enough and the ivy wound around her legs. She tumbled to the ground. Snow watched as the evergreen wrapped around her upper torso, pinning her arms against her sides.

Snow turned to face the onslaught and raised her arms to the sky.

"Cease your siege!" she called. "I am Snow White, crown princess and heir to the throne of the Mystic Vale. And I have come to reclaim my birthright."

All movement on the ground stopped. She peered down, watching as one lone rider moved forward. Several joined him from the glowing circle of elves. The man on the horse glanced their way and then looked up at her. From the distance, she only made out he had a bearded face and wore full plate armor.

"We have come to aid you, princess," he called. "The walls are breached and my men have entered the castle to apprehend the false queen."

Snow gripped the railing, realizing she had left a smear of blood from her still oozing palm. "Who are you, sir?"

"I am King Alfred of the Feywood, your majesty."

Suddenly, a fluttering of wings buzzed her face. She lifted her uninjured hand. Annilen alighted on her palm, collapsing in a heap. Her breath was labored.

"Annilen?"

"Snow..." she panted. "We came to help you. Roderick said..." She paused to catch her breath. "Roderick said you needed our help."

"Roderick?" She glanced back at his still sleeping form on the floor. "You can explain later. Tell the king—"

"And the elves," she interjected. "They helped him get here."

Snow blinked surprise. So many questions fluttered through her mind but there wasn't time to ask them all. "Tell the king to secure the castle while I deal with the queen."

Annilen climbed to her feet again and then dipped a deep cour-tesy. "By your command, your majesty."

She fluttered away.

Once she was gone, Snow took a deep breath and turned back toward the bedchamber. She had a mirror to destroy.

# CHAPTER 39

The ivy had taken over the balcony, crawling along the stone floor and then inching into the bedchamber. Seraphina was still on the ground, wiggling to try to free herself but it was no use. Snow checked to make sure the ivy was snug around her struggling form and binding her hands.

"What are you doing?" Seraphina said, watching with wide eyes as Snow stepped through the ivy.

Snow snatched up the brass candleholder. She swiped the enchanted blade from the floor near it and stuck it in the empty sheath on her belt. Then she headed for the alcove with the mirror. The mirror's eerie face jerked to and fro inside the cracked looking glass, as though trying to get away.

"Stay away from there!" the queen shouted.

Snow lifted the candleholder and smashed it against the mirror. It cried out, as if in pain. Seraphina echoed it.

"Please! I beg you!" she said. "Please stop!"

"Please stop?" Snow glanced at her over her shoulder.

The queen managed to wiggle into a position to see Snow smashing the mirror. Good. She was glad the queen would see it destroyed.

"Yes, please." She sniffed. Tears pooled in her eyes. "You don't know what you're doing."

"I know exactly what I'm doing," Snow said. "I know you worked with a dark wizard to kill my mother to become queen. I know you murdered my father. I know you used the dark wizard to become all powerful. I know you also tied the essence of that dark wizard to the Magic Mirror."

Seraphina's face paled as she stared at Snow in disbelief. "How do you know all that?"

"Because I found the essence of the dark wizard you left in the Wyldwood Forest. You tethered his soul there and have been siphoning his magic for your use ever since," Snow said. "Do you deny this?"

The queen sucked in a breath, nearly choking on a sob. "Snow, please. I was young when I met Govan. He seduced me, made me promises he didn't keep."

"And so, you repaid him by stealing his magic and trapping him for all eternity?" Snow glanced at the mirror, wondering then if the visage floating there was what was left of Govan. "You saw nothing wrong with murdering my parents in cold blood and stealing my throne. You would have killed me, too, but hoped I would die alone in the forest, didn't you?"

Her response was nothing more than a wracked sob. "Snow, I'm sorry. I was consumed with my wrath and drunk on the magic."

"I do not accept your apology."

With that, Snow smashed the mirror again. This time, pieces broke off and fell to the stone floor with a tinkling. The mirror itself groaned.

"I release you, Govan, from your eternal fate," Snow whispered.

One more blow to the mirror and it shattered completely. Shards fell from the ornate oval frame, sprinkling the floor around where she stood. Pale blue smoke curled upward from the empty frame, dancing a moment over her head in a swirl, and then dissipating into nothing. Seraphina's wail was deafening as she cried out.

Slowly, Snow turned to face the queen who still writhed on the floor in apparent agony. The same smoke lifted from her body in a hiss of steam and swirled over her. It churned as though realizing it was finally free and then floated upward, disappearing. Snow dropped the candleholder with a thunk.

"I release you from your bonds," she said with a wave of her hand.

The ivy retreated back to the balcony. Snow held her breath as the queen got to her feet, her face wet with tears. In a fit of final rage, she clenched her fists as if to conjure a spell and then flung her hands outward. Nothing happened.

"You may have taken my magic, but I still have your throne. You swore a blood oath."

Snow nodded and approached the queen slowly, relieved to see she no longer had magic. "That's true. I did. But I am not willing to go without a fight."

In one fluid motion, she whipped the enchanted blade from her belt and charged the queen. The blade in her hand sprang to life, the steel shimmering and glowing and humming, as if it knew what she intended to do.

She cried out when Snow crashed into her and managed to put her arms up in defense. The blade was inches from the queen's face.

But Snow was determined. She wanted to avenge her parents. Revenge for a life of living in solitude. Vengeance for all the things the queen did to keep her away from the Mystic Vale, for torturing the villagers, for taking and taking and taking.

Frustration edged through her as she shoved the queen back toward the balcony. Even as she shoved her backward, the point of the blade inches from her face, the queen smirked.

"You can't kill me, Snow. You don't have it in you."

Snow thought of the ivy lining the floor and sent a command to it. It crept upward, lifting just enough for Seraphina to stumble over. It was enough to make Snow release her grasp on the queen. She regained her footing and gave her a wicked grin.

"Nice try," she taunted.

Snow was not to be defeated, though. She charged again, this time crouching a little lower. She gripped the blade tight in her slick palm. It continued to glow and hum against her hand. The ivy wound around Seraphina's ankles, obeying Snow's command to keep her in place. A whisper of a voice flickered through her mind. The words were in concert with the humming of the blade. *She is not the rightful ruler.*

She crashed against the queen, who was unable to defend herself this time. Snow plunged the dagger deep into the queen's chest. A hiss emitted from the blade and black smoke seeped out from around the wound, much like when Ardan had stabbed her.

Seraphina's eyes widened with shock as she stumbled, glanced down at the dagger sticking out of her chest. The very one she had commissioned to kill Snow White. She tripped over the ivy on the balcony, stumbling toward the railing.

With a little help from the greenery, Seraphina was hoisted over the railing. A muffled thud resounded.

Snow moved to the railing and peered over. Seraphina's broken body was on the ground.

The evil queen was dead.

A tingling sensation was in her cut palm. She glanced down at it to see a swirl of purple magic. It lifted from her palm and flickered into nothingness. The wound knitted itself back together, fully healed. The blood oath was broken. All her promises to Seraphina were erased.

Turning from the railing, she stood a long moment in the silence. The ivy wound around the balcony moving upward toward the turret over her head. The castle had grown completely still.

Roderick still slept in the center of the room. Neither destroying the magic or killing Seraphina had released him from the sleeping curse.

She walked to him, dropping to her knees at his side. She brushed back a lock of hair from his forehead. He looked as though he were merely sleeping peacefully. Whatever poison the queen gave him had taken a deep hold on him.

"I will find a way to release you from this sleeping curse," she said, her voice low, as if he was able to hear her. She knew he didn't. "I swear this to you."

On impulse, she leaned down and pressed a long, sweet kiss against his cool lips. She sat back on her heels, trying to push away the sharp grief punching through her. She failed him. She'd find someone to help move him to the bed until she was able to find the antidote.

He groaned then, his brows drawing together as if in pain. His blue-green eyes fluttered open and met hers, piercing her. Snow sucked in a sharp breath as she gazed down at him. With a grunt, he pushed to a sitting position and ran a hand through his hair.

"You're..." Snow started but she wasn't sure how to put it into words.

Roderick reached for her, cupping her face in his hands. His eyes were like summer lightning on a warm day igniting a faint smoldering flame that startled her. Her heart fluttered. He pulled her closer, only a breath between them.

"You broke the sleeping curse." His lips brushed hers as he spoke.

And then he kissed her. His lips captured hers in a timeless kiss that seemed to go on forever, sending spirals of warmth through her. She slipped her arms around him. In that one moment, she felt as though she floated on a wispy tender breeze and everything was right and perfect in her world for the first time in her life.

When he released her, he held her face in his hands. Light smoldered in his eyes. He pressed his forehead against hers and for a moment, there was nothing but peace between them. Despite everything they'd been through since they met, Snow was certain he was the one for her.

When he pulled away, he still held her face in his hands. There was a tenderness in his gaze that made her weak.

"Snow, this sounds odd to even me, but I knew the first moment I met you that you were the one for me."

She smiled. "I felt the same. I need you by my side always."

"For as long as you'll have me."

He took her hand. He glanced around the chamber, question deep in his eyes. He took in the shattered mirror in the alcove and the ivy that had crawled across the floor.

"I take it you were successful." The corner of his mouth lifted in a grin.

"I destroyed the mirror, yes," she said. "Seraphina is dead."

He nodded, as though he had expected that. They helped each other to their feet. He was still a little wobbly. She wrapped an arm around his waist to steady him.

"And," she added, "King Alfred is here with his army. Know anything about that?" She tilted her head back to look at him.

He gave her his best innocent look. "I'm afraid I don't know."

She nudged him in the ribs with her elbow. "Yes, you do. Annilen already told me."

"Ah, then, it appears I have some explaining to do."

She laughed. "Yes, right after we greet them."

"We?" One brow lifted.

"Yes. You will be joining me, won't you?"

"If that's what you wish, I will."

"Good."

She took his hand in hers and led him out of the bedchamber, leaving the destruction behind.

# CHAPTER 40

King Alfred's men had used the battering ram to bash in the large oak door at the front of the castle. Two of his men now stood to the side of it while others were stationed within the great hall. A few dead—presumably Seraphina's guards—littered the ground. The captain of the guard was being held by one of Alfred's men, his hands bound by rope.

Much to her surprise, Tasnia and a few of the other Elders stood behind the king. To her right, Elator. Elation soared through Snow as she broke free from Roderick and rushed to him. She flung her arms around his neck and hugged him tight. Tears flooded her vision.

"You're all right," she whispered.

He hugged her back. "The forest—"

"I know," she said.

He pulled back, holding her at arm's length. "You saved us, didn't you?"

"I tried," Snow said.

"You did." He gripped her hands in his, squeezing them.

Tasnia stepped up to her then. Elator moved aside as the Elder looked over Snow. "Most of the village burned but because of you, Snow White, the rest was saved. For that, I will be eternally grateful."

Then the Elder did something that utterly shocked Snow. She dropped to one knee and bowed her head.

"You have the loyalty and gratitude of the elves forevermore, your majesty."

Uneasiness swept through Snow. "Please rise, Tasnia. I did what needed to be done to save those in the forest and the village."

She stood up, thanks glittered deep within her eyes. Snow suspected that it was difficult for the elven woman to admit to a mere human.

"I will help you rebuild," Snow promised.

In a rare moment, a smile lifted the corners of her mouth. "We can manage. It appears you will have your own rebuilding to oversee."

King Alfred cleared his throat.

"Apologies, your majesty." Snow turned her full attention on the king who had come to her aid. She dipped a low curtsy. "I want to express my deep thanks for you coming to my aid, though I'm not entirely sure how you got here or knew I needed aid."

"I received a message from a little sprite who insisted I needed to answer the call. Apparently, she knew I had an enchanted blade with the initials of my family engraved on the hilt." His gaze flickered to Roderick who stepped up next to Snow.

"I sent her," he admitted.

"Seraphina had no intention of invading Feywood, did she?"

Roderick shifted next to her, uncomfortable. But it was Erick, the captain of the guard, who answered.

"She planned to invade all the kingdoms and claim them for her own."

King Alfred glanced his way, his brows raised in surprise.

"It was her plan as soon as Snow White was dead," he added. His gaze was full of sorrow and regret when he looked at her. "I'm glad to see she did not succeed."

Everyone understood the queen wanted Snow White dead because she was a threat to her throne and would always be as long as she lived. Snow thought of the cut on her palm, the blood oath she made, and how close she came to losing that throne.

King Alfred said, "As am I. As for how I got here, the elves had a hand in that."

Snow gave Tasnia a questioning glance.

The Elder said, "I did what I had to do and used elven magic that has not been used in over a thousand years."

"And what was that?" Roderick asked, curious.

"Why, I opened a portal, of course." She said it as though she were speaking of nothing more than the fine weather. "And, now,

Snow White, we elves will return to our forest to continue our efforts to rebuild what was lost."

Snow reached for the Elder, taking her hand in hers. "I cannot express what it means to me that you came. Thank you. I hope we can continue to be friendly."

Tasnia lifted her chin. "The elves will consider an amicable coexisting with the Mystic Vale, if your majesty agrees to it."

Snow tried hard to hide her grin. "I do."

She nodded and turned away, gathering her Elders and motioning them out of the great hall and into the night. But Elator hung back and approached Snow. He took her hands in his.

"I'm glad you have your throne back," he said. "I'll tell Yirrie."

"Yes, and that I miss her."

"Of course."

He released one of her hands as his gaze lifted. He touched the circlet still on her head, which she had forgotten about. Amazement flitted through her that it had remained on her head during the entire ordeal with Seraphina.

"I was wrong. Not fit for a princess." He paused, smiled, a twinkling of admiration and pride deep in his blue luminescent eyes. "Fit for a *queen*."

"I will wear it always."

He kissed her cheek then bid her farewell and left with the others.

Alfred watched them go, clearly confused by the interaction. "I must say, I don't understand why the elves came to our aid. When we started our trek through the Wyldwood Forest, they were more than happy to get us here through the portal. An odd experience, that."

"How so?" Snow asked.

"Hard to describe, but I would say it was like walking through a hole in space. At any rate, now that everything is settled, we'll round up Seraphina's men and arrest them. It will be up to you to decide what to do with them. For now, I'll leave a few men stationed inside and around the castle."

"I appreciate that," she said. "Thank you."

"And, uh, if you don't mind, we'd like to set up camp outside the castle walls for the night," Alfred said.

"Please stay as long as you like," she said.

"I thank you." Then to Roderick, he said, "I knew the message was from you. It's the reason I came. However, it would appear I've lost my best blacksmith to the Mystic Vale."

He gave Snow a surreptitious wink, which made Snow blush to the roots of her hair. Then he and a few others headed out of the great hall through the destroyed door and into the night. Roderick moved to stand by her side, wrapping an arm around her shoulders.

"Now that you have your throne back, your majesty, what will you do first?"

"Try to get used to everyone calling me *your majesty* for starters."

He chuckled at that. "And next?"

She took a deep breath, expelled it, then glanced up at him. "I don't know, really."

A smile tugged at the corner of his mouth. "I'm sure you'll figure it out in no time."

As the weeks passed, Snow oversaw the rebuilding of the castle, which didn't sustain too much damage from Alfred's trebuchet. He broke down camp, but left a few men behind to assist in the rebuilding.

Snow found the family portraits Seraphina had stashed in an unused bedchamber and restored them to the gallery. The queen had also removed much of the furniture, stashing it away in parts of the castle that were unused. Snow spent a lot of time putting things back to the way she remembered when she was a girl.

She'd offered the position of advisor to Roderick, but he refused. He was more comfortable with a hammer in his hand pounding out steel. He never found his enchanted dagger and so he resolved to make another one. Snow, however, had retrieved hers from the dead queen but refused to keep it. She asked Roderick to melt it down and remake it into something else.

The Captain of the Guard, Erick, pledged allegiance to Snow and asked to regain her trust. Snow agreed since he helped them gain access to the queen's chambers, much to Roderick's objections. But Snow trusted him and allowed him to interact with Alfred's men and saw he had changed and was willing to fight for his new queen.

When it came time for her and Roderick to visit the villages, she left the care of the castle in his hands as steward. They told the villagers of the queen's death and that she had taken her rightful place as ruler of the Mystic Vale. There was much rejoining within the villages and they were treated with feasts and festivals and tournaments. Snow was happy to learn the innkeeper's son, William, was still alive and well and happy to see them again. And Snow made good on her promise of paying the innkeeper in gold. He was shocked and grateful.

After weeks of traveling, they returned to the castle to find things progressed and Erick had not betrayed her in her absence. The rebuilding of the castle was almost complete.

Snow found she could not stop thinking about the dark wizard deep within the Wyldwood Forest and wondered if his essence had also died with the mirror. There was only one way to find out.

She fell easily back into old habits by slipping out at night to spend time in the castle gardens, which were overgrown and ignored. She vowed to bring them back to their former glory. But in the meantime, she managed to find a piece of grass under an old oak tree. There, she sat cross-legged, her eyes closed and her palms flat on the ground.

She attuned herself to nature, feeling it inhale and exhale every breath as it moved under the canopy of stars. Night creatures were busy foraging. Frogs sang in the creek beds. Crickets chirped the night away. The elves were busy rebuilding their burned village. Some regrowth began to spring from the ashes, which made her smile.

And deep with the Wyldwood there was an abandoned cabin that once belonged to the dark wizard, Govan.

She used her senses to push deeper into nature than she had ever been. There was Faradill, standing strong and sure as always. In the meadow, the unicorn grazed on blades of grass bathed in the blue-white veil of moonlight.

Past that, she pushed deeper until she was in that place where the abandoned cabin was. The place where there was silence and no creature stirred. She stretched her senses deeper, recalling the ivy climbing the walls and smiling at the alias she gave the disembodied voice of the dark wizard. Her mind stretched into the cabin, where it was overrun with plant life and nothing more.

The dark wizard was gone.

She sensed no other presence aside from nature and nocturnal creatures. And so, he told her true. Destroying the Magic Mirror released him from his bonds, allowing him at last to rest.

Snow pulled back to herself, passing by Faradill. A faint fluttering brushed her cheeks. She opened her eyes to see Annilen hovering. She held her palm out to let the little sprite land. She dipped a curtsy.

"Your majesty."

She laughed. "I'm Snow to you. And I didn't get a chance to thank you for helping bring King Alfred here."

"No thanks necessary. I was happy to do it." She stifled a yawn. "Snow, can we take our morning walks again?"

Snow leaned back against the tree. "Yes, we can."

"Good, because I missed them." Which also meant she missed Snow. "What happens next?"

"What do you mean?" she asked.

"With you and the Mystic Vale?"

"Well..." she said. "I suppose I'll do my best to be a good queen."

Annilen yawned and settled down in her palm. "You will."

"I hope you're right."

"I am," she said, sounding confident. "You'll be a kind and just ruler."

And she was.

# Epilogue

"The end," Hilde said. She took a swig of water from the bottle she held in her hands, her throat parched and her voice tired from telling the story.

Marigold blinked sleepy eyes. "But what about Roderick and Snow? Did they live happily ever after?"

"Yes, they did," she said.

"Did they get married?" she asked around a yawn.

"They did. And Snow created a beautiful garden with all sorts of flowers. Roderick became the master blacksmith for the Mystic Vale. Eventually, he hired an apprentice who would learn how to make enchanted blades like he did."

"Was he an Artificer?"

"He was," Hilde said. "Roderick was happy to find others like him."

"What sort of flowers were in the garden?" she asked.

The girl was always full of questions when she finished a story. Almost as though she thought the stories were real and the people in them lived on. Well, she wasn't wrong.

"Roses, tulips, peonies and—"

"A hedge maze?" the girl asked.

For a moment, Hilde was taken aback. She peered down at the girl wondering where she had seen or heard of a hedge maze.

"I've always wanted walk through a hedge maze," she said, closing her eyes and slipping her hand under the pillow.

It struck her then how grown up her niece sounded when she said that.

The Mystic Vale gardens were some of the most spectacular, cultivated and overseen by Snow White herself. The lawn was immaculate. The hedges trimmed to perfection. The roses fragrant and colorful. There was a gazebo with climbing ivy and an arbor with pale blue morning glories winding up and around it.

"Yes, there was a hedge maze." Hilde rose and tucked her into the hospital bed. "Now, you get some rest. Your mum will be here soon."

"And will you stay?"

"I will for as long as I can." She kissed her forehead. "Now, sleep."

Moments later, Marigold was out. Hilde sat back in the chair and watched her sleep. Perhaps she shouldn't tell the girl fanciful stories, but then what fun was that?

# ACKNOWLEDGEMENTS

Writing can be very lonely. Especially when you sit and stare at a computer screen for hours on end trying to figure out what your characters are doing. Sometimes they tell you. Sometimes they go completely rogue. Most of the time you have to figure it out on your own and the characters are really no help whatsoever.

In this book, Snow White doesn't have a Prince Charming and there is no poisoned apple. For her, I wanted her to have a hero who was more than just some dude who kissed her to wake her up (I'm thinking of the original Disney cartoon). While I loved the TV version of her and Charming in *Once Upon a Time*, I also wanted to do something different. I wanted a fresh, new twist. Having the hero be a blacksmith was challenging and also fun to write. Having him be the one who falls under the sleeping curse was even more fun.

First, thanks to **Jennifer August** for her devilish ideas about how to get the elves to back Snow White! Those margaritas at lunch really pay off. LOL

To my sister, **Kathy**, who reads everything I write and helps proofread. Not only does she read, she listens, too. I'm a perfectionist, so it really bothers me when there are typos!

To my **husband** for all his patience and support. He is the best and reminds me we are in this together.

And to you, **readers**, who read my books and support this indie author. It means the world to me.

# Also by Michelle Miles

**Age of Wizards (Epic Fantasy)**

In the Tower of the Wizard King

On the Hunt for the Wizard King


**Dragon Protectors (Paranormal Shifter Romance)**

Desiring the Dragon Lord

Seducing the Dragon Knight

Tempting Her Dragon Bodyguard

Dragon Protectors Book Collection, Books 1-3


**Dream Walker (Urban Fantasy)**

Call of the Dark

Blood and Bone

Flame and Fury

Smoke and Ashes

Light of the World

Dream Walker Collection (Books 1-5)


**Dream Walker: Origins (Fantasy)**

Provenance

**Enchanted Realms (Fantasy Romance)**

Once Upon a Midnight Clear

Once Upon True Love's Kiss

Once Upon an Enchanted Kiss


**Five Towers (YA Fantasy)**

The Sorcerer's Daughter


**Ransom & Fortune Adventures
(Time Travel Action/Adventure)**

Highland Fling, Vol 1

Dead of Winter, Vol 2

The Citadel, Vol 3

Lord of the Underworld, Vol 4


**Realm of Honor (Fantasy Romance)**

One Knight Only

Only for a Knight

A Knight to Remember

A Knight Like No Other

Shadows of the Knight

Realm of Honor Collection (Books 1-5)

**Guardians of Atlantis (Fantasy Romance)**

Tempting Eden

Seducing Eve

Ravishing Helene

Guardians of Atlantis Box Set


**Shorts and Anthologies (Fantasy/Paranormal)**

A Dance Among the Faeries, Short Story

Eorwulf, Short Story

The Soul of Sharah, Short Story

Sinfully Sweet, Short Story

Flights of Fantasy: A Collection of Short Stories

# About the Author

MICHELLE MILES believes in fairy tales, true love and magic. She writes heart-stopping urban fantasy, epic fantasy and paranormal romance with an action/adventure twist that will leave you breathless. She is the author of numerous series that includes everything from angels and demons to fairies, dragons and elves.

She is a member of Romance Writers of America (RWA) and Science Fiction and Fantasy Writers Association (SFWA). A native Texan, in her spare time she loves reading, listening to music, watching movies, hiking, and drinking wine. She can be found online at Facebook, Instagram, Pinterest and Goodreads.

**Your Adventure Awaits**

*Read more at MichelleMiles.net*

9 79898 9854219